MW01145835

Sorceress
Super Hero

DARIUS BRASHER

Copyright © 2018 Darius Brasher

All rights reserved.

No part of this book may be reproduced or transmitted in any form or by any means, electronic or mechanical, including photocopying, recording, or any information storage and retrieval system without prior written permission of the author. Your support of authors' rights is greatly appreciated.

All characters in this novel are fictitious. Any resemblance to actual persons, living or dead, is purely coincidental. The use of any real company and/or product names is for literary effect only. All other trademarks and copyrights are the property of their respective owners.

ISBN: 1723092207
ISBN-13: 978-1723092206

DEDICATION

To my higher level Patreon patrons, Michael Hofer, Paul Krause, and Flint L. Miller. Thanks for your support!

CHAPTER ONE

I was wistfully eyeing the swanlike neck of the gorgeous television star and secret fairy I was supposed to protect and thinking about how good it would feel to punch her in the throat when the gargoyles attacked, changing my life forever.

"I'm thrilled to be here in Washington, D.C. to receive the United States Institute of Peace's Humanitarian Award," my client Willow Wilde said to the assembled throng of reporters and cameramen. "I know I don't deserve this great honor."

You've got that right, I thought, wisely keeping the sentiment to myself. First not punching Willow in the throat, and now not saying aloud every thought that popped into my head. Maybe, after twenty-six years of impulsiveness, I had finally learned some restraint. Sage Hawthorne of Capstone Security Consultants was my name, self-control was my game.

Willow was conducting a press conference on the top floor of the Institute of Peace building before the awards ceremony began on the ground floor. A few dozen members of the media clustered around her in a semi-circle. Willow's show *Born to be Wilde* was the biggest on television and had been for years. Willow was rich, an international celebrity and socialite, and had the kind of beauty men would kill their brothers over and launch a thousand ships for. Willow was A Big Deal. She would be the first person to tell you so.

I stood out of the range of the cameras trained on Willow, but close enough to her that I could get to her if there was danger. Or punch her in the throat if my newfound restraint slipped.

My eyes scanned the surrounding area, alert to any hint of danger, magical or otherwise. An earbud was in my ear, feeding me status reports from the members of Willow's mundane permanent security detail I had positioned throughout the five-story Institute of Peace building. Since I was an independent contractor brought in a few weeks ago rather than an employee of Willow's like her permanent guards, they resented the fact they had to take orders from me. The fact I was a woman didn't help.

Oh well. As long as they did what I told them, I didn't care what nasty names Willow's mundane guards called me under their breath. Little did they know I could hear the name-calling. We Gifted humans had enhanced senses, reflexes, and strength, as well as the ability to wield magic. The guards' ignorance of my abilities was understandable. Few mundanes knew the magical world even existed.

The Institute of Peace was on Constitution Avenue, near D.C.'s iconic National Mall. The building's curved roof, fashioned to resemble the wings of white doves, glowed faintly overhead. Willow and I stood on a limestone floor near a waist-high, clear protective barrier which overlooked the George P. Shultz Great Hall, a massive atrium on the ground floor facing the National Mall.

A large crowd of people who had flocked here to see Willow receive her award mingled in the atrium below, awaiting the start of the ceremony. The sounds of their voices wafted up to us, including the high-pitched squeals of children. A lot of folks had brought their kids so they could see Willow. Kids made up a healthy percentage of Willow's fanbase, though I couldn't fathom why. Probably because their brains hadn't fully developed yet.

I continued to look around as Willow droned on to the media about how awesome she was. I saw the Lincoln Memorial off in the distance through the atrium's floor-to-ceiling glass curtain wall. It was nighttime, and the memorial glowed thanks to its internal spotlights. I wondered if Honest Abe would have bought what Willow was selling if he could hear her. Lincoln once said of a political opponent that "he can compress the most words into the smallest ideas better than any man I ever met." Clearly he had never met Willow.

Willow was saying, "I have dedicated my life to making a difference, improving lives, brightening days, and bringing people together." Flashbulbs and video camera lights reflected off her jewelry, sequined gown, and porcelain skin, almost making her glow like the Lincoln Memorial outside and the wing-shaped roof overhead. With firm flesh and tight, flawless skin, Willow appeared to be in her early twenties. Appearances were deceiving, as they often were when it came to a citizen of the hidden magical world.

If Lincoln had never met Willow, it was not because they had not been contemporaries. They had been. Willow was well over three hundred years old. One would think that if Willow really were dedicated to bringing the world together, she would have done it after three centuries of devotion to it, with time to spare to fix global warming. I knew for a fact Willow recently leaked on the Internet a sex tape of her participating in a foursome. I wondered how it fit into her dreams for worldwide kumbaya. Maybe she intended to tame the world's savagery one horny hung dude at a time. Ambitious, though unsanitary. I'd bet fixing global warming would be less messy.

"It's so important that we all work toward making our planet better for the next generation." Willow's world-famous voice was low and breathy, reminiscent of Marilyn Monroe's, somehow simultaneously implying innocence, worldliness, a big rack, and its availability to all comers.

Comers. I swallowed a giggle, earning me a quick but sharp glance from Willow before she turned her attention back to the assembled media throng. None of them paid me any mind. After all, Willow was a star and the reason why they were all here; I was merely one of her bodyguards. I might as well have been a piece of furniture. If they knew I could perform magic, maybe they would have paid me more attention.

Then again, maybe not. They were transfixed by Willow, hanging on her every word, as if she was divulging the secrets to cold fusion rather than mouthing platitudes I knew she didn't mean. But really, who could blame them? She was stunning, though slightly plastic-looking and otherworldly, like a sex doll built by aliens who'd only seen human women in *Juggs* magazine: all breast, butt, pouty lips, thin limbs, and perfectly sculpted blonde hair. She looked like a million bucks in her glittering jewels and form-fitting evening gown, which might not be too far off from how much the ensemble had cost.

Though I had been known to turn heads from time to time, next to Willow I looked like sun-parched dog-doo with eyes. Tall for a woman, I had pale skin, shoulder-length black hair, and piercing blue eyes. My ex-boyfriends all told me my arctic blue eyes were my best feature. Though I considered myself a liberated woman, just once it would be nice to hear that my best feature was my butt. I would have to ease up on the breakfast pastries for that to ever happen.

As Willow blathered on, I wondered which of her many suitors had bought Willow's duds and baubles for her. Or maybe it had all been gifted to her. Willow publicly wearing a company's clothes or jewels would blast sales through the roof. I doubted Willow had paid for any of it out of her own pocket. I had learned in the weeks I'd been leading her security detail that, despite her fabulous wealth, she was as tight-fisted with it as a leprechaun with his gold. The only reason she gave so much money away, she had told me on the ride here from the hotel, was because otherwise she'd be eaten alive in taxes.

"As far as I'm concerned, if the pits of Hell open tomorrow and demons gobble up every mundane on the planet, it won't be a moment too soon," Willow had sniffed disdainfully in the limousine. "And that goes double for their crotch spawn. Filthy, screeching, snot-nosed, disease-carrying little brats. Living arguments for the wisdom of abortions." The voice she used in private was dramatically different than the one she used in public, like coarse sandpaper compared to velvet.

"Because our greatest resource is our precious, innocent, pure, beautiful children," Willow was cooing now to the microphones. "I believe the children are our future . . ." Disgusted, I stopped listening to her again. If she started belting out Whitney Houston's *Greatest Love of All*, I'd likely choke on my own vomit.

Tuning Willow out brought my aching feet into focus again. I longed to kick off the idiotic high heels Willow had talked me into wearing with my black pantsuit. "How my chief of security looks is a reflection on me," she had said, and threatened to call my boss Oscar if I didn't submit to her foot torture. Every step threatened to send me toppling. My calves burned. My pinched toes felt like they were being slowly pulled through a funnel.

Willow had said they were Louboutins when she pulled the red-soled shoes out of her massive shoe collection. Though I had expensive tastes, I wasn't a shoe gal. I preferred a Louisville Slugger over a Louboutin. More useful in my line of work. How female superheroes kicked butt while wearing heels was beyond me. One of their Metahuman powers, maybe.

I was the only one not listening to Willow. The male media members were slack-jawed as they hung on her every word. The women were almost as enthralled. Even my eyes kept being drawn to Willow, and I knew she was so bewitching only because of her fairy glamour. Fairy glamour was why so many supermodels and movie and TV stars were closeted fairies—when you laid eyes on them, it was almost impossible to look away, especially if you were a mundane who did not know what was going on.

Standing this close to Willow and getting the full brunt of her glamour, something primal deep inside of me stirred, whispering enticingly to my lizard brain and parts farther south that despite my lifelong glandular bias in favor of men, maybe it was time to put down the balls and bats and start caressing catcher's mitts. Or at least one catcher's mitt in particular.

I suddenly found myself caressing Willow with my eyes.

My conscious mind shuddered at the thought. I literally shook myself, trying to shake off the effects of the glamour Willow constantly projected like an eel's electric field.

My movement caught Willow's eye. Her mouth tightened in an almost undetectable frown. In her mind, all the world was her personal stage, and no one had better dare do anything which might take the spotlight away from her. Willow shot me a quick look of pure venom while she continued to mouth saccharine inanities.

I winked at her, knowing the impertinence would drive her nuts. Despite the fact Willow relied on me to protect her against the threats she had been getting from the magical world lately, to her, I was just the help who should stay in her place. Before those magical world threats, Willow's security chiefs had been licensed Heroes. One such Hero, a young one fresh out of Hero Academy, had been murdered a couple of years ago, though in an incident unrelated to Willow. I hoped I would not suffer the same fate.

Avoid dying. One should always set ambitious goals.

Knowing I could not afford to let my senses and reflexes be dulled by Willow's glamour, I opened my Third Eye. To do so, I did not need to use the Word, the Will, and the Wave as I did when I cast spells. Once you were used to opening your Third Eye, triggering it was as easy as riding a bike. I had stumbled into how to do it before I got my first period, long before I had any formal magical training.

The mundane world I perceived through my biological eyes drained away like water in a sink with the stopper removed. It was replaced by a vision of the magical world my mystical Third Eye permitted me to see.

A 360-degree panorama unfolded and displayed in my mind. Vivid colors of every shade swirled around me in eddies of strong magical current. Since magic drew its power from life, and especially sentient life, magic was particularly potent in major cities. Sometimes I wondered if urban fantasy novels, which were almost always set in cities, were written by Otherkin or Gifted humans, the two general types of citizens of the magical world. Gifteds like me wielded magic; Otherkin like Willow *were* magic.

With my Third Eye open, now I saw Willow for who she truly was. Rather than a blonde bombshell, I saw before me a pinch-faced mousy brunette who looked like she had just sucked on a bushel of lemons. Her skin had so many fine lines that it looked like parchment paper. Willow's tight dress hugged the lumpy rolls of her body. She looked overindulged, overfed, and under-exercised.

I closed my Third Eye. I staggered slightly in my infernal heels as the dull mundane world returned and snapped back into focus. Now that I had peeked behind the magical curtain, Willow's glamour would have no effect on me for a while and I could focus on my job. The lizard part of my brain had needed the reminder that Willow's looks and allure were no more real than her name was.

Willow had used a lot of different names over the years: Madame de Pompadour in the 1700s when Willow seduced her way into becoming the official chief mistress of King Louis XV of France; Lola Montez in the 1800s when Willow was the mistress of King Ludwig I of Bavaria, eventually ruining him and nearly ruining Bavaria; and Mata Hari in the late 1800s and early 1900s when Willow was a stripper who parlayed what she called "sacred Hindu dances" (hah!) to international fame and fortune before being arrested in Paris during World War I and tried, convicted, and executed as a German spy. Obviously, it had not been Willow who had been executed by a firing squad. A sorcerer smitten by Willow had animated a golem in Willow's likeness, replaced Willow with it, and teleported Willow away before the bullets hit her. Fairies were vulnerable to iron, so the firing squad's bullets would have surely killed Willow if the golem had not taken her place.

I only knew all that about Willow because I read it in the dossier on her the gnomes in Capstone's research department had prepared. On my own, I did not know much about history, unless you were talking about what happened during season one of *Game of Thrones*. I was a butt-kicker, not a nerd.

I didn't have to be a history buff to know Willow had forged her path throughout the centuries with her looks and on her back. It was one of the reasons why I did not like her. Women who relied exclusively on their looks and sexuality irritated me. If my mother knew Willow, she would call her "a do-nothing bitch." I did not agree with Mom on much, but that description hit Willow on the head.

Willow probably knew I was not her biggest fan since I have never been known for my subtlety and tact. She likely thought I was jealous of her. Jealousy was the go-to explanation for attractive women when less attractive women did not like them. I was not jealous. Well, not of

Willow's looks. I *was* a tad jealous of her money. Whoever said money was the root of all evil had never been behind on her rent and in credit card debt up to her eyeballs. I was both. Financial discipline, like historical knowledge, was not one of my strengths.

Willow seemed to be wrapping up her soliloquy of clichés when I saw, out of the corner of my eye, dark forms swoop out of the darkness of the night into the brightness cast by the Institute of Peace's outside lights.

My pulse starting to race, I spun to look at the flying figures through the clear curtain wall.

Before I could raise my voice in warning, the flying forms crashed into the curtain wall, ripping through the thick glass like it was tissue paper. The breaking glass sounded like crashing cymbals. People below us in the atrium screamed. Some pointed up in the air at the monsters beating their wings there.

For that was what they were: monsters. Three of them. Each the size of a Mini Cooper, each with the body of a different animal—a dog, a ram, and a rattlesnake—and each with giant bat wings that beat the air so powerfully they generated gusts of wind. Their wings were crimson red and leathery, with long sharp talons on the ends. Their bodies were bluish-black. They glistened evilly with an oily sheen.

Gargoyles. The only gargoyles I knew of in the city adorned the Washington National Cathedral, over three miles away in the northwest quadrant of the city. I didn't understand what was happening. Gargoyles protected the buildings they perched on from demons and evil spirits, which was why they were often placed on churches. They simply did not sprout wings, become animated and oversized, and crash into buildings miles away from their roost.

Clearly nobody had told these gargoyles that.

The dog gargoyle suddenly swooped down. Shrieking, the people in the atrium scattered like ants. The dog gargoyle's massive jaws clamped down around the waist of a man who had tripped and fallen in his haste to get away.

The gargoyle rose into the air with the screaming man. Blood spurted from him like fuel from a ruptured gas tank. The gargoyle shook the man like a terrier who had caught a rat. The man's bones cracked loudly enough to be heard over all the pandemonium. The man's screaming died as he did.

The dog gargoyle opened its jaws, spitting the man out like bad tasting candy. The man's torso hit the floor, followed a second later by his lower body. His guts oozed out of him like a mound of spaghetti drowning in red sauce.

The gargoyle's powerful bite had ripped the poor man in two.

Jaiden Burnham

CHAPTER TWO

People's screams got louder. They trampled each other in their haste to get away from the monsters and out of the building.

The sound of gunshots rose above the cacophony as Willow's men opened fire on the gargoyles. Their bullets had no noticeable effect.

My earbud exploded with sound, the men under my command all yelling at once.

I grabbed Willow's bare arm. Dragging her alongside of me, I moved as quickly as I could in my stupid heels away from the area overlooking the madhouse that was the atrium. We left the media behind. They all just stood there like dumb mutes, their eyes following Willow, not even looking up at the gargoyles, still under the spell of her glamour.

I yanked open an office door. This was the panic room I had supervised the preparation of before I escorted Willow on site. I shoved Willow inside. She went sprawling on the floor. Her heels flew off and one of her boobs popped out of her low-cut gown. In my haste, I had pushed her harder than I meant to. Sorry, not sorry.

"Stay here," I commanded. "The room is fully warded. Nothing will be able to get in without your permission." I started to close the door on her.

"Wait!" Willow shrieked, climbing to her feet unsteadily. "Where are you going?" The screams in the atrium had not lessened. If anything, they had increased.

"I'm going to go help those people." I tried to close the door, but Willow put her hand on it, stopping me.

"You're not leaving me alone." It was an order, not a question. Willow's sex kitten voice was gone, replaced by a tone more like the crack of a whip.

"Just watch me," I said. "There are innocents out there. Kids. You'll be safe here." I tried to remove her arm, but she shifted it and still blocked the door.

"I don't give two shits about those mundanes and their drooling little STDs," Willow said. Her green eyes were unyielding emeralds. "And neither should you. I pay you to protect me, not a bunch of slack-jawed mundanes. You're staying here with me." She shook her head at me in disgusted disbelief. "In over three hundred years, I've never met a stupider human than you."

"Three hundred years? Wow, you don't look a day over a hundred."

Willow recoiled as if I'd slapped her. The vainer someone was, the more insecure she was. "You take that back!" she screeched.

I smothered a smirk and brushed her hand off the door. I wasn't gentle about it.

"If you don't stay here and protect me you ugly, big-assed witch, you're fired," Willow swore, her face red with anger. Witches and warlocks practiced black magic. Actual witches wore the label like a badge of honor. For those of us who did not walk on the dark side, calling a Gifted woman a witch was the equivalent of calling a mundane woman the C word.

Willow's slur broke the camel's back. Willow's throat beckoned me like a bullseye beckons a marksman. *Dear*

Lord, I silently prayed, *lead me not into temptation . . . tomorrow. But not today.*

I punched Willow in the throat. Willow doubled over, gagging, clutching her neck. I'd hit her hard. But not too hard. I was irritated, not homicidal. I could've punched a hole clean through her neck if I wanted to.

"You can't fire me," I said. "I quit. That's my letter of resignation." I wanted to yank her godawful shoes off and fling them at her as well, but I resisted the impulse. I thought it demonstrated phenomenal restraint, yet no one showed up to give me a humanitarian award. A clear double standard.

I slammed the door on Willow's hunched over form. "Claudo," I murmured as I waved my hand in front of the door in the necessary pattern while I exerted my will, activating the wards a Capstone ward specialist had placed on the panic room. The door shimmered for a quick moment as the wards snapped into place. *Claudo* was Latin. Latin was the language of magic, much like math was the language of science.

I turned away from the door, kicking off my despised heels as I did so. I had struck Willow without thinking in the heat of the moment. Acting impulsively was nothing new for me. Now, I was starting to regret the punch. Not because Willow didn't deserve it, but because of what Oscar might say and do about it when he found out.

Oh well. I'd burn that bridge later.

In bare feet, I raced back toward the area overlooking the atrium. I peeled off my pantsuit jacket and dropped it on the floor as I ran. It hindered my movement too much. The transmitter and earbud attached to it fell away as well.

I skidded to a stop at the railing and hastily assessed the situation.

Things had gotten worse in the short time I'd been dealing with Willow. More people lay on the atrium floor, injured or dead. Blood stained the light-colored floor like red paint on a canvas. The gargoyles were still in the air over the atrium. They were swooping down onto the hapless people below like birds of prey.

A couple of Willow's mundane security guards were trying to shepherd people to the only exit on this side of the building. The other guards were gone. I guessed they'd pushed their way to the front of the crowd fleeing the building in the face of these flying nightmares which were apparently immune to their bullets. Cowards. Willow should fire them, not me. Then again, in their defense, they had never faced magical creatures before.

Most of the media were gone. They must have snapped out of the effects of Willow's glamour and run away. The remaining two cameramen had their cameras trained on the gargoyles and the carnage they caused.

Evidence of the hidden magical world was going to be on the nightly news. Fantastic. The Conclave, the magical world's ruling body, was going to be pissed. And when the Conclave got pissed, the people who had gotten them pissed tended to disappear.

A woman howled like a banshee as the ram gargoyle swooped down, hitting her with its big head, sending her flying into a wall. A miniature version of the woman wailed as the girl watched with wild-eyed horror. The woman's daughter, obviously.

Where the heck was one of those blasted costumed Heroes when you needed them? Licensed Heroes always seemed to be there when you didn't need them, and they were nowhere to be found when you did need them.

Somebody had to do something before all these people got slaughtered.

Since there was no Hero handy, I guessed that somebody was going to have to be me.

And yet, I hesitated for a split second. There was no way I would be able to deal with the gargoyles without violating the Conclave's First Rule of Magic.

Screw the Rules, I thought, chiding myself for my hesitation. More innocent people would get hurt or killed if I did not step in and do something. Dad had taught me that right was right and wrong was wrong. I'd worry about the Conclave later.

I backed away from the railing to give myself a running start. Aiming for the dog gargoyle, which was the one hovering in the air closest to me, I took off running.

I hurdled the railing like a track star. My Gifted legs sent me shooting through the air toward the dog gargoyle like I had a jetpack on my back. I was vaguely aware of one of the cameramen filming me flying through the air like no mundane was capable of.

Yeah, the Conclave was definitely going to be pissed.

I arced through the air above the atrium, my arms windmilling, my head almost grazing the glowing white ceiling. Then I started to drop. The air whistled in my ears.

My aim was true. I landed astride the dog gargoyle's back with a bone-rattling thump, right in front of where the thing's bat wings were attached to its body. Pain shot through my nether regions. My lady parts weren't going to be happy with me tomorrow. Assuming there was a tomorrow.

Now that I was up close and personal, I saw the dog was some sort of mastiff. A bulldog, or maybe a Rottweiler. It didn't matter. Perhaps I'd investigate its pedigree later.

There was a dark flash in the corner of my eye. I ducked down low, flattening my torso against the dog's body.

The ram flashed by overhead with a rush of disturbed air. The ram gargoyle had claws instead of sheep hooves. Those claws grazed my back, slicing through my blouse and into my flesh. Pain erupted like a volcano on my back. Still, it could have been worse. If I had not ducked in time, the ram would have smacked headfirst into me with its horns, which were large and curved like those of a male bighorn sheep.

Trying to ignore the pain, I shoved myself back upright. I slammed a fist down, striking the canine gargoyle's big head with a blow that likely would have decapitated a real dog. My magic made me strong. Not as strong as some Metahumans, but stronger than the strongest non-Meta mundanes and stronger than most Gifteds.

Ow! Pain rippled through my fist and up my arm. Despite the fact the body my legs were wrapped around felt like flesh, punching this thing's head felt like punching a concrete block.

The gargoyle shook my blow off like it had been a mosquito bite. It twisted its neck, snapping at my hand with canines as long as my forearm. I snatched my hand back before I was forced into a Captain Hook impersonation.

Uh-oh. What now? I hadn't planned past leaping and punching. Story of my life. Should I now pat him on his head soothingly and ask, "Who's a good doggy?"

Before I could implement the lamest plan ever, I felt the gargoyle's muscles bunch up under my legs. Instinct made me grab the scruff of the gargoyle's neck.

I'd barely grabbed the scruff when the gargoyle started bucking and flipping in the air, trying to shake me off. I held on for dear life. If I had known I'd be going through this, I would have gone to more rodeos in preparation. By more rodeos, I mean I would've gone to a rodeo. I'd never been to one before. I was a city slicker, not a cowgirl.

In just a few seconds of being bounced around, my legs' and hands' grips started to slip. If I hit the ground from this high up, I'd be so dazed I would be easy pickings for the gargoyles, assuming the fall didn't break my fool neck.

Desperate, I waved my free hand in a long-practiced gesture as I waggled my fingers and exerted my will. "Ignis!" I said through clenched teeth.

My hand burst into flames. The fire was warm, but it didn't burn me. A sorceress was immune to her own spellfire.

I shoved my burning hand against the gargoyle's flesh like I was branding a bull.

The gargoyle let out an inhuman shriek that was a bizarre mix of a wolf's howl and a rooster's crowing. It set my teeth on edge. It was an unmistakable cry of pain. Good.

Emboldened, I gathered my will and released it in a torrent through my arm instead of in a steady stream.

Whoosh! Both the gargoyle and I were engulfed in fire, as if we had been drenched with gasoline and set ablaze.

The gargoyle's shrieks of pain increased in intensity, deafening me, making me want to cover my ears. I did no such thing. I instead kept shoveling my will into the blaze, increasing the intensity of my spellfire.

The gargoyle spun wildly in the air, out of control, falling like a shot bird, making me dizzy.

The gargoyle and I smashed into the stage Willow was supposed to accept her humanitarian award on.

The gargoyle was on its side, struggling like an injured cockroach to right itself. My leg was pinned under the beast, making me cry out in pain. I didn't let go of the monster though, nor did I let up on my spellfire. I took care to confine my spellfire to me and the gargoyle, and not let the stage catch on fire. It would be horrific if I destroyed this human-chomping gargoyle, only to also kill everyone else in a raging inferno.

The gargoyle started to crumble, bits of it flaking away, collapsing under the force of my spellfire like it was a sand castle pounded by a wave.

Then, suddenly, the gargoyle fell completely to pieces. The weight on my leg lessened dramatically. I was no longer pinned down.

Cautiously, I withdrew my will, canceling my spell. The raging bonfire of my spellfire went out like it had been deprived of oxygen.

I stood up. Black fragments like super-sized grains of sand fell off me, joining a larger pile of the stuff all around me. I was no forensic magician, but my guess was my spellfire had burned off whatever magic had animated the gargoyle, not to mention destroying the integrity of the gargoyle's body. It was good to see the gargoyles had a vulnerability.

Magicians like me stored magic like a battery, and that big expenditure of magical will had tired me, draining me of a good bit of my magic. My chest heaved with exertion. I got a flash of naked flesh. I glanced down.

I was as naked as the day I was born. Though I was immune to my spellfire, my clothes were not. They had burned off in the inferno, leaving only soot stains on my otherwise bare body.

I flushed in embarrassment, then tried to shove the silly emotion aside. People seeing me in my birthday suit was the least of the bad things that had happened today. Even worse things would happen if I didn't do something about the two remaining gargoyles. Even so, the vain part of me wished I had salad for dinner last night instead of a double cheeseburger with bacon and fries.

A high-pitched scream cut through the tumult in the room. The scream came from a kid dressed in his Sunday best. The ram gargoyle had latched onto the boy with its claws and was flying toward the high ceiling with him. A woman, presumably his mother, stood underneath them, looking up, wailing almost as loudly as the kid.

I didn't know if the ram intended to rip the kid apart or drop him from the ceiling. I couldn't let either happen.

Wishing I knew how to fly, I twisted my head around frantically. I spotted a microphone stand nearby on the stage. I lunged for it. I knocked the microphone out of it, causing screeching feedback from the atrium's speakers that temporarily drowned out the screams of mother and child. Holding the vertical metal part of the stand in my right hand, I stomped hard on its base. With a metallic pop, the circular base separated from the vertical metal.

I focused my will on the metal in my right hand, waved my left hand in the necessary pattern, and said "Ignis." The metal pole burst into flames. If your will was strong enough, spellfire could burn just about anything. Magic was not subject to the usual laws of science.

I took three quick steps forward, and then I flung the flaming microphone stand like it was a javelin. It zoomed through the air with a hiss, toward the ram gargoyle. If I had stopped to think, I probably wouldn't have thrown it out of fear of hitting the boy by accident. It wasn't as though I was an expert javelin thrower. I was no Olympic athlete.

Dread over what the gargoyle would do to the kid must have aided my marksmanship. The flaming metal hit the center of the ram's chest like it had been guided there by a laser. With a whizzing sound, the metal sliced through the center of the ram like a hot knife through butter. The flaming metal continued upward and poked a hole through the white glowing roof of the building.

The ram bleated in agony, like a sheep being slaughtered. Green ichor shot out of its chest, like a giant infected pimple had been popped. The ram dropped the kid. The boy fell like a stone, tumbling and screaming.

"Ventus!" I cried, exerting my will again as I waved my hands around and around each other in the required pattern.

A small whirlwind twisted into existence on the atrium floor underneath where the boy fell. It grew, stretching upward like a Slinky.

The boy fell into the wide top of the whirlwind's funnel. The twirling air currents slowed the boy's descent. He went from falling like a stone to falling like a feather. By the time he was a couple of feet off the floor, he was no longer falling at all, but rather, hovering, held up by the air currents.

I relaxed my will, and the whirlwind faded, then disappeared. The boy landed lightly on his feet. His mother rushed up and smothered him in her arms. The boy looked dazed, there was green goo on him, and his hair looked like Einstein's, but he seemed unhurt.

The same could not be said of the ram gargoyle. Despite it beating its bat wings ever more weakly to stay aloft, I had apparently hurt it too badly. It touched down on the atrium floor like a hot air balloon with a leak.

It turned into stone as soon as its claws touched the floor. The collision with the floor broke up the gargoyle's now stone body. Bits of stone flew everywhere.

Two gargoyles down, one to go. I turned, looking for the remaining gargoyle, the rattlesnake one.

No need. The rattlesnake reared up in front of me like an ambush predator. Its beating bat wings made it hover only a few feet from the floor, with its body slightly above the stage I was still on.

Before I could react, the tip of the snake's tail began to move faster than my eyes could follow. The tail's tip rattled so loudly, I wanted to cover my ears.

I wanted to cover them, but I did not. I *could* not. I could not move at all. I was completely mesmerized, struck dumb and motionless.

The snake opened its mouth and hissed. Drops of venom glistened from the bottom of sharp fangs the length of my forearms. I knew I was about to be bitten. And yet, I still could not move. Clearly the snake's rattle was some form of immobilizing magic. As strong as my magical will was, I could not resist the snake's potent power. I didn't think I could have resisted it even if my magical reserves were at full power, which they most definitely were not after the energy I had expended destroying the dog gargoyle and saving the boy from the ram.

The snake's eyes glittered like the blackest of onyx. Quick as a wink, its head surged forward, its mouth gaping as it prepared to sink its fangs into me.

The snake's surge toward me broke its spell. There was no time to cast a spell of my own. I threw my arms up in a last-ditch effort to save myself.

By sheer instinct, my hands grabbed the snake's upper and lower jaws. The snake's momentum forward pushed me backward.

I slammed into the back wall of the stage. My already lacerated back erupted in fresh pain while I struggled to keep the snake's mouth from getting closer and biting me. Thank heaven for my magically fueled strength. I never would have come close to holding the snake off if I weren't Gifted.

The snake and I struggled against each other, each of us pushing mightily, vying for supremacy. I couldn't cast a spell. The Wave was as important as the Will and the Word. If I freed up one of my hands to perform the Wave, the snake would pump me full of venom.

The snake's gaping head was so big, it could've swallowed me whole. No longer airborne, the gargoyle's wings beat against me. It was like being whipped by a massive leather belt. I almost lost my grip. A drop of venom the size of a baseball dripped from a fang. It barely missed my leg and hit the stage. The venom sizzled against the wooden stage like water dropped on a hot skillet.

The snake's forked tongue lashed my face. It was rough, wet, and disgusting, smelling like two-week-old fish that had been left out in the sun. Fortunately, it did not seem to be coated in venom.

The snake was winning our reverse tug of war. Its head crept closer and closer.

Desperate, I changed tactics.

Instead of merely pushing against the snake's mouth, I started pulling it apart too, like opening the jaws of a bear trap.

Almost imperceptibly at first, then more and more obviously, the snake's mouth got wider and wider. Staring into its fleshy, bluish-black mouth felt like staring into the pits of Hell.

I felt, then heard, the snake's jaw begin to pop and crack.

The snake struggled against me, but in the opposite way than before. The tables had turned. I had gained the upper hand, and now the snake was trying to get away from me. Obviously panicked, the rest of the snake's body whipped at and thrashed against me as the snake tried to escape.

With a sound that was like the world's biggest crab cracking open, the snake's lower jaw ripped away from the rest of its body.

Instantly, the snake transformed into stone. Its coils froze in place. They looked like an elaborate slide the Addams Family might have kept in their backyard.

I dropped the snake's lower jaw, which was now as stony as the rest of its body. It landed on my bare foot. I yelped in pain and cursed my carelessness. I was strong, but sometimes stupid.

Panting like a locomotive that had just chugged up a steep incline, I climbed out from within the stone coils of the immobile gargoyle. My adrenaline was draining away, making me feel like an emptied glass. Exhausted and in pain, I stumbled to the front of the stage.

A bunch of people had not made it out of the building. Some lay on the ground, either not moving at all or writhing in pain from injuries. Now that the gargoyles were gone, Good Samaritans started to tend to the injured. Others were looking up at me with their mouths agape, astounded by what they had just seen and experienced. A couple of guys pulled out their smartphones and pointed them at me, no doubt recording videos.

It was then that I remembered I was as naked as a jaybird. Plus, I had used magic in front of a bunch of mundanes. I was exposed in every sense of the word.

Suddenly self-conscious, I covered my crotch with a hand and my chest with an arm. Alas, covering my chest was all too easy to do. A woman as busty as Willow never would have been able to do it. Darn her bodacious body. Okay, I guess I was jealous of both her money and her boobs. If I had to choose between the two, I'd pick the former. With the former, I could buy the latter.

An adorable little girl who could not have been more than seven approached the stage. She wore a denim overall dress over a shirt with the Hero Omega's silver logo on it. Omega had become very famous very quickly, and his shirts were all the rage these days. The child was alone. I wondered where her parents were, and hoped they weren't lying on the atrium floor.

I got a mental image, as vivid as if it had happened ten seconds instead of ten years ago, of my father lying dead on a different floor, his body twisted, part of his head missing. He had shot himself in the head to save me when I was sixteen.

Tears welled up in my eyes. With an effort, I pulled my mind out of the past and back to the present. I wiped away my tears with the hand that wasn't shielding my so-called chest.

The girl in the denim dress stared at me with brown eyes as big as saucers. She looked up to me like I had hung the moon in the sky.

"Are you a superhero?" she asked with wonder in her voice.

I hesitated for a second. Aw heck, after all she had just seen, what would it hurt to tell her the truth? Besides, if she repeated it, who would believe a little kid?

I got on one knee so I was close to the girl.

"No honey," I whispered confidentially. "I'm a sorceress."

CHAPTER THREE

Oscar Hightower, a Halfling and the founder and owner of Capstone Security Consultants, drummed his thick fingers on top of his desk. He stared at me, his big head as silent and blocky as the stone heads of Easter Island.

Oscar wore a tieless gray suit that probably cost more than everything I owned, and I owned some expensive stuff thanks to my spendthrift habits. As for me, I was dressed in dark jeans, a short-sleeved dark green blouse, a ruched sleeve collarless yellow jacket, and black loafers with no socks. Sorceress casual elegance.

It was two days after the attack of the gargoyles. *Attack of the Gargoyles* sounded like a 1950s B movie. While it had held my interest, I'd have to give it two thumbs down.

Oscar most definitely gave my part in the show two thumbs down. I did my best to look contrite as he stared at me. It was a look I was unaccustomed to, so I wasn't sure if I was doing it right.

I waited patiently for Oscar to resume berating me again. When I'd been summoned to Oscar's office earlier, I had taken a few fortifying belts from the flask of Elven wine hidden in my desk. The wine had bolstered my patience immensely. You could patiently await a trip to the guillotine with Elven wine coursing through your veins.

I knew Oscar wasn't finished; he was merely taking a break from ripping me a new one. Not literally of course, though Oscar was fully capable of doing it since he was half Orc. His father was the human one, which proved that human men would screw anything that would hold still long enough. Orc women were so ugly that their portraits hung themselves.

Oscar loomed over me like a mountain thanks to his Halfling heritage. He wasn't as big as a full-blooded orc, but he was far larger than the average human. He looked like a retired professional wrestler who had taken too many steroids back in the day. Other than his size and the fact he was hairier than normal, you would never guess he was half Otherkin. He had gotten his tusks filed down and his pointy ears bobbed years ago so he could pass as a mundane. He kept his gray hair closely cropped because otherwise it looked like a bird's nest. He avoided staying out in the sun for too long. Oscar didn't tan; his skin turned as green as the Hulk's.

If he wanted to, Oscar could tear someone in half without breaking stride. Everybody in the company was afraid of him, myself included. I just hid it better than most. I think that's why he liked me—I didn't walk on eggshells around him. He respected that. I also hid from him the fact I was attracted to him. Oscar was an older male authority figure. That meant he was right up my alley. I was not terribly self-aware, but even I knew I had daddy issues.

I was being dressed down in the Fishbowl. We employees called Oscar's office that because its walls were a clear, thick glass like an aquarium's. They allowed Oscar to keep an eye on the rows of desks, including mine, arrayed outside his plush office. It was the middle of the workday, and all the agents who weren't in the field were at their desks. About half of the employees were Gifteds, and the other half were Otherkin. The Otherkin who could pass as human worked on this floor, which presented the public face of Capstone. Those who could not pass as human, such as the gnomes in the research division, were under the building, in Capstone's underground annex. The twelve-story tall building housing Capstone was in D.C.'s Golden Triangle district, just a few blocks from the White House.

Oscar's hairy fingers continued their staccato beat on the desktop. Office scuttlebutt claimed the light-colored desk was made of the laurel tree the nymph Daphne was turned into to help her escape molestation by the lesser god Apollo, but I wasn't sure I believed the rumor. I did not believe everything I heard, especially when the imp who worked in the sales department was doing the telling. Imps were notorious liars.

"What am I going to do with you?" Oscar finally asked. His voice sounded like the rumble of an earthquake. His eyes were so dark, they were almost black.

"Give me a raise?" I suggested hopefully. I had stitches in my back, so I was careful to not lean back in Oscar's chair. Fortunately, I hadn't broken any bones in the hand I had punched the dog gargoyle with. It still ached though, as did the foot I dropped the snake's stone jaw on. The Elven wine helped with that too. Was there any problem Elven wine could not solve? I wondered if the North and South Koreans knew of it.

Oscar's thick fingered drumbeat continued. On the antique wood desk, it sounded like galloping horses approaching. The Elven wine made me desperate to cry *Hi-Yo Silver! Away!* Self-preservation made me not do it. And people said I had no self-control. Ha!

Oscar said, "I'm far more likely to fire you than to give you a raise."

"My vote is for door number two."

"You don't get a vote."

"Um, have you heard of a little thing called the Nineteenth Amendment?"

Oscar's finger drumming stopped for a second, then resumed. "Do you really think this is a good time to be sassing me?"

"No sir," I said, my eyes downcast. I aimed for demure this time since contrite hadn't worked out so well.

Oscar wasn't fooled. "Knock it off with the sirs. You only sir me when you're kissing my ass." I winced slightly at the curse word. In honor of my clean-mouthed father who had been as close to a saint as you could find on this side of the afterlife, I didn't curse, at least not out loud. I didn't like even hearing it if I could help it. Oscar knew I didn't like cursing, though he didn't know why. I suspected his use of the vulgar word had been deliberate. All part of the taking Sage to the woodshed experience.

Oscar sighed. It sounded like the rumbling of a volcano. "Since you obviously need a reminder, what's the First Rule of Magic say?"

"The First Rule of Magic is you don't talk about Fight Club." The Elven wine had perhaps been a mistake. I was awfully lippy for someone a brownie's hair away from losing her job.

Oscar's finger drumming stopped again. "What did I tell you about sassing me?"

"You didn't come right out and say don't do it, but you strongly implied it."

"Exactly. I'm stupefied you were listening. It's an unexpected change of pace." More finger drumming. "As you well know, the First Rule of Magic says, 'There is no magic.' Meaning, you don't expose mundanes to the hidden magical world. We can't let it be widely known that magical creatures and magicians walk among the mundanes. Every psychological study the Conclave has commissioned and every diviner they've consulted have concluded that knowledge of the magical world would trigger oppression of magical folk the likes of which haven't been seen since the Salem Witch Trials. And the oppression would be far worse now than it was then because the mundanes have Metahumans to back them up."

Oscar paused, then let out a sigh that sounded like the whistle of a steam engine. "When I started this firm . . ."

Oh boy, here we go, I thought. I had heard this story many times before.

"I was the only employee, and I skipped countless meals to pay the bills."

I had to walk fifteen miles to school, I thought.

"I operated out of my rat-infested apartment in the projects of southeast D.C."

In the snow.

"I had to go through people's garbage to get cans and bottles to take to the recycling center to help make ends meet."

Barefoot.

"Rejected by orcs because of my mixed-race heritage, everyone else was uncomfortable around me because of my size."

Uphill.

"The business almost failed more times than I can remember."

Both ways! I added silently.

"From those humble beginnings, I scratched and clawed my way to where I am now—the owner of one of the preeminent security providers in the country, and *the* preeminent provider of magic-based security. Orc women who teased me when I was struggling would now give their eyefangs to be with me. I employ hundreds of people. The company is worth millions. Our office space here on K Street is some of the most expensive commercial real estate in the city. We provide security for heads of state, captains of industry, movie stars, Otherkin royalty . . . I could go on."

I felt a yawn coming. I admired Oscar, but sometimes he got too caught up in his own Horatio Alger story. I held the yawn back. The Elven wine hadn't dulled my wits so much that I was stupid enough to let it out.

"And in a single day, you've jeopardized everything I've worked decades to build. You assaulted our Otherkin client you were supposed to protect, who also happens to be one of the most famous women in the world."

"She deserved it," I blurted. Oscar's face darkened like a storm cloud, making me regret my words. I needed to muzzle myself.

"Or I should say our former client. She's terminated Capstone's contract. A sizable contract, I should add. She's threatening to sue you. More importantly, she's threatening to sue me and Capstone."

"Willow's not going to sue anybody," I scoffed. "She wouldn't risk it becoming public that she tried to stop me from helping those people. She won't do anything to tarnish her public image. Her entire career is based on it. Not to mention the fact the Conclave would never let her draw even more attention to the incident."

Oscar lifted an eyebrow. "So, you actually are capable of rational thought. It's a shame you didn't bring your brain to bear at the Institute of Peace." Oscar drummed his fingers some more. He was likely to dig grooves into the desk's surface. "I think you're right about how Ms. Wilde is not going to sue. She's just posturing. What she's more likely to do is file a complaint against you with the Conclave. You did strike her, after all. Ms. Wilde is not a turn the other cheek kind of fairy."

My stomach turned cold. The Conclave's Enforcement Bureau was no joke. Innocent until proven guilty was a mundane legal concept, not a magical one. The CEB was more a "you're probably guilty, so let's smite you with a spell first and send flowers to your descendants later if it turns out we were wrong" kind of organization.

"And speaking of the Conclave," Oscar continued, "there is the not so small matter of your violation of the First Rule. As your employer, I'm as much in the Conclave's crosshairs as you are. The only exception to the no public use of magic rule is when you're acting in self-defense or the defense of others."

"What do you think I was doing?" I demanded, starting to get irritated. "If I hadn't done something, more people would have been killed or injured." It turned out that only two people had died, one being the man who was bitten in half by the dog gargoyle. My only regret was that I had not acted quickly enough to save those two as well. About a dozen people had been injured, but none of the injuries were life-threatening.

"The exception applies to the defense of Otherkin and Gifteds, not the defense of mundanes. As you well know," Oscar snapped. "The Conclave thinks it's the job of Heroes to protect the mundanes, not ours." Then he paused. His voice softened slightly. "On the other hand, if I had been there, I don't know if I could have stood idly by when a bunch of mundanes were being hurt either, First Rule or no First Rule. That is the only reason why you're still sitting here instead of pounding the pavement, looking for another job. And with your checkered past, good luck in getting someone else to hire you."

I was so annoyed, I almost said I wished I were walking around in the fresh air and not cooped up here being lectured to. I swallowed the undiplomatic remark in the nick of time. You had to be careful what you wished for, because you might get it. I had lots of unpaid bills and debts, so I needed this job.

Oscar sighed again. "Sage, you have a lot going for you. You're tough, aggressive, fearless, you have a big heart, genuinely care about people, and you have more raw magical capacity than almost any other Gifted I've ever encountered. That magical capacity is why you're so strong and have such quick reflexes. In ways, you're the best field agent I have. Plus, as a sorceress, you're as rare as hen's teeth. I've landed a lot of high-profile, big-money clients by emphasizing the fact I have a sorceress on staff. It's why I've cut you so much slack in the past."

I didn't bother saying thanks for the kind words. I didn't have to consult a diviner to know a *but* was coming.

"But," Oscar added, "you're also impulsive and woefully lacking in self-control. You're immature, stubborn, insecure about certain things, foolishly arrogant about other things, and too much of a smart-ass for your own good. And while aggression is a good trait for a bodyguard to have, sometimes you go overboard. You're about as diplomatic as a wolf at a sheep convention. Also, you're undisciplined and intellectually lazy. You're a sorceress. You're supposed to be good at all forms of magic. Especially at your age. You're no spring chicken, yet you're still uncertified. Most magicians have gotten their Conclave certifications long before they're your age."

All Gifteds were born with an inherent knack for a certain magical specialty—alchemy, for example, or elemental magic, necromancy, divination, druidry, illusionism, voodoo, or any one of numerous others. All Gifteds, that is, except for those with the potential to be sorceresses and sorcerers. They were magical generalists. Jacks and Janes of all magical trades, but the masters of none. Gifteds were a tiny sliver of the human population. Sorceresses and sorcerers were in turn a tiny sliver of the Gifted population, so they were the rarest of the rare.

Unlike Gifteds, magicians were made, not born. A Gifted had to train and study to unlock her inherent talent for magic. A Gifted who had undergone some magical training earned the title of magician, though often she was instead called by the name of her particular magical specialty. For example, a Gifted who was born with a knack for illusionism could go by the title of magician, or more specifically, illusionist, once he had trained in the use of his magic. If that magician then earned his Conclave certification, he was called a Master Magician or Master Illusionist and became a voting member of the Conclave. For Master Magicians, the First Rule was somewhat relaxed, the idea being a Master Magician was wise enough to know when to and when not to use his magic where mundanes might see him. In the magical world, all men were most definitely not created equal.

I was a sorceress—that is, a magician with no specialized knack—but not yet a Master Sorceress since I had not yet earned my Conclave certification. Millennium, the famous former licensed Hero, was a Master Sorcerer, and perhaps the most powerful magician the world had ever known. He was also the only magician I knew of whose abilities were public knowledge. He had gotten a special dispensation from the Conclave to practice magic openly despite the First Rule. Considering all the shady stuff he had been exposed for doing, I bet the Conclave regretted making him an exception to the general rule.

Oscar said, "But despite all your potential, the only type of magic you're really proficient at is elemental magic. I suspect it's because the capacity of air, fire, water, and earth to make things go boom appeals to your inner child. Unfortunately, your inner child seems to sit in your psyche's driver's seat more often than not. You're terrible at just about every other magical discipline because you refuse to put in the work to master them. You're not living up to your potential. At the rate you're going, you never will."

"Boss, please stop. Such a sweet-talker." I made a show of fanning my face. "You're making a girl blush."

Oscar slapped his palm down on his desk, making me jump. The wood of the desk cracked loudly. He pointed a thick finger at me. "That's exactly what I'm talking about," he snarled. "You don't know when to keep your big trap shut."

I opened my mouth to respond, then abruptly closed it. Didn't know when to keep my big mouth shut, huh? I guess I showed him.

After staring at me for several long, uncomfortable beats, Oscar lowered his finger. He leaned back in his chair. It creaked ominously under his weight.

He said, "Hopefully the Conclave can cover up the nature of the gargoyles and your use of magic. We still don't know who animated the gargoyles and why, but that's something the Conclave will look into. As is usually the case when magic slips into the public eye, the Conclave is trying to explain away what happened by attributing it to Rogues and Heroes. I don't know how we'd hide magic so well if we didn't have Metahuman superpowers to point the finger of blame at. The Conclave's Magic Suppression Division is spreading the word through Fox News, CNN, Twitter, and all the other usual disinformation outlets that a Rogue's Metahuman powers were responsible for the gargoyles. They're doctoring all the footage of your exploits they can get hold of to change your features. Unfortunately, they're sending me the bill for the entire disinformation campaign since you were on site as an agent of this company.

"The Conclave also opened a First Rule violation investigation. You'll be under their microscope. As will Capstone Security." Oscar frowned at the thought. "I've got to show the Conclave I take this matter seriously, otherwise there's the danger they'll revoke my operating license. Though your smart-aleck tendencies tempt me to fire you, I won't. Like I said, in ways you're one of my best agents. But I can't let you off scot-free, either. What message would that send to the Conclave while they're going over my business practices with a fine-toothed comb?

"Here's what I'm going to do," Oscar said. "I'm going to suspend you for three weeks."

I leaned back, relieved. Oscar had me worried there for a while. Three weeks? That wasn't so bad. I could use the free time to get my nails done for the first time in years, clean my apartment for the first time in forever, crack open that copy of *Alchemy for Dummies* I had bought during a short-lived spurt of ambition a few months ago . . .

"Without pay," Oscar added.

. . . and scrounge around in my couch cushions for spare change to buy bread and water. I was already behind on all my bills and living from hand to mouth. I couldn't go three weeks without pay.

I shot up straight in my chair. "That's not fair!" I objected. Dismay burned away my Elven wine buzz.

"What's not fair is that you exposed this company to liability and that I have to clean your mess up for you. I'm letting you off easy."

"Maybe you should ask all the people I saved if they think you should suspend me. They'd probably say you should throw me a party, give me a corner office, and make me vice president of the company."

Oscar's skin flushed green and his eyes narrowed to black slits. "Make that a month's suspension."

"But—"

"Make it two months. Say one more word, and you're fired."

My jaw clenched. I stood so abruptly, my chair turned over. I didn't pick it up.

I stalked to the Fishbowl's glass door. I opened it, then hesitated. I turned my head back to Oscar. The devil within opened my mouth. I was about to say *Word*.

I closed my mouth before the job-killing syllable escaped. When Oscar said he would do something, he always did it. My better judgment had tackled the devil within in time, gagging and hog-tying it before I wisecracked myself out of a job. I needed this job. With my background, it would not be easy to find another, especially not one that paid as well as this one did.

I stormed out of Oscar's office. I left the door wide open behind me.

That would show him.

CHAPTER FOUR

I hurried past Oscar's longtime secretary Alice, a Gifted whose knack was inscriptive magic. I went back to my desk, feeling people's eyes on me the whole way. Many of the Otherkin species here had preternatural hearing, and no doubt had heard everything in the Fishbowl.

Seething with anger and embarrassment, I struggled to not slam my drawers as I cleaned out my desk. I dumped my belongings into a nylon bookbag. I made sure to grab the leather flask containing the rest of my Elven wine. I would definitely need to drown my sorrows later.

I approached Loopy's desk on the way to the elevator. A field agent like me, Blake Longtooth was his real name. Or at least that was the name he went by; I suspected his birth name was unpronounceable by a human tongue. Loopy was his office nickname, a bastardization of his Otherkin species' scientific name Lupus Mutabilis.

Loopy's feet were propped up on an open drawer. The long fingers of one hand were spread wide on top of his wood desk. His other hand casually tossed an open pocketknife into the air. The knife rose five or six feet, then descended. The sharp blade impaled itself between Loopy's outstretched fingers with a dull thunk. He had been at this for a while judging from the countless gouges in the desk between his fingers. I prayed he'd slice a finger off with the knife, but I knew he wouldn't.

Loopy was an intense guy, so much so that much of the office thought he was insane. Hence the nickname Loopy. Few people had the balls to call him that to his face, though. He was muscular and square-jawed, with thick curly black hair most women longed to run their fingers through. When I first met him, I thought he was one of the hottest guys I had ever seen. After getting to know and dislike him, his male model good looks became immensely irritating instead of intensely alluring.

Loopy's knife thunked into the desk again as I passed him. Without looking up at me, he said, "Has the teacher's pet finally gotten her tit slammed in the principal's office door?"

Darn his Otherkin hearing! My fists balled up. I took a step toward him. Then I realized Loopy was deliberately goading me into a fight. I was already on thin ice with Oscar.

"Bite me, Loopy." I winced. Not a great retort. My rapier wit needed sharpening.

Loopy looked up. He smiled happily. It was a normal human smile, not the canine-filled one he had when he transformed into his werewolf form. "One day, human bitch. One day." The way he said it, *human*, not *bitch*, was the insult.

The knife thunked into the desk again. I fought back the urge to grab it and perform impromptu plastic surgery on Loopy's face. And Oscar said I had no self-control? Hah! I oozed self-control like zit-faced teens oozed pus.

Okay, maybe similes were not my strong suit.

Suppressing violent thoughts, I swept past Loopy and got on the elevator. I didn't flip him off as the car door's contracted. Self-control yet again. I could teach a master class on the subject.

I exited the building through the revolving doors. I squinted against the brightness. The summer sun beat down like a hammer on an anvil. The city's humidity hit me like a hot, wet wall. Who needed steam rooms when you had D.C. in the summer? The city was below the Mason-Dixon line, which meant that it was a part of the American South. And the South got so hot during the summer that it felt like Satan's armpit. I needed to cool off with some iced sweet tea and drown my troubles in Elven wine, not necessarily in that order.

All the buildings around me were multi-storied, but none were taller than the twelve-story building I had walked out of. Washington, D.C., unlike many major cities, was not a city of skyscrapers. I'd heard it was because, by law, no building could be taller than the Washington Monument, the 555 feet tall obelisk on the nearby National Mall. It was just like men to pass a law saying nothing could be bigger than their giant phallic symbol.

Traffic crawled by on K Street, all the vehicles' exhaust adding to the heat. I dropped my knapsack on the sidewalk and peeled off my jacket, earning me an irritated glare from a middle-aged guy in a suit who had to step out of the way to avoid my bag. His suit looked like it cost about as much as Oscar's. The pricey suit and his *I'm more important than God and all His angels* attitude made me think the guy was a lobbyist, probably one with a law degree. He likely drove a late model BMW, had a pre-med son who played lacrosse at Harvard, was on a first name basis with the White House Deputy Chief of Staff, and had a five hundred dollar a week coke habit. People like him were like roaches in this part of K Street. Lawyers in general were like roaches all over the city, not just on K Street. There were more lawyers per capita in D.C. than any other place in the United States. All the legal brainpower was needed to figure out how to legally screw the rest of the country.

K Street was not only a major D.C. thoroughfare, but this part of it was also ground zero for D.C.'s lobbying industry. "Lobbying" was a euphemism for "Senator, I'll give you a boatload of money, and in exchange you'll let me write the bills benefitting my industry that you will then vote into law under the guise of helping the American people." It was legalized bribery. The fact I was the one in trouble when criminal activity was going like gangbusters out in the open showed there was no justice in this world. Maybe there was some in the next, though I doubted it. I had been to enough seances during my magical training and spoken to enough dead people that I wasn't holding my breath.

I stuffed my jacket into my bag, pulled out a pair of designer sunglasses, then slung the bag over my shoulder again. I tugged on my blouse, detaching it from where the humidity had pasted it onto my skin. I had just gotten out here and was already sweating. Before she abandoned me and Dad when I was very little, my mother used to say girls didn't sweat, they glistened. I was glistening like a pig. If I stood in this heat much longer, I'd be putting on a wet t-shirt contest.

That gave me an idea. Maybe stripping was what I'd do for the next couple of months to bring in much needed cash.

I looked down at my potential moneymakers. I sighed. My chest wasn't impressive enough to support a new career. I was again envious of Willow's rack.

I hesitated in the middle of the sidewalk. I didn't know what to do with myself. I wasn't used to getting off work this early. There were a lot of things I could do in the District in the middle of the day, but a lot of them involved money, something I had a limited supply of. With no cash coming in for the next two months, I needed to tighten my belt.

I could always go to one of the nearby Smithsonian Museums, all of which were free. I was one of the rare

Washingtonians who was born and raised here, rather than having moved here from elsewhere for work like so many other people. My father, who had been far more cultured than I, had taken me to the Smithsonian all the time when I was a kid. I still went a lot. Going reminded me of Dad. I also often went to the Smithsonian for first dates so those dates wouldn't think I owed them something. A lot of guys thought buying you a burger and a beer also rented your vagina for the night.

Not that I dated much, anyway. Human/Otherkin relationships were taboo. Halflings like Oscar were rare. I didn't often date other Gifteds, either. Gifted men often acquired money and status with their magic, meaning they had their pick of the female litter, both Gifted and mundane. As a result, I'd found most Gifted men to be insufferably arrogant. I mixed romantically with them as well as oil and water. And mundane men? Yuck. The mundane world was full of weaklings and crybabies who'd wet themselves if they caught a glimpse of what was going on under society's hood.

Oops, I had almost forgotten about Metahuman men. The idea of being with a Hero was intriguing. Then again, they came with their own set of issues. Grown men running around fighting crime in masks and underwear? Really? I didn't have to be a professional therapist to know that anybody who did that had some deep-seated psychological issues.

I shook my head, and I shoved thoughts of dating aside. I didn't need a man right now, unless he was going to be my sugar daddy. I needed a job. More to the point, I needed money.

I didn't feel like going to a museum. I was still too mad about getting suspended to pay attention to exhibits. I'd just go home.

My decision made, I started walking. As I moved, I got the weirdest feeling I was being watched, like when the nape of your neck tingled, and you looked up to find someone staring at you.

I looked around. No one on the street seemed to pay me the slightest bit of attention. Forced idleness was making me paranoid.

Trying to shake off the strange feeling, I walked toward the nearby bus stop to catch the bus that would carry me to my apartment in Columbia Heights. I did not own a car. A car would be yet another monthly expense I could ill afford. Assuming I could even buy one. The last time I had tried to finance something, the guy who checked my credit had laughed me out of his office. I didn't need to own a car to get around, anyway, thanks to ride sharing services, cabs, and the District's extensive public transportation system. Also, D.C. was not that big as far as major cities went and had sidewalks everywhere. It was a very walkable city.

I weaved my way through a throng of men and women who walked purposefully, spoke on their cell phones like they were planning world domination, and were dressed for success. Dodging them all made me feel like the star of a video game. *Frogger: The Lobbyists Dodging Edition.*

Hmmm. Maybe all these well-dressed guys and gals were onto something. I could become a lobbyist instead of a stripper. How hard could it be? Buy an expensive suit, walk up to a congressman and say, "Here's some money. Now dance, monkey, dance."

Now that I thought about it, being in Congress and being a stripper had a lot of similarities.

"I don't think I've ever seen you out and about this time of day, child," a voice said, interrupting my reverie and making me jump.

I tensed, turned my head, then relaxed when I saw who it was.

"Hi Daniel. I'm . . . just taking a walk." I stopped myself just in time from admitting I had been suspended. Daniel and I were friendly, but not friends. He didn't need to know all my business. It was not as though I really knew anything about him. I didn't even know his full name. I would just chat with him when I encountered him on the street, which I had been doing from time to time the past few weeks, usually near my apartment.

Besides, I would feel like the world's biggest jerk complaining to Daniel about anything. My job problems paled to insignificance compared to Daniel's life problems. He was homeless.

I could not begin to guess how old Daniel was. Though he had the clear brown eyes, moderately unlined face, dark brown hair, and upright gait of a man in his thirties or forties, his long gray beard belonged on an old man. An air of sorrow hung around him like a dark cloud, like he had lived longer than he had expected to and was none too pleased about it. I supposed life on the streets would do that to you. His hair was long and unkempt, his nails unclipped and dirty, and his white skin was dark with grime. He wore pants than might have started off as khaki-colored, but that had been many years and stains ago. Too big for Daniel's wiry frame, the pants were held up by a dirty rope around Daniel's waist. He wore a tattered black blazer over a holey t-shirt.

As far as I knew, the rusting shopping cart Daniel pushed around contained everything he owned. A thick stick stuck out of one end of the cart. The gnarled, dark wood was so long it was more like a staff than a walking stick. I had no idea why I always saw Daniel with it; he walked around just fine without using it. Maybe it had some sort of sentimental value, or maybe he used it to defend himself. Lowlifes saw homeless people as easy prey.

Daniel had a hand in his pocket, playing with unseen coins there. Daniel played with those coins every time I saw him, like they were a reminder of something. Some sort of tic, or maybe simply a nervous habit.

"Mighty hot day for a walk, child," Daniel said, the jingling of the coins in his pocket providing background music to his words. The non-patronizing way he always called me *child* added to the impression he was far older than I. The people walking by us pointedly ignored Daniel like he was invisible.

"I laugh in the face of heat stroke," I said, though I was more concerned about Daniel getting heat stroke with that black jacket on.

Daniel bent over to rummage through a trash bin. He pulled out a half-eaten donut. He squeezed and sniffed it. The pastry must've passed inspection, because Daniel dusted dirt and ants off and put it on a piece of carboard on top of his cart. Tonight's dinner, maybe.

I pulled my bag off my back again and rummaged through it for my wallet. "This is not the best place for you to be, Daniel. The people around here are too hoity-toity. I'm surprised the police haven't already hassled you." The cops usually made sure D.C.'s sizable homeless population stayed out of wealthy areas and the areas tourists frequented. The cops funneled the homeless to the poor areas, especially Southeast D.C., and let them run wild there.

"I fear only the Almighty Father, not men and their weapons," Daniel said as he played with the coins in his pocket again. His brown eyes were intelligent and knowing, like they had seen everything.

"Uh-huh," I grunted noncommittally as I pulled out my wallet, not wanting to get into a religious discussion, though I wondered what kind of father would let so many of his children live on the street like animals. I also wondered how Daniel had become homeless. He did not seem crazy or like he had substance abuse problems like so many other homeless people did.

I looked down. I had forty-six dollars in my wallet. With all the bills I was behind on and with no money coming in for the next couple of months, I needed to hold onto all the money I could. However, I always made a point to give Daniel some money when I saw him. I sighed. Why couldn't one of these rich douchenozzles around here hook Daniel up?

I pulled out a couple of ones. I started to hand them to Daniel, but I hesitated when my eyes fell on the half-eaten donut. Yeah, I had debts and bills to pay, but this guy was sifting through garbage for something to eat. *I cried because I had no shoes until I met a man who had no feet.* Helen Keller said that. That guilt-tripping blind bitch.

Before self-interest changed my mind, I pulled all the money I had out of my wallet and thrust it into Daniel's hands. "Buy something decent to eat. Water too. It's a hot day. And I'd suggest you move on to another part of the city. I'd hate for you to get arrested for vagrancy."

Daniel's eyes moved from the money in his hands back to my face. "May God bless you, child." The money disappeared into his pants pocket.

"Thanks," I said, slinging my bag over a shoulder again. "I need all the help I can get." I turned away before I changed my mind and snatched some of the much-needed money back. Nobody likes an Indian giver.

Daniel and I separated, with me continuing up the street toward the bus stop. I wondered how much money I had left on my Metro card. I hoped I had enough to pay for the bus home. Though I didn't regret giving Daniel money, I wished I had held onto a couple of bucks to make sure I could cover bus fare. Maybe Oscar had been right about me being impulsive.

"Help! Somebody help!" a woman's voice cried, piercing my thoughts of how broke I was.

A stoop-shouldered old black woman was being pulled into an alley up the street by three young men in t-shirts and sagging jeans. The old woman swatted at the young men with her purse ineffectually. The black and brown-skinned youths looked like extras from a bad movie, some racist casting director's idea of what a big-city thug looked like.

The thugs and their victim disappeared into the alley, with the old woman's cries for help trailing behind them. There were plenty of pedestrians and passing cars, but no one stopped to help the woman, or even looked in her direction. Maybe everybody was too busy making money and amassing power to make time for a little old lady. So many lawmakers to bribe, so little time.

Where's a Hero when you need one? I thought for the second time in just a few days. I groaned as I pulled my knapsack over both shoulders, knowing I'd have to step up again. First Daniel, now this. Was I the only person in this selfish, self-involved city who did the right thing?

My bag secure, I ran up the street toward the alley the woman had been pulled into. People turned to stare as I dodged around them. They noticed me, but not an old lady screaming her head off. I guess the old lady's mistake was in not being a white woman wearing a half-wet blouse containing bouncing boobs and who was running like a demon was chasing her.

I darted into the alley. The alley was shrouded in shadow thanks to the tall buildings on either side of it. I was swallowed by gloom, like I had entered a different world.

I blinked, my eyes adjusting to the comparative darkness. Garbage and trash bins lined either side of the alley. The smell was a potent mix of rotten vegetables, decaying meat, and moldy coffee grounds.

The alley dead-ended against the side of another building. The old woman was on the ground, cowering with her back against the end of the alley. Her eyes were wide with fear. The three thugs stood around her. Their backs were to me.

I skidded to a stop a few feet behind the three yahoos. I was breathing hard thanks to my sprint. My back ached where the gargoyle's claws had raked me.

The little old black lady was tiny compared to the three thugs. I said, "Didn't anyone ever teach you knuckleheads to pick on someone your own size? Really, hassling an old lady? Did you run out of puppies to kick?"

The three turned around to face me. Two black, one Hispanic. They were my height or taller, no older than twenty. Lean guys, corded with muscle. They were risking imprisonment to rob someone unlikely to have much. D.C. street thugs at their finest.

Oscar's ear beating about not using magic in front of mundanes still rang in my ears. No matter. I didn't need spells. Me against three mundanes? I liked my chances. This was actually just what the doctor ordered. I'd take my frustrations out on these criminal masterminds, and maybe pound some sense into them at the same time. Win, win.

The old woman rose to her feet. Surely she wasn't trying to help me. While I admired her spunk, she was liable to get hurt.

"Get out of here lady," I said. "I got this."

The woman didn't flee. Instead she lifted a hand to her throat where an amulet hung from a chain. "Help! Somebody help!" came the voice I had heard on the street. The lady hadn't moved her mouth; rather, the voice came from the amulet itself. Magical ventriloquism, no doubt on a frequency only a citizen of the magical world could hear. No wonder no one else had reacted to the woman's screams.

The woman's lined black face split into a wide, satisfied grin. Her teeth elongated, becoming yellow fangs. She dropped to all fours, her body shimmering as it transformed, becoming bestial.

In the blink of an eye, the supposed little old lady changed into a giant, furry, hissing, terrifying rat. It was the size of a Rottweiler on steroids.

The young men transformed too. They shimmered into two-legged creatures with rat heads. The heads had beady black eyes, and long narrow mouths full of rows of fangs, with four sharp, discolored incisors poking out the front. The three had humped backs. Their legs were angled at the knees, making them stand at a half-crouch. Even stooped over, they still stood taller than I. Their hands were four-fingered and ended in claws that looked like they could disembowel you with a swipe. Their long, brownish-orange tails looked like steel cables. The two who had been black men had pitch-black fur; the formerly Hispanic one had matted dark brown fur. Short leather loincloths concealed their bulging private parts.

Wererats. Part man, part rat, all nightmare. I knew them by reputation but had been fortunate enough to not have encountered them before.

The wererats shifted position so they were in a diamond shape, with me in the center. They moved gracefully, flowing like water, despite how clumsy their bodies looked.

I was disgusted with myself. So much for rescuing an old lady. I didn't need Admiral Ackbar to tell me this was a trap. Like an inexperienced fool, I had fallen for the helpless little old lady trick. What was next, me smelling someone's finger? There was a village somewhere that was missing me, its prize idiot.

I had been confident when I thought these guys were mundanes. But me against four wererat Otherkin? I did not like my chances.

So, I did what any butt-kicking sorceress bodyguard on unpaid leave would do in this situation:

I pointed over the shoulder of one of the wererats. "Oh my God! Look at all that cheese!" I cried.

I didn't wait to see if they were as gullible as I was. I feinted to the right, spun to the left, juked around one of the monsters, and took off running toward the alley's exit.

CHAPTER FIVE

I only made it a few steps away from the wererats when
something whipped around my ankle. It went taut. I
tripped. I toppled over like a felled tree. I caught
myself with my hands before I face-planted. The sore hand
I had punched the gargoyle with howled in protest.

I rolled over. The end of the brown wererat's tail was
wrapped around my leg like a boa constrictor. I kicked at
the coil, trying to free myself. Despite giving it a couple of
solid whacks, the tail did not budge. If anything, it
tightened, making me gasp in pain.

I waved my hand, starting to trigger a spell. Before I
could get it off, the brown wererat twisted its body,
picking me up by my leg and flinging me into the air. His
tail fell away from my ankle. I went spinning like a fastball.

I slammed into an alley wall. The wind was knocked
out of me. I saw stars. I bounced off the wall, collapsing
into a pile of trash below.

The giant rat leaped on me. Its fangs snapped at my
throat. Instinctively, I threw my arm up, getting my
forearm under her neck, keeping her from biting my face
off. She was strong. Heavy too. Her squirming weight
pressed down on my chest like a pestle on a mortar. I

gagged in desperation mixed with disgust—her breath smelled like a rotting corpse stuffed with putrefied garlic.

I couldn't get her off with brute force. I desperately focused my will, waved my hand, and gasped, "Ventus!"

Trash swirled in the air as concentrated gale force winds lifted the giant rat off me. She hurtled through the air, smashing into the wall on the other side of the alley with a loud thump and an inhuman squeal. She stuck on the wall for a split second before sliding down into the garbage below like she was a wet spitball. Now she knew how it felt.

I struggled unsteadily to my feet. I used the summoned wind to pelt the male wererats with garbage, hoping to get a chance to catch my breath.

No such luck. They sprang out of the trash storm and at me like monsters out of a bad dream. They attacked, slashing at me with their claws, all three at once. Chivalry truly was dead.

The windstorm died as I lost my concentration. I struggled to keep the wererats from landing a lethal blow. Claws raked my forearm, drawing blood. My foot shot out, connecting with the leg of the offending black wererat. There was a satisfying crunch. Screeching in agony, the wererat toppled to one knee, his leg no doubt broken.

I clouted another on the side of the head. Holy hard heads! I hurt my arm probably as much as I hurt the wererat. He staggered but immediately recovered. He counterattacked in a blur of fur and claw, accompanied by his fellows. I blocked and avoided some of their blows, but not all.

They didn't let up for a second, not giving me time to cast a spell or room to escape. Hand-to-hand and three-on-one, I was outmatched. I knew it, and they knew it. It was only a matter of time before it was night-night Sage.

In my dangerous line of work, I had often thought about what might eventually get the best of me and take me out. Wererats had never even occurred to me. What a revolting way to go.

A big blur of white dropped out of the sky, landing in the alley behind the wererats. The large, white-garbed figure grabbed the arm of a wererat that was about to swing down on me like a sword.

An angel?

The all-white figure didn't have wings, but he did have a mask and cape.

Not an angel. A Hero.

The Hero yanked on the wererat's arm. The Otherkin shifter went flying. The giant rat, having recovered from me slamming her against the wall, leaped at the Hero's face, snarling at a high pitch that made my ears hurt. The Hero, moving faster than I would have thought such a big man could, dodged out of the way. The Hero grabbed the rat's foreleg as it sailed by. The Hero spun, using the rat's momentum against it to slam it against a wall.

I kicked the face of the wererat who had only one working leg. Blood sprayed. The wererat's head twisted sharply, and his body hit the ground. The other wererat, the one with the dark brown fur, slashed at me with his claws. I blocked his arm, grabbed it, twisted, and turned. I slammed him face-first into the alley wall. He bounced off it and fell heavily. On his way down, a bit of his fur got caught on a jagged piece of metal sticking out of the trash.

Thanks to the Hero, the tide had dramatically and quickly turned. Obviously seeing the writing on the wall, one of the wererats let out a sharp whistle that sounded like a train's. He and all the others shimmered again, turning into normal-sized rats.

Before I or the Hero could react, all the wererats scurried for a nearby sewer grate. The one whose leg I had probably broken dragged his foot as he scampered away, but even he was too quick for me to grab before he disappeared down a slit in the grate after his faster friends.

Just like that, the Hero and I were suddenly alone. The Hero's face was turned toward the sewer grate.

"Well, that's certainly a new one," he said in a deep voice. He sounded bemused. "And I thought I'd seen everything." While he faced away from me, I bent over and quietly pocketed the bloody tuft of wererat fur that had snagged on the piece of metal.

Now that I was no longer fighting for my life, I got a better look at the Hero. He was pro basketball player tall, perhaps as tall as seven feet. He was broad-shouldered, and well-muscled. Something ancient and primal stirred within me at the sight of his powerful body. His costume, which covered him from head to toe, was more off-white than lily-white. His matching cape was so long it almost touched the ground. His costume completely covered his face, not even having holes for his eyes, mouth, and ears. A utility belt was around his waist.

I felt something on my head. I pulled something green, squishy, and smelly out of my hair. Gross. My clothes were a mess, like I had been doing exactly what I had been doing—rolling around in the trash with vermin. I looked and felt like a bag lady. I felt embarrassed this big, strong Hero was seeing me this way, then chided myself for the stupid emotion. I had bigger fish to fry than the first impression I was making.

I glanced at the sewer grate. I didn't like the fact the wererats had caught me with my pants down. I was eager to settle the score. If I was at one hundred percent and a Hero wasn't breathing down my neck, I might have been dumb enough to follow the wererats and find out why they had attacked me. But I was not at one hundred percent. My arm bled, my back felt like the stitches had opened, and I was as well-shaken as a cocktail.

I ached to sit and catch my breath, but this was no place to linger. I was already in enough trouble with the Conclave without getting into a conversation with a Metahuman mundane about wererats.

"I'm hurt. I need to get to a hospital," I said. I took a couple of steps toward the mouth of the alley.

"Not so fast," the Hero said, blocking my path. "I want to talk to you." His voice was slightly muffled from his mouth being covered. It was like talking to a pillowcase.

"Later," I said, sidestepping him. I'd only gotten a few more steps before I felt his vise-like grip on my shoulder, stopping me.

My adrenaline already sky-high thanks to the wererats, my temper was on a hair-trigger. Besides, Hero or no Hero, hunk or no hunk, you did not get to put your hands on me without permission.

Before I consciously thought about it, my elbow shot out. It struck the Hero in the groin. He grunted in pain and surprise. His hand fell away from me. I took off running for the alley's opening.

I had almost made it out of the alley when I felt an explosive pain in my chest. Fireworks seemed to go off right behind my eyes. I looked down to see the costumed hand and forearm of the Hero sticking through my chest. There was no blood. His arm was now translucent; I saw the dirty ground of the alley through it. It was as if the Hero had turned into a phantom and shoved his arm through me.

"I've ached to have a man inside of me before, but this isn't what I meant," someone said, as if from far away. As my eyes fluttered closed and I slumped to the ground, I realized that someone had been me.

An expanding darkness in my mind swallowed me whole.

* * *

I dreamed of wererats, street thugs, Heroes, my body being torn apart at the seams and put back together again, and of me being poked and prodded. I had dreamed of being poked and prodded before, but those dreams had involved fewer medical instruments and a lot more nudity.

I felt a sharp prick in my arm. I was jolted awake as if I had just mainlined a pot of coffee. My eyes snapped open. A woman in a white lab coat with a needle in her hand opened the door to the room I was in. She closed the door behind her, and I was alone.

Alone, but alone where? The room I sat in gave me no clue. It was completely nondescript with white, windowless, featureless walls. The floor was metallic, and a dull silver in color. A small, four-legged table was directly ahead of me. My backpack was on it. The door the woman had walked out of was beyond the table.

I looked and smelled like the trash the wererats had thrown me into. I sat in a black padded chair. I was strapped into the chair with leather bands around my ankles, wrists, and waist.

I tried to move. I could wiggle, but that was all I could do thanks to the leather restraints. The slight movement made my stomach flip and my head feel like it was about to slide off my neck.

The claw wounds on my arm had been treated and bandaged. It felt like the cuts on my back had been freshly treated too. And unless I missed my guess, I had been given painkillers. Considerate, except for the tying me up part.

Putting aside my treated injuries, I felt weird. I felt hollow, weak, and achy, like I was getting over the flu.

The last thing I remembered was that Hero's arm sticking through me. Or at least I had assumed he was a Hero since he had helped me fight off the wererats. Maybe he had been a Rogue. What kind of Hero went around kidnapping people?

For it was clear that was what I had been: kidnapped. How else had I gotten to this strange place?

I could not move my arms and hands enough to cast a spell. Fortunately, I didn't need to cast a spell to get out of this chair. I examined the leather straps again. They were thick enough to restrain a mundane, but not someone like me. My magic-based super strength would make short work of them.

I glanced around again, this time looking for cameras. I did not see any, but that did not mean there were not any around. Oh well. I certainly was not going to stay here, waiting for God only knew what to happen. If someone saw me do something no normal woman could, then I hoped they enjoyed the show.

I flexed, trying to raise my arms. I expected the leather bands to rip free of the chair. They did not. The bands did not do as much as quiver in fear.

I struggled and strained against my confines, completely befuddled.

Then I realized why I felt so weird and was so weak.

I had lost my magic.

CHAPTER SIX

Bound to a chair and unable to free myself, I felt like a damsel in distress. I hated feeling that way. I *loathed* damsels in distress. I liked to think of myself as the heroine who rushes in to save the day, and on the way there slaps the damsel in distress upside the head for being such a weak bitch.

By the time the door opened again and the big costumed man in white who had fought the wererats with me walked in, I was ready to claw his hidden eyes out for making me feel so helpless.

"What's the meaning of this?" I demanded. "Let me out of here this instant." It was not hard to play the role of an indignant mundane. Though I was no mundane, I had the indignant part down pat.

"In time, Ms. Hawthorne," the deep-voice man said. He carried a computer tablet that looked like a toy in his massive hands, and a manila folder containing a bunch of paperwork. Facing me, he cocked a hip over the corner of the table. "Or may I call you Sage?"

"You may call the cops so they can arrest you. You kidnapped me and strapped me to a chair. We're certainly not friendly enough to be on a first name basis. How do you know my name, anyway?"

"I know a great deal about you, Ms. Hawthorne." He flipped open the manila folder. "Born and raised in Washington, D.C., you currently live in a basement apartment on Tobacco Place in the District's northwest quadrant. You're behind on your rent, something that is not at all unusual. You have substantial credit card debt. Your checking account is nearly empty; your savings account is empty. You have no assets to speak of. You served three years with the D.C. Department of Corrections for assault and battery, threatening an official, and contempt of court, and you were released two years ago. Since then, you've been employed by Capstone Security Consultants. Age, twenty-six. Height, five-nine. Weight—"

"Okay, okay, I get it," I interrupted. Some things were best left unsaid. "You know all and see all. Who the heck are you? And where are we?" The nearly complete loss of my magic shook me to my core.

"Where we are is not important. My name is Ghost. I am a licensed Hero. I am also the chief investigator of the Heroes' Guild." His voice was that of an educated man.

"Bully for you. I hope your liability insurance is all paid up, because I'm going to hit you and whatever the Heroes' Guild is with a lawsuit so big, your great-grandchildren will still be paying off the judgment." Despite the bluster, I was scared and confused. Not only had I been abducted by a Hero who somehow knew all this stuff about me, but I had never been without my magic since it had manifested when I was a child. Despite what I had thought earlier, it was not completely gone. Just mostly. The magic I usually drew on from all around me was mostly absent here. Wherever *here* was. I thought I might still be able to open my Third Eye, but that was about the extent of my magical capacity right now.

"The Heroes' Guild is the organization that sanctions and regulates Heroes." Ghost paused. "How much do you know about the U.S. Hero Act of 1945?"

"Other than having heard of it, not much. I'm guessing it doesn't suggest Heroes should go around assaulting and kidnapping private citizens and scaring them out of their wits. Just wait until my lawyer hears about this." I didn't have a lawyer, but decided it was something a mundane woman would say in this situation.

Ghost proceeded as if I hadn't spoken. "In 1945, an American Metahuman named John Tilly grew concerned about the mounting casualties of World War Two. Based on news reports, he came to believe that the Allies were losing the war." Ghost recited all this as if it were rehearsed, like he had said it many times before. "On his own initiative, Tilly used his powers to fly to Japan. There he used his powers again to set off nuclear explosions in the cities of Nagasaki and Hiroshima. Japan surrendered shortly thereafter, bringing the war to a rapid close."

I vaguely remembered what Ghost was saying from school. Recess, not history, had been my best subject. "What in the world does all that have to do with anything? If John Tilly isn't about to use his powers to blast me free from this chair, why should I care about him?"

"Metahumans had existed before 1945 of course, but not in sufficiently large numbers that the government had seen fit to regulate them," Ghost said, ignoring my comments again. Rude. "And before Tilly's actions in Japan, none of them had done anything quite so . . . dramatic. What Tilly did made the powers that be realize Metahumans were potential loose cannons with the ability to change the course of history. As a result, the Hero Act sailed through Congress. It established a system for the regulation and control of Metahumans for the safety and protection of the rest of society.

"The Hero Act established the U.S. Department of Metahuman Affairs. Under the dictates of the Hero Act, any person who manifests Metahuman abilities must register with the USDMA. Further, Metahumans are prohibited from using their powers unless they are first trained in their use and receive a license granted by the USDMA and the Heroes' Guild. Such people are licensed Heroes like me. Or as we're often called by laymen, superheroes. Anyone who uses their Metahuman abilities without a license is a Rogue under the terms of the Hero Act. A supervillain, in more common parlance."

"The history lesson is fascinating," I said sarcastically, "but it still doesn't explain why you, a so-called Hero and supposedly one of the good guys, has abducted me and tied me to a chair. If a guy wants to tie me up, he usually has the decency to buy me dinner first."

The fabric around Ghost's mouth twitched. He was smiling. When I got free, I'd wipe the smile off his face with a brick.

Ghost said, "It's my understanding that a few nights ago you had an encounter with some, how shall I say, unusual creatures at the Institute of Peace in Washington."

Uh-oh. If I admitted he was right, I would be violating the First Rule. Again. Maybe I could bluff my way out of this. "I have no idea what you're talking about."

Ghost poked at his computer tablet. He moved to stand directly in front of me. He held the tablet up to my face. A video started to play. It was of me fighting off the gargoyles. So much for the Conclave's Magic Suppression Division having gotten hold of and doctoring all the footage.

The video finished playing. I said, "It's amazing what they can do with CGI these days." It sounded lame, even to me.

"You deny it is you in the video?" It was disconcerting to not see this guy's eyes. How were you supposed to know how a lie was going over if you couldn't read someone's face?

"Sure, it looks like me. But I didn't get into a fight with those . . . whatever they are." I had been about to say gargoyles before I caught myself.

Ghost perched on the table again. "The USDMA is constantly on the lookout for reports of unregistered Metas. When news of this incident at the Institute of Peace crossed my desk, I decided to investigate it myself. It was consistent with certain other incidents I have heard of. Incidents that cannot be explained away by Metahuman involvement.

"Using the footage I just showed you, I ran your face through federal and state databases. Thanks to your criminal conviction, I got a ping. Locating you after that was child's play. I have been discreetly following you for a little over a day now." I remembered that nagging feeling of being watched when I left Capstone. "I was trying to get an understanding if you're simply an unregistered Meta, or if you are something I do not quite understand. When those rat creatures seemed to be getting the best of you, I intervened."

"And thanks for that. I don't know what those things were, but whatever they were, they were terrifying." I wasn't about to tell this joker what I knew about wererats. They were a mercenary race. Wererats wouldn't piss on you unless someone paid them to do it. I wondered who had sicced these particular ones on me. The Conclave for violating the First Rule? Maybe, though it didn't seem the Conclave's style. The Conclave wasn't big on due process, but there was usually some attempt at an investigation before they rubbed someone out. Willow Wilde? I wouldn't put anything past her. Unfortunately, there were several additional people I had annoyed over the years who'd be happy to see me six feet under. My personality was not such that everyone fell madly in love with me.

I'd worry about the wererats later. First things first. I said to Ghost, "This is all one big misunderstanding. I'm not Metahuman. If you let me go now, maybe I won't sue after all. From what you were saying, you were just doing your job."

"I agree that you are not a Meta. While you were unconscious, I took the liberty of having your blood drawn so it could be tested for the Metahuman gene. You are no more a Meta than the lab tech who awakened you a short while ago."

"You drew my blood? You had it tested? You've got no right!" I was outraged by the invasion of my privacy.

"I have every right. The terms of the Hero Act are quite clear—anyone who appears to have Metahuman abilities must be tested. Normally we seek that person's consent before testing them, but considering your recalcitrance in the alley, I had you tested without it."

"Let me guess—my blood proves I'm not a Metahuman. I could've told you that. I'm just an ordinary and increasingly pissed-off woman. I guess I won't have to pick out a mask, cape, and sidekick. And here's a news flash: Even if I were a Meta and needed to select a sidekick, it wouldn't be you."

The fabric of Ghost's mask twitched again. "Since, as you say, you are not a Metahuman, that begs the question of how you were able to do the things you did at the Institute of Peace and in the alley against those powerful rat creatures."

I didn't respond. The room fell quiet. Neither of us spoke for minutes. Though I couldn't see Ghost's eyes, I felt the weight of his gaze as he stared at me, motionless and silent.

I wondered if Ghost worked as a lawyer when his costume was off. This was an old lawyer's trick, keeping quiet in the hopes the person you were questioning would fill the silence and say something she should not. I had played this game before, back when I had my tangles with the law. Since this was not my first rodeo, good luck in getting me to talk. Loose lips sank ships and sorceresses. Lousy lawyers and their tricks! *The first thing we do, let's kill all the lawyers.* Shakespeare had known what he was talking about.

Ghost was the first to break the silence. I felt smug for a moment. Sage, one; Ghost, zero. Then I remembered I was bound to a chair, and he wasn't. Perhaps my scorecard was inaccurate.

Ghost said, "I assume you've heard of Millennium, the licensed Hero gone Rogue?"

I just glared at him and kept quiet. Stick with what works, that was my philosophy.

Once he saw I wasn't going to answer, Ghost said, "Millennium is an Omega-level Meta, meaning he is one of the most powerful Metas in the world. He has sullied the title of Hero by conspiring to kill another Metahuman. That conspiracy resulted in several deaths, not the least of which was that of a young Hero a couple of years ago who had barely begun her career." As coincidence would have it, that Hero had been Willow's security chief back in the day, but I wasn't about to tell Ghost I knew that.

"Maybe Millennium took a page out of your criminal handbook, Captain Kidnap," I blurted. So much for keeping quiet. My mouth had a mind of its own.

Ghost again continued as if I had not spoken. I wished I were married to him so I could divorce this ill-mannered clown. He said, "Millennium has always said that he drew his powers from the mystic plane, whatever that means. In short, he billed himself as a magician. For a time, I thought that was merely an affectation. Schtick. Like the Rogue Ares insisting he is really the immortal Greek god when I know for a fact he's just a Jewish man from New Jersey.

"Over the years though, I have heard of and seen things that cannot be explained through conventional means: Wolves transforming into men. The persistent Bigfoot and ghost sightings, in a few instances by people I know and trust. When it rained frogs in Astor City, Maryland for a solid forty-five minutes last year."

I obviously was not going to tell Ghost this, but Bigfoot was very much real. I had dated him briefly in my wild late teens when I spent a summer in the Pacific Northwest. Actually, "dated" is perhaps overstating things. Mainly I had been curious if there was truth to the old wives' tale correlating foot size to penis size. Sister was there ever!

And as for the raining frogs thing, that had been the talk of the magical world. John Woxell, an uncertified magician specializing in demonology who thought he was more powerful than he was, had tried to summon Baal, one of Satan's chief lieutenants. The downpour of frogs had been a side effect of opening a portal to Hell. It had taken the combined might of the Conclave's Inner Circle to close it again. The only remains of Woxell the Conclave later found was a film of greasy residue next to Woxell's smoking summoning circle. To my eternal dismay, I knew all too well the dangers of summoning a demon you were ill-equipped to handle.

I blinked away sudden tears at the memory, willing myself to not cry in front of Ghost. It was bad enough I had been kidnapped and tied up by this guy. I'd be darned if I embarrassed myself by bawling in front of him too.

If Ghost noticed me getting emotional, he gave no indication. He said, "In my years of work for the Guild, I have either witnessed or heard from reliable sources of other unusual things I cannot reasonably attribute to a conventional source or to a Metahuman. Interestingly, when I checked into some of those unexplained phenomena out of curiosity, some opposing force always seemed to spring into action to throw me off the scent." The Conclave's Magic Suppression Division at work, I thought. "I began to wonder if I had misjudged Millennium, and if the miraculous feats he performed were indeed magic and not subject to conventional laws of reason and science.

"Now that Millennium's criminal conspiracy has been exposed, he is apparently on the run. I say 'apparently' because he is simply nowhere to be found. The Guild has focused its considerable resources on apprehending him, as have the governments of several world powers. To no avail, despite the fact we've looked for him for over two years now. It is as if Millennium has dropped off the face of the Earth.

"If magic was indeed real as I had begun to believe and since superpowers were proving ineffective in locating a magician, I started to think that perhaps I need a magician to track a magician," Ghost said. I saw the direction he was headed, and since it was toward a certain broke and bound sorceress who was already in trouble for flaunting her magic in front of mundanes, I didn't like it the least little bit. "So, for the past several months, I have kept an eye out for any new unexplained phenomena, hoping it would lead me to another magician who could in turn help me locate Millennium."

Ghost leaned forward. "And then the footage I just showed you of the incident at the Institute of Peace came across my desk. Your abilities evidenced in that footage could be explained easily enough it you were a Metahuman. Those creatures you fought? Not so much. However, footage can be doctored, and eyewitness testimony is notoriously unreliable. That is why I placed you under surveillance, thinking that perhaps the incident at the Institute of Peace was some sort of trick or hoax. But what happened in the alley with those rat creatures I saw with my own two eyes. Those were not tricks or hoaxes I helped you fight. And now that I know for a scientific fact you're not a Meta, I can only conclude that you are a part of this mysterious magical world that Millennium is also a part of."

The room fell quiet again. Then, I began to laugh. Part of it was me acting, reacting how I thought a mundane would react if she were accused of performing magic. Part of it was near-hysteria from the pain I was in, from being bound like a mental patient, and from the nearly complete loss of my magic.

"You're as nutty as all those Bigfoot hunters," I said once my laughter had died down. "Maybe this Millennium guy is a magician as you say. Maybe magic is real. Maybe the Easter Bunny and Santa Claus and the Tooth Fairy are too. I don't know. All I know is I don't know the first thing about magic, magicians, or how to go about finding the one you seem to have misplaced."

"You and I both know better," Ghost said. I sensed he was frowning.

"I don't know any such thing," I said fiercely, not having to pretend to be angry. "I'm the victim of an attack by creatures straight out of a nightmare. I'm hurt, I'm hungry, I'm tired, I'm dirty, I smell, I've got a headache the size of your nerve, and yet all you can do is throw around wild accusations and treat me like I'm a criminal. Sure, I had some anger issues in my youth, but I served my time. You've got no right to treat me this way. You apparently have the legal authority to detain someone long enough to find out if they are a Meta. Well I'm not. You said so yourself. Now let me go. If you don't, you're as much of a criminal as Millennium apparently is. If you're a hero, I'd hate to meet a villain."

The room was quiet again for a while. I didn't mind. I was starting to find the long patches of silence soothing. I had not been lying about that headache.

Finally, Ghost let out a long sigh of resignation. "Very well. I will release you. As you say, I no longer have the legal right to detain you."

He stepped forward, so he stood directly in front of me. He bent over, putting his big head right in my face. If he was trying to intimidate me, he was barking up the wrong tree. I was too pissed to be intimidated.

"But know this: This is not over," Ghost said. "I do not know if you know where Millennium is or how to locate him. But I do know you know about magic. I suspect you can point me in the right direction as to how to find Millennium, or at least give me the name of someone who can. We Heroes take our obligations to use our powers for the benefit of the public very seriously. Or at least most of us do. What Millennium has done is a black stain on the rest of us. I will find him, and I will bring him to justice. No matter what it takes to do it. There is simply no way I am going to let a lead to his whereabouts—no matter how tenuous—slip through my hands simply because you are an accomplished liar and play the role of innocent victim well. From this moment on, I'll be watching you. If you don't want me as your shadow, you'd be wise to help me find Millennium."

Even when he was still, Ghost's presence was like a force of nature. The fervent way Ghost spoke of Millennium and his crimes made me see Ghost for what he was. He was a fanatic for justice. I had dealt with fanatics before. Religious fanatics, political fanatics, sex fanatics (Bigfoot again—he was insatiable), sports fanatics . . . I could go on. They were all the same—single-minded, dogged, and stubborn. I knew Ghost would do whatever he had to do to bring Millennium to justice. Including trampling all over the civil rights of little ol' me.

The truth of the matter was that I could probably point Ghost in the right direction. Though I was not particularly skilled at location magic, I knew people who were. A sorcerer as powerful as Millennium shouldn't be allowed to run around scot-free if he was guilty of the crimes Ghost said he was. Would it kill me to help Ghost track him down?

Yes, it literally might if the Conclave found out I helped a mundane find a magician. Snitches got stitches. I was in enough trouble with the Conclave as it was without adding fuel to the fire. If I knew what was good for me, I needed to mind my own business.

So I said, "Now you listen to me, Javert. You can chase this Millennium character until your cape falls off for all I care. Just leave me out of it. And if I ever catch you following me, I'll have you arrested for stalking. Despite what you seem to think, Heroes aren't above the law. I've got my rights."

"Javert?" Ghost stood up straight, taken aback. "The police inspector obsessed with the pursuit and punishment of the convict Jen Valjean in Hugo's *Les Misérables*? You surprise me, Ms. Hawthorne. I would not have thought you a reader of the classics."

"I'm chockful of surprises." I had never read the book, and only knew the reference because I'd seen the musical on TV. I wasn't about to admit that to this smug know-it-all. "Now are you going to let me out of here, or not? And again, where is here, anyway?" I still had no clue why my magic was mostly depleted.

"That information is classified." He pulled a piece of cloth from his utility belt. "Hence the blindfold." Ghost sounded annoyed I wouldn't tell him what he wanted to know. He could join the annoyed club I was the founder of.

I did not struggle as Ghost blindfolded me. Weak and bound, struggling would have been futile. Besides, I was just happy to finally get out of here.

Once blindfolded, I was as blind as a bat with glaucoma. Ghost unstrapped me from the chair and had me stand up. Then he cuffed my hands behind me. Even blindfolded, I knew handcuffs when I felt them. Men had cuffed me before, and not in a sexy fun way.

Ghost led me out of the room. Based on the echoing of our footsteps, we went down a narrow hall. Ghost's massive hand was on my shoulder, guiding me as he walked alongside me.

Then the echoing stopped even though we still walked. I surmised we were in a much larger area now. I heard the faint murmur of others' conversations.

Burning curiosity finally got the better of me. I just had to know where I was and why my magic was so depleted.

I dug deep, tapping into the dregs of magic that my body was still absorbing from my surroundings. I tried to open my Third Eye. Normally opening it was as easy as whistling. Now, though, it was hard, like picking up a dumbbell far heavier than the one you were used to.

It was like waking a stubbornly drowsy bear in the middle of its winter hibernation. Finally, though, my Third Eye opened. I went from not being able to see anything at all to being able to see everything around me, after a fashion.

The last time I had opened my Third Eye, at the Institute of Peace, multicolored swirls of magical current had been all around me. Here, things were dramatically different. The magic I saw was faint and almost unsubstantial, manifesting as dull flashes of light in the air, like an empty canvas had been dabbed at by a mostly dry paintbrush.

There was little magic in this environment. That explained why I had so little magic to draw from. It did not explain why there was so little magic in the first place.

Ghost was a glowing form next to me, his strong life force making his body distinct. As I had guessed from the low hum of conversations, others were in the area we walked through. No more than a dozen total, the glowing forms of the people stood either alone or in small groups. Black shadows of varying shapes were all around us, including the floor, indicating inorganic material. A wall of shadow was on the left, curving around all of us for as far as I could see.

I stopped walking and ducked my shoulders down, feigning a sneeze. Ghost's firm grip left my shoulder for a moment. A moment was all I needed now that I could see well enough to maneuver without losing my balance.

I stepped to the side, planted a foot, raised the other leg, and pivoted sharply. Even with my super strength gone, my roundhouse kick slammed into Ghost's midsection like an ax biting into a tree. The air whooshed out of him with a loud grunt, and he doubled over. It served the big galoot right. Kidnapping me, tying me up, and taking my blood to see if I was a Meta? Maybe it was legal like he said, but it wasn't right.

Before Ghost could recover, I darted toward the wall of blackness that surrounded us all. My arms being bound behind me made the sprint awkward.

I tripped over something in the black murkiness of the floor. I went sprawling.

I struggled to my knees. I rubbed the side of my face against the edge of the blocky black shape next to me. My blindfold peeled partially off, freeing my eyes. I closed my Third Eye. The magical world—what there was of it here—faded away, replaced by the mundane one.

The thing I had rubbed my face against was a brown couch, rumpled and well-used. Other couches and chairs were haphazardly arranged in the area, reminding me of what I might see in a heavily patronized clubhouse or a college dorm. Costumed men and women were scattered around the area, some masked, some not. I recognized a few: Dynamite Dan based in Los Angeles, Myth from Astor City, and Astonishing Woman from Chicago. All Heroes. The Heroes gaped at me like I had escaped from an asylum for the criminally insane.

The most striking feature of the area, though, was the massive curved window that was before me and that all the seats were arranged in front of. Or maybe it was a crystal clear viewscreen. It didn't matter. What mattered was what it displayed: The entire Earth, with green land and blue water and white clouds. The glittering orb was so beautiful that it made my throat tighten looking at it. The void of space surrounded it, serving as an inky black backdrop that made our planet even more gorgeous by comparison.

Holy celestial bodies! I was in space. For the first time in my life, I was not surrounded by teeming humanity and its combined life force that generated pools of magic. No wonder I was as magically weak as a newborn Sphinx kitten.

Movement and a deep-voiced curse behind me roused me from my gawking. Before I could react, I felt an explosive pain in my chest again. I looked down to see Ghost's well-muscled, translucent arm sticking through my chest like a stake through a vampire. This was the sequel to a movie I'd seen before.

My eyes closed as my body slumped to the floor. My last thought was of how sick I was of Ghost shoving his hulking limbs through me.

I wished I had kicked him harder.

CHAPTER SEVEN

I opened my eyes, and immediately regretted it. My chest hurt. My head throbbed, like the drumline of a historically black college was really going to town inside my skull.

My vision, blurry at first, slowly came into focus. I sat with my legs sprawled in front of me. My back was against a hard wall. The air was warm, humid, and fetid. Trash surrounded me like a play fort built by the Garbage Pail Kids. Tall buildings rose around me. It was almost night. The moon was bright overhead.

I recognized my surroundings. I was in the alley the wererats had attacked me in. I blinked, confused. Had the wererats knocked me out? Had I been sitting here comatose for hours? Had Ghost abducting and somehow taking me into space all been a dream caused by my bell getting rung?

I looked down. A folded piece of paper was pinned to the front of my shirt, like the note a preschool teacher might send home pinned to a kid. The thick glob of red wax that sealed the note shut had the imprint of a masked man on it, like a signet ring with that shape on the face of it had been pressed into the wax when it had still been warm and pliable.

I pulled the note off me and opened it. In bold handwriting, it read: *If you change your mind about helping me, give me a call. And remember, I'll be watching you.* A telephone number was printed underneath. The note was signed *Javert.*

That cheeky Heroic schmuck.

The note was certainly not a dream. I really had been kidnapped by Ghost and spirited away (hah!) to some sort of space ship or space station with a bunch of Heroes on it.

I got shakily to my feet. My legs were as unsteady as a newborn foal's. A loafer was missing, baring my left foot. It hurt. I didn't even remember hurting my foot. Correction: I didn't remember hurting my foot today. My other foot still ached a little from when I'd dropped the snake gargoyle's stone jaw on it.

My blouse and jeans looked like someone messy had used them as a napkin. Where the wererat had raked my arm was still bandaged, and the rest of my arms were bruised. They looked like they would be mottled black and blue by tomorrow. I smelled like week-old fish.

I had started the day off with sorceress chic and was ending it with sorceress shabby.

Despite not feeling the best physically, I was enormously relieved to feel that my magic was back. I had lived with its presence most of my life, like music that was always quietly playing in the background. It was as much a part of who I was as my eyes or my arms. Being mostly without it in space had been like looking in a mirror and seeing an unfamiliar face stare back at me. It had been both unsettling and more than a little frightening. I did not know how mundanes walked around feeling so weak and vulnerable all the time.

My knapsack was on the ground next to me. How thoughtful. Maybe Ghost had left two months' salary inside it, along with a polite but firm note ordering muggers to not molest me or steal my stuff while I was comatose.

I pulled my cell phone from the bag and checked the date and time. It was the same day Oscar had suspended me. How in the world—or off the world, as the case was here—had Ghost taken me off planet and back in a few hours? I had seen him fly, toss wererats around like they were pieces of cheddar, and become intangible like the spirit whose name he shared. Could Ghost teleport too? I knew of a few powerful magicians who could.

A sudden dark suspicion overcame me. Maybe that big jerk had invisibility in his power set too. I opened my Third Eye and took a careful look around. There were no ghosts of either the Heroic or spiritual variety.

Fortunately, my wallet was still in my knapsack, as was my Metro farecard. I slowly walked out of the alley and made my way toward the bus stop again. This time no little old ladies set traps for me. Things were looking up. Besides, I had learned my lesson. If a little old lady was attacked by the entire cast of *The Sopranos* tonight, I wouldn't lift a finger to help.

I boarded the bus that was eastbound toward Fort Totten. I was relieved to find when I scanned my farecard that I had enough money to make it to my apartment. If I had been forced to walk the three miles to my apartment, my aching feet's little piggy toes would not cry *Wee! Wee! Wee!* all the way home.

Though the bus was crowded, the well-dressed young passengers who looked like they had just left work parted like the Red Sea as I pushed my way to the back of the bus. Between my dirty clothes, my smell, and the pissed-off look on my face, no one wanted to mess with me.

I was pretty angry, and I got more so as I stewed about things while the bus swayed and lurched around me. Not only was I suspended from the job that I liked and desperately needed, but the Conclave would soon knock on my door asking uncomfortable questions about First Rule violations, someone had sicced a bunch of wererats on me, and I was under the microscope of a Hero who had a hard-on for someone in the magical world.

The whole thing was a mess, no doubt about it. Why did everything always happen to me? If I were watching shooting stars in a crowd of people, I'd be the one to have a meteorite cave in my skull.

I felt like punching something. Instead, I fished my Elven wine flask out of my bag and took a long pull from it. The potent, magic-laced brew quickly spread through my system and washed my aches and cares away. I smacked my lips with satisfaction. Whoever said laughter was the best medicine had never tried Elven wine.

A woman standing nearby frowned in disapproval. She looked pointedly from me to the no food and beverage sign. I stuck my tongue out at her. I have always been the very soul of maturity.

I transferred buses, getting on a new one heading north on 7th Street. Farther north, 7th Street turned into Georgia Avenue, the street I lived off of. The people on this bus were different than the ones on the first bus. Those on the first bus had all looked like white-collar workers and had been mostly white with a sprinkling of blacks and Asians. The people on this bus were a mix of white-collar, blue-collar and the no-collar poor, and every race was represented. The demographics reflected the neighborhoods this bus serviced. The D.C. of my youth had been majority black, just as it had been for decades before my birth. Though there were still plenty of black people, they no longer made up a majority of the city now. The District's longtime nickname of Chocolate City was no longer accurate. I guess Rainbow Swirl City did not sound as good.

I giggled at the thought. By now, the wine had hit my system like a nuclear bomb, blowing most of my worries to bits. I felt better about things. I was in a mess all right, but I'd muddle through somehow. I always did.

I would start by gathering some intel.

I opened the *National Inquiry*'s news app on my phone. The *National Inquiry* was a supermarket tabloid headquartered here in D.C. It was known for headlines like *Severed Arm Claws Its Way To Hospital*; *Horse With Human Head Found, Says "Nay" When Asked For Comment*; *Giant Woman Uses Washington Monument As Toothpick*; *I Kissed A Girl Bigfoot (And I Liked It)*; *JFK Faked Own Death: Lives in Cuba With Marilyn Monroe*; and *God Converts To Atheism, Saying "I No Longer Believe in Myself."* No one in the mundane world took the *National Inquiry* seriously. They thought it was parody or satire. Some of what appeared in the newspaper's pages was indeed fictional—the John F. Kennedy and God stories were completely made up, for example. The other stories and so many others which sounded outlandish were in fact one hundred percent true.

The *National Inquiry* was the paper of record for the magical world, at least in this country. Its stories were slanted to seem preposterously ludicrous so mundanes would not catch on to the magical world's existence. Mundanes read it because it was funny. Those of us in the magical world read between the lines of it to get the news.

Its publisher Devin Copeland was a big muckety-muck with a seat on the Conclave's Inner Circle, which was how he got away with his paper's constant First Rule violations. In the magical world, as in the mundane, people with money and power were held to a different standard. I interned in Devin's office before Dad died, and Devin had told me then that he had started *National Inquiry* to acclimate mundanes to the idea of magic and magical creatures, so that one day the magical world could operate in the open. Devin also owned the District's professional basketball franchise, and him getting mundanes used to the idea of magic was also why he had changed the team's name from the Washington Bullets to their current name, the Washington Wizards.

Devin had grabbed my boob one morning during my internship. I broke his finger. It had seemed a fair exchange until someone from human resources visited me that afternoon. She said I was insubordinate. Since I was fifteen, I told her Devin was a child-molesting creep. I lost my internship, yet Copeland was still humming merrily along as the *National Inquiry*'s publisher. I was a trailblazer for the #MeToo movement.

I skimmed *National Inquiry*'s articles on my phone as the bus rumbled around me. I looked for any news about increased wererat activity or the gargoyle attack on the Institute of Peace. I found an item in the Wizard's Whisperings gossip column that penetrated the numbing effects of the Elven wine:

> *A certain naughty sorceress is in hot water after publicly destroying three of Chocolate City's most iconic gargoyles without so much as a "What's a nice goyle like you doing in a place like this?"*

> *I won't name names because of pesky libel laws, but the sorceress shares the name of an herb and an author, so let's call her Dill Twain. She's under investigation by Those Who Must Not Be Named, so Dill might soon land in the soup. Those Who Must Not Be Named have already made a preliminary determination of a First Rule violation. PETA (People for the Ethical Treatment of the Animated) has condemned Dill's actions as well. Dill really is in a pickle.*

> *"I hope that witch topples off her broom and then a house falls on her," commented a prominent fairy we'll call Tinker, since she spoke*

to this scribbling scribe on background. Dill reportedly rang Tinker's bell during the gargoyle incident. Tinker looks forward to Dill being punished with relish.

This statuary lover and annoyed author cannot help but conclude this entire gargoyle incident is grotesque.

I groaned, both at the terrible puns and the information. If the Conclave had already made a preliminary determination of a First Rule violation, that meant I would go to sleep in my own bed one night and wake up to find I was in a Conclave prison awaiting trial, a trial in which I was presumed guilty and would have to prove my innocence. And since I *was* guilty, proving I was innocent would be like proving the sky wasn't blue.

I was tempted to drown my mounting dread in more wine, but I resisted the notion. With everything in my life spiraling out of control, I needed to keep my wits about me. Such as they were.

I tugged on the stop request cord, and the bus ground to a halt at my stop. I got off, and the bus continued up Georgia Avenue with a loud hiss and the smell of exhaust. The Maryland state boundary line and the town of Silver Spring were farther north. I looked at the bus wistfully, dreaming of getting back on it and escaping from the District and my troubles. Alas, the Conclave did not care two diddly-squats about mundane jurisdictional boundaries. If I knew where Millennium was successfully hiding from Ghost and the Heroes' Guild, maybe I'd go there.

I walked down Tobacco Place. The entire tree-lined street was occupied by rowhouses of differing colors and levels of upkeep. Like the surrounding area, the street was transitioning from being poor and mostly black to middle class and racially mixed. The local news called it gentrification. Longtime residents who were being priced out of their own neighborhoods and displaced called it something far more vulgar.

Two structures were stubborn reminders of what my entire block used to be like years ago: Chocolate Thunder on the corner of Georgia and Tobacco, and a run-down house on the other end of the block that the local drug dealer operated out of. Chocolate Thunder was a strip club with only black dancers. I went in there once, for a goof. Never again. I don't shock easily, but I had been so mortified by what I saw I had a hard time looking black women in the eye for a while afterward.

The evening had cooled off considerably, and a lot of people were out, enjoying the mild temperature. On the other side of the street from the house I lived in, a young black accountant sat on his porch, reading something on a computer tablet. In the property next to him, a white teacher played in the yard with his young son. Ebony and ivory, living together in perfect harmony.

Or not, I thought when I saw my black landlady sitting on the porch of the well-maintained gray rowhouse I rented the basement of. Though the Conclave was a problem, getting into my apartment without the formidable Vidalia Leverette harassing me about my unpaid rent was suddenly the more immediate problem.

Mrs. Leverette was a woman in her seventies who'd lived on this block since she and her husband Vernon moved here from the Deep South as newlyweds over fifty years ago. Vernon was a courtly old gentleman who was as sweet as pie. His wife was as hard and tart as raw cranberries. A Vidalia onion was a sweet onion. Whoever had named it that had never met this human Vidalia.

I wished my knowledge of magic was advanced enough that I could cast an invisibility spell. Maybe if I walked really quietly, Mrs. Leverette wouldn't see me.

Nope, no such luck. Mrs. Leverette looked up as I crept up the stairs to the house's small yard. I froze like a deer who had just been spotted by a hunter.

"Hiya, Mrs. Leverette," I said, forcing a cheeriness I did not feel. "Mighty nice weather we're having this evening."

"Be nicer if my bank account weren't emptier than it should be," she harrumphed pointedly. She folded the newspaper she had been reading and impaled me with her steely gaze. Why did I get the feeling she had been sitting here for hours waiting for me to show up? Ambush predators could learn a lot from this lady.

I laughed nervously. "Yeah, well, money's tight for everyone these days." Even the rare times I wasn't behind on my rent, Mrs. Leverette still somehow made me feel like I was a jewel thief with a pocketful of loot who had run into a cop—nervous and eager to not draw attention to herself.

Feeling like a cockroach scurrying away when the light has been turned on, I tried to hasten down the walkway leading to my apartment door on the side of the house.

With speed that belied her age, Mrs. Leverette glided off the porch and blocked my path. Less than one hundred pounds dripping wet, even at her age she was as lithe as a dancer. She had short salt and pepper natural hair, brown eyes that missed nothing, and dark skin dotted with moles. She had a knack of making me feel tiny even though I was much taller and heavier than she. Maybe it was a trick she mastered over decades of teaching in public schools.

Mrs. Leverette looked me up and down with obvious disapproval. Her broad nose wrinkled as she got a whiff of me. I felt like what the cat dragged in under her gaze.

"What in the world happened to you?" Her teeth were white and perfectly even. Dentures, probably.

"You wouldn't believe me if I told you. Well, it's been nice chatting. Good night." I tried to sidestep her. She blocked me again. Maybe Ghost should sic Mrs. Leverette on Millennium.

"Where's the money you promised you'd have for us? You're already two months behind on your rent." It looked like the small talk portion of the conversation was over. I mourned its passing.

"A few things came up. I'll have it for you as soon as I can. I already worked out a grace period with your husband." I tried moving around her again, and she blocked me again. It was worse than trying to shake a cold.

"As soon as you can is not good enough. It's always the same story with you. 'I'll have it for you tomorrow.' 'I'll have it for you next week.' Yet tomorrow and next week never seem to arrive. I know you have a good paying job. What in the world do you spend your money on? It's certainly not your rent." Mrs. Leverette shook her head in disgust. "As for Vernon, you leave him out of this. He's a good man. Too good for his own good sometimes, I fear. You bat those pretty blue eyes of yours at him, give him a sob story and a backside wiggle, and suddenly he's looking out for you more than he is for himself."

"I don't bat my eyes. And I certainly don't wiggle my backside," I protested, outraged. Who was I, Willow Wilde?

"Please," she scoffed in disbelief. "I haven't always been old. In my time I did my fair share of eye-batting and backside-wiggling to get what I wanted, so I know what it looks like. I'm not as innocent as my Vernon. Or as vulnerable to your wiles and sob stories. In the time you've lived here, you haven't paid your rent on time. Not once." She shook her folded-up newspaper at me. I felt like a dog who had taken a crap on her carpet. "I've had enough of your freeloading. You have exactly one week to get current on your rent, plus all the late fees our lease calls for. It's a week more than you deserve. If you don't pay up, I'll throw you out. Given your record and your rental history, it'll be tough for you to find another place, especially a place as nice as this one. But you can go live on the street for all I care. At least then you'd be somebody else's problem."

Something inside of me snapped. Being spoken to like this after the day I'd just had was too much.

I stood up straight so I towered over Mrs. Leverette even more. If she found me intimidating, she did not show it. "Listen, I realize that I'm in the wrong here. But I'm doing the best I can to get the money together. I'll get it to you guys eventually." Now seemed a bad time to admit I had been suspended from work. Occasionally—but only occasionally, unfortunately—I was capable of self-editing. "But in the meantime, I know something about D.C. landlord-tenant law. If you want to evict me, you must first give me thirty days written notice. This browbeating you're giving me right now does not count as such notice. After the thirty-day notice period passes, only then can you file an eviction action with the court. It will take a while for the court to schedule and then hold a hearing. Then, and only then, can I be evicted. Call it four or five months from now.

"So you can go through the time, expense, and stress of jumping through all those hoops, or you can be a little more neighborly, stop hassling me, sit back in your rocking chair, bounce your grandkids on your knee, and take it easy while I finish getting the money together." If I had a mic handy, I would have dropped it.

Unfortunately, Mrs. Leverette was not as impressed with my speech as I was. Her eyes flashed with anger.

"You're right about how the landlord-tenant system works," she said. "But you're wrong that I'm going to wait that long. If you have not paid up in a week, I'm going to have my three sons come over here and have every stitch of your things thrown out on the street. Then we'll change the locks." She punctuated her words by tapping me in the chest with her newspaper. If she were not an old woman, I would have put her in the obituary section. "Then you would be in the position of suing me over your stuff and to get back into your space. By then, your stuff will be long gone, taken by your fellow ne'er-do-wells wandering the streets who'll take anything that's not bolted down. And I wonder how much sympathy a court will have for someone who can't be bothered to pay her rent due to her elderly landlords."

"You wouldn't dare," I hissed.

"Watch me."

We stood there for a moment, glaring at one another, neither of us wanting to give an inch. Then, before I completely lost my temper and did something I couldn't undo, I stepped around Mrs. Leverette and continued toward my apartment.

I seethed. I'd been bested by a mundane septuagenarian. Thank God my coworkers weren't here to see this. Loopy would never let me hear the end of it. First Oscar, then the wererats, then Ghost, now this. Some days it did not pay to get out of bed.

"One week from now, I said. And not a second longer." Mrs. Leverette's voice trailed after me like a banshee's cry.

I fumbled for my keys, muttering darkly to myself about Mrs. Leverette and her sons as I went down the short patch of stairs to my apartment's front door. She brandished her boys like they were a weapon. Nonetheless, I knew I could handle three brawny mundanes as long as they didn't bring a few wererats or an intangible Hero along with them to help. I could not handle, however, without exposing the fact I was no ordinary woman. I remembered what the *National Inquiry* column said about the Conclave. This dill was already in a pickle without adding to the brine by sending a bunch of mundanes to the hospital. On top of that, I did not know if I could bring myself to rough up three guys who would only be trying to rid their parents of what they perceived to be a deadbeat.

I took a long, calming breath as I stood in front of my door. Mrs. Leverette was right—I did have a good paying job. Unfortunately, I couldn't seem to stop myself from spending a ton of money on non-essentials like designer clothes, absurdly expensive Elven wine, and eating out at pricey restaurants. I didn't need to consult a therapist to know I was trying to fill a hole in my heart with stuff I didn't need.

I'd deal with my collapsing financial house later. Tonight, I would take a nice hot bath, one or two or two dozen aspirin, and get some sleep. My ever-expanding list of problems would wait until tomorrow.

I gave the door a quick glance to make sure nothing had been disturbed. A horseshoe hung above the heavy wood door, and above the shoe was a large cross. I was not particularly religious. When I walked into a church, God probably elbowed Saint Peter and asked him who I was. Plenty of other people were religious though, and those billions of believers gave religious symbols like the cross lots of protective magical power.

A small bundle of rowan twigs and a sprig of wolf's bane hung from nails on the left doorframe; a small bagua mirror and a head of garlic hung on the right. The Leverettes thought I was just overly superstitious of things that went bump in the night. Little did they know I'd seen the things that went bump in the night, and those things did not always confine themselves to just the night.

Also, every three months or so I sprinkled on and around the door holy water from the Basilica of the National Shrine of the Immaculate Conception, a mouthful of a church that was about a thirty-minute walk from here. The Basilica was the largest Catholic church in the country and the second largest in North America. God never smote me during one of my jaunts to the Basilica, so I guess Saint Peter vouched for me.

I waved my hand, exerted by will, and said "Resero." I felt the wards on my apartment unlock and slide away. The same Capstone ward specialist who had put the wards on the panic room at the Institute of Peace had done me a favor and warded my apartment for me.

Now that the wards were deactivated, I used my keys to unlock the door's three locks. I went inside and deactivated the burglar alarm before it started shrieking at me. Despite being a sorceress, I did not sneer at technology's usefulness.

Between my alarm, locks, wards, door talismans, holy water, and the residual protective threshold magic built up over the years of the Leverettes living in this house and raising a loving family in it, good luck to any person or creature who tried to get in here without my consent. I was as well-protected as a secret sorceress could be. As the last few days showed, I made enemies as easily as a baby made diaper doo. My apartment being so hard to get into let me sleep easy at night.

Tired, I yawned so wide that my jaw cracked. I stretched, and I regretted it. My whole body ached. It had been a long, eventful, stressful, and strange day. The adrenaline I had been operating on much of the day was receding, leaving exhaustion in its place. Sleep would not be a problem tonight.

I dropped my keys on a stand by the door. Seeing a glow of lights, I chided myself for leaving the lights on in the room that served as everything but kitchen, bedroom, and bath. Someone with my money problems needed to be more frugal.

I stepped out of the gloom of the short hallway and into the light of the room.

"Hi!" a middle-aged stranger dressed in only my crimson bathrobe said cheerily. He sat in one of my kitchen chairs with his bare feet propped up on another chair. He was surrounded by empty beer bottles.

The man looked me up and down. "You look terrible," he said. "Oh, I had a few of your beers. Home invasion makes me thirsty."

CHAPTER EIGHT

Cursing, I sprang for my end table. I ripped its drawer open and shoved my hand inside.

The man said, "Looking for this?" He brandished the Smith and Wesson 629 revolver my father had shot himself with. He didn't point it at me; he held it as if it were a baseball, with his fingers around the barrel and trigger guard. The fact this guy was touching Daddy's gun made me madder than the fact he had broken in, and I was plenty mad about that.

I leaped over my small couch like it was an Olympic hurdle. In a wink, my hands were on the stranger—one on his hand with the gun, one around his throat. Beer bottles went flying.

I jerked him off my chair, surged forward, and slammed him against the wall. My robe parted, exposing the stranger's hairy chest and naked white flesh. There were scars all over his body, but especially on his torso. Five silver coins fell out of the robe's loose pockets and hit the linoleum floor with a clatter. Though shiny, something about the coins made them seem ancient. On the face of the coins was a man with laurel leaves on his brow; on the back was an odd-looking bird. It's weird the little details your mind noted in the heat of the moment.

I sharply smacked the man's wrist against the wall twice. He dropped Dad's gun with a pained cry. The weapon clattered on the linoleum floor. I kicked it across the room.

The man was slightly taller than I and wiry. I had him pinned to the wall like he was a bug in a collection, holding him up so his feet were off the ground. My fingernails dug into his neck, drawing blood. My palm shoved hard into his Adam's apple. His neck's skin was soft and smooth, like it was freshly shaved.

The man struggled against me, kicking. I brought a knee up, ramming it into his exposed genitals. He yelped and stopped struggling as hard.

"You've got five seconds to tell me who you are and what you're doing here, or I'll ram your balls into your throat," I snarled.

"My child, I can explain," the man gasped hoarsely. His brown hair was damp, making it look almost black. He smelled of lavender. The scent was all too familiar. Unless this guy shopped at the same high-end soap store I did, he had taken a shower in my bathroom. His breath was minty, like he had just gargled with mouthwash. It smelled like mine too.

Breaking into my place, using my things, touching Dad's gun . . . everything about this guy was a violation.

"Two seconds." My knee lifted on its own accord. I was pissed, acting on auto-pilot.

Out of the corner of my eye, I saw something fly across the room. It smacked into the man's hand I had knocked Dad's gun out of. It was a long staff of gnarled, old wood, so dark it was almost black. It started shimmering slightly in the man's hand in all the colors of the rainbow, like rainbow swirls on a soap bubble's surface.

I slid my hand across the man's wrist, intending to snatch the staff out of his hand. The staff's rainbow colors flashed brightly when my hand touched the wood. A massive invisible force hit me like a tidal wave. I was flung backward through the air, head over heels.

I slammed into my couch. Cushions went flying. The couch tipped over backward, spilling me onto the floor. I hit the linoleum hard. The couch added insult to injury by falling on top of me. Jarred, I felt the wererat wound on my arm reopen.

I stood, stiff-arming the couch off me. My head swam for a moment before the world snapped back into focus. The man was still by the wall where I had held him. He was doubled over, coughing, clutching his throat. He looked at me through teary eyes. His hands were up in what was probably meant to be a pacifying gesture. I was not pacified, though, especially not with that staff in his hand. I wanted to pick the couch up and shove it down his throat.

"Touching this is not a good idea," the man said between coughs, gesturing with the still-shimmering staff. "Especially not when you intend violence. Good Lord, you're strong. Are you all right?"

"I'm fine," I snapped. In truth I felt like I had just stepped out of a snow globe some hyperactive kid had shaken up. That staff was no joke. I had been hit with a lot of things in my time, but I had never felt something like the staff and its raw power before. It had made me feel like an ant being flicked off a giant's shirt. Was I dealing with a Meta, or a member of the magical world?

Keeping a wary eye on the guy, I retrieved Dad's gun. I went for the gun because I did not want to use magic around this guy until I knew who he was.

Stainless steel with a wood grip, the gun felt heavy in my hand. After checking to make sure the man had not taken the bullets out, I disengaged the safety. I didn't point it at him yet; I just let its barrel point toward the ground.

I said, "You're the one who won't be fine if you don't tell me right now what you're doing here and how you got in, Daniel. Assuming that is your real name." I realized now that was who this was: Daniel the homeless guy. The wooden staff Daniel always had with him and the fact this man had called me child had clued me in. Daniel looked radically different cleaned up and without his long gray beard. Handsome, even. And, not a bad body for a supposedly homeless guy I had seen scrounging for donuts in the trash hours ago. An air of sorrow still clung to Daniel like a storm cloud, though.

"I'm more than happy to answer your questions," Daniel said. His cough was subsiding. He stood up straight, then grimaced in pain, no doubt due to me kneeing him in the groin. "And Daniel is my real name. Well, it's the name I go by these days. I've had so many. Why don't you put the gun down, sit down, and we'll talk?"

I eyed the gnarled wood in his hand. "You first." Once swatted like a fly, twice shy.

The corners of Daniel's mouth curled. Part smile, part wince. "Prudence. I admire that," he said. He could shove his admiration where the sun didn't shine, and I was more than happy to assist if he did not drop that staff. Since my robe was askew, exposing Daniel's backside, I had a nice white round bullseye to aim for.

Daniel put the wood staff on the floor. He did it gently, like the wood was something sacred. The staff stopped its gentle rainbow shimmering as soon as Daniel's hand was off it.

Daniel pulled his robe closed—or rather, *my* robe, the expensive silk one I had spent too much money on, the cheeky creep—and bent over to pick up the coins that had fallen out of its pocket. Once the coins were back in the robe's pocket, Daniel was visibly relieved, like being without the coins was almost painful.

Daniel righted the overturned kitchen chair he had been sitting in before. He sat again. He winced, his bait and tackle probably still tender from where I had kneed him.

"Better?" he said. His voice was hoarse from the pressure I had applied to his throat. "Now come. Let's smoke a peace pipe together."

If he thought I really was going to drop the gun, he was smoking something a lot stronger than a peace pipe. Still holding the weapon, I moved my other kitchen chair farther from Daniel. I kicked broken beer bottles, empty food containers, stacks of old magazines and other junk out of the way and sat.

"Have you considered cleaning this place?" Daniel said.

"I don't take home improvement tips from burglars." I put my father's big gun between my legs. Freud would've had a field day with that one. "You're going to be smoking on the end of this gun instead of a peace pipe if you don't tell me what's going on right this second." My hands rested on my thighs where I could get to the gun in a hurry. Now that I had calmed somewhat, I noticed an old green duffel bag on the floor near the television. It was not mine. Daniel's, I supposed. Sherlock Holmes had nothing on me.

"It's kind of a long story, but I'll give you the *Reader's Digest* version." Daniel's brown eyes bored into mine intently. "I am an angel. The world is in danger. I need your help to save it."

Daniel's words sank into my brain. I didn't respond right away. I never had been at a loss for words before, but there was a first time for everything.

"You, the guy who was scrounging in a trash can earlier today and whose windpipe I almost crushed, are an angel? And you need my help to save the world?" I made no effort to keep the disbelief out of my voice. I couldn't believe how absurd my life had become lately.

"Yes."

"Aren't you supposed to have wings? Or is that just an urban legend?"

"It's no legend. I do have wings. Well, I did. They were removed."

"By who?"

"As the object of the preposition, it should be *by whom*, not *by who*."

The temptation to shoot Daniel grew almost irresistible. "Do you really think now is a good time to correct my grammar?"

Seeing the look on my face, Daniel hastily said, "You're quite right. My mistake. Who, whom . . . what does it matter between friends?"

I was starting to envision a bullseye on Daniel's forehead. If I shot this nutjob and buried him in the Leverettes' backyard, who would know? "We're not friends."

"Yet. We're not friends yet. You'll find I'm quite charming."

"Unlikely."

"As for *who* my wings were removed by," Daniel said, emphasizing my incorrect word with a placating smile, "who do you think? The Big Guy, of course."

"The Big Guy?" I repeated slowly. "The Big Guy meaning—"

"God." Daniel blinked, as if it was a stupid question. "Who else?"

"Oh, I don't know. The center for the Washington Wizards. The Incredible Hulk. A leprechaun if you were being ironic."

Daniel frowned. "I feel as though you're not taking this seriously, my child."

"It's because I'm not. And stop calling me 'My child.' I only stood for that before because I thought you were a guy down on his luck. Now I see you're just a robe-stealing cuckoo bird."

"Sorry. About both the robe and calling you child. The latter is habit. I'm considerably older than you. I'm considerably older than everyone on Earth, come to think of it."

"So you say. And I say I'm the Queen of England, but saying it doesn't make it so. What's that thing?" My eyes flicked over to the length of wood on the floor. "The world's biggest lockpick? Or maybe you heard I'm the Queen and decided to present me with a royal scepter. I don't like it. Not enough bling."

"That?" Daniel waved at it in a casual manner that said *This old thing?* "That's a fragment from Noah's Ark."

"Of course it is. Why would it be anything else? How stupid of me to not have recognized it. I assume you have the Shroud of Turin stuffed in the duffel bag over there. And those coins in your pocket must be a portion of the thirty pieces of silver Judas got paid off with." My robe was sliding open at Daniel's throat, exposing the scar tissue on his chest. I was curious despite myself. "How did you get all those scars? Did the knife slip in God's hands when he was removing your wings? So much for Him not making mistakes."

If Daniel noticed the boatload of sarcasm, he gave no indication. "The coins are a reminder from God of my sin. I must carry them everywhere I go. As for the scars, they're from various injuries I've gotten over the years, my ch—um, Sage. I don't remember all of them, but I can tell you about some. This one," he said, shifting in the chair to expose a pucker of flesh on his upper thigh, "is from where Al Capone shot me during Prohibition." He lowered his voice conspiratorially. "He went mad from syphilis, you know. Horrible way to die. I wouldn't wish that fate on anyone, not even someone who shot me."

Daniel shifted again, showing the side of his left calf where there was a crimson scar about the size of my hand. "This is where I got hit by French grapeshot during the Battle of Waterloo. It would make for a great story if I could say Napoleon himself shot me, but alas, no. Just some random soldier. He's taller than people give him credit for, by the way. Napoleon, not the soldier. The soldier was actually quite small."

Daniel pulled my robe down, exposing a long scar on his upper chest. "And this is where a Roman centurion slashed me with his sword in Gaul." He paused, frowning in thought. "Or was it in Constantinople? I can't remember. Cities and countries tend to blend together after a while."

A wave of exhaustion mixed with exasperation washed over me. I picked up Dad's gun and pointed it at Daniel.

"It's been a long day. I've tangled with bosses, landlords, Heroes, and vermin, and I'm not about to add to the list a burgling whack job who says a religious artifact is his homie. I'm tired, I'm hurt, I'm dirty, I smell, and I'm growing a headache the size of the Pentagon. I just want to take a bath, a fistful of aspirin, and go to bed. I had hoped to figure out how you managed to get in here first, not to mention how you flung me across the room. Now I find I've stopped caring. De-winged angels? Noah's Ark? The Battle of Waterloo? A Roman centurion? Me help you save the world?"

I shook my head in disbelief. "Either you're crazy, a con artist, or both. Either way, I'm in no mood to add your particular flavor of wacko to today's absurdity stew. I've got enough problems already. Get out and never come back. Take your kooky stories and rainbow stick with you. Leave the robe, though. That thing's expensive."

Daniel didn't get up. He seemed unfazed by the gun. He started playing with the coins in the robe's pocket. "I can see we've gotten off on the wrong foot. It was a mistake to let myself in and wait for you."

"You got that right. Add using my bathroom, mouthwash, robe and drinking my beer to the list of mistakes." I waved the gun. "Now beat it before I give you a brand-new scar."

Daniel waved breezily at the gun with his free hand. "You're not going to use that gun. You don't have the heart to shoot an unarmed man. If there's one thing I've learned while observing you these past few weeks, it's that you're no killer."

"Oh, so you're not just a crazy con artist. You're a crazy con artist stalker. One who's about to come down with an acute case of lead poisoning."

Daniel proceeded as if I hadn't spoken. That did not make him more endearing. "Your good heart is one of the reasons I'm here. Besides, you couldn't kill me even if you wanted to. Whether you believe it or not, I am in fact an angel. Which means I'm immortal." He gestured at his scarred chest. "It's how I survived all these wounds over the years. I can be hurt, but I can't be killed. Now put that thing down before you shoot your big toe off." He blinked, looking down, as if his conscious mind registered for the first time one of my feet was bare. "Why are you wearing only one shoe, by the way?"

"To make it easier to shove my foot up your—" I stopped myself, having almost violated my resolution to not curse. I brandished the gun. "Leave. Now. Or so help me, I'll field test your so-called immortality by shooting you in the head."

Daniel raised a restraining hand. "Calm down," he said. Why was it the most infuriating thing a man could say when you were mad was *Calm down*? "I can prove the truth of what I'm saying. Or rather, you can. Just open your Third Eye and take a gander."

Caught off guard, I hesitated for a beat. "Third Eye? What's that?"

"Oh please. I'm no mundane. There's no need to maintain the First Rule masquerade around me. I'm an OG member of the magical world." Daniel made flapping motions with his hands. "An angel, remember? I know you're a magician. More specifically, a sorceress. So, stop pretending you don't know what I'm talking about, and use your Third Eye."

I was still dubious. Obviously, Daniel knew the magical world was real and that I was a part of it. It didn't mean he was telling the truth about everything else, though.

Still pointing the gun at Daniel, I opened my Third Eye. The non-magical world faded away as it always did, replaced by the swirling, colorful, mystic currents of the magical one.

A white aura surrounded Daniel, like a full-body halo. It was the same sort of aura that surrounded the holy water I got from the Basilica and that was around some churches, mosques, temples, and synagogues. It was as if Daniel had been infused by the holy power of something eternal and unspeakably powerful.

That aura was not the only unusual thing about Daniel. Normally when I looked at people with my Third Eye, I could see them decaying, their life force flaking away from them. It was like watching a stopwatch that was slowly, almost imperceptibly, but inevitably ticking its way down to zero. The rate of decay was much slower with Otherkin who had long lifespans—Willow, for example—but even with people like that, the decay was still visible.

That decay was completely absent in Daniel's life force.

There was but one conclusion: Daniel was immortal.

Daniel clearly was no mundane. But, he wasn't a Gifted or Otherkin, either. He was something else entirely, something I had never encountered before.

That went double for the piece of wood Daniel said came from Noah's Ark. It throbbed like something alive with a white light similar to Daniel's aura. It was suffused with the same holy power as holy water, yet several orders of magnitude more powerful. It reminded me of a dam, holding back countless tons of water pressure. The sheer breadth of its pent-up force stabbed at my brain like a serrated knife. Looking at it with my Third Eye was akin to staring at the sun with my biological eyes—blinding and painful. It felt as though looking at it too long would cause permanent damage.

I hastily closed my Third Eye. The glimpse I had gotten of the wood's power made my head throb. I panted, like I had just sprinted through the neighborhood. It took a few seconds for my biological eyes to come back into focus.

When they did, I saw Daniel looking at me. Smugness played around his lips.

"Now do you believe me?" he asked.

My hand was empty. I had been so overwhelmed by looking at the staff, I had dropped Dad's gun. It was a good thing the gun was designed to not discharge when dropped. Accidentally shooting myself would put the cherry on top of a bizarre day.

I picked the gun up, engaged the safety with shaky hands, and put it between my legs again.

"You I'm not sure about," I said, breathless. "But that," I pointed at the piece of gnarled wood on the floor, "I believe. It feels like the Vatican on steroids."

I wanted to leave the room, crawl into bed, pull the covers over my head, and pray Daniel would get bored and just go away. Suspended from work, attacked by wererats, surveilled by a nosy Hero, and now this. Why was all this happening to me? I didn't know what I'd done to deserve someone leaving this big box of bizarre on the porch of my life, but whatever it was, I regretted it.

I sighed in resignation mixed with equal parts of weariness, wariness, and curiosity.

"Now what's this about saving the world?" I asked.

CHAPTER NINE

aniel leaned forward in his chair. His eyes burned with zeal. "What do you know about the Spear of Destiny?"

"The British rock band?" I said. "Not much. But British rock is not really my cup of tea."

Daniel's mouth fell open. He stared at me like I had started spouting Greek. "You can't possibly be serious."

I flushed with embarrassment. I felt like a child who had given the wrong answer in front of the class. "I guess you're not talking about the band. Is there another Spear of Destiny?"

"How are you a magician and you don't know what the Spear of Destiny is?"

"How are you an angel and you don't know better than to break into people's houses?"

Daniel leaned back. "Touché. Alright, let's take a step back and start from square one." He took a deep breath. I felt like I was about to be the victim of a lecture. "There are various Relics of great magical power. Some are of holy origin, some are of unholy origin, others are neutral. This fragment of Noah's Ark is an example of a holy Relic. The thirty pieces of silver Judas was paid to betray Jesus you

95

referenced earlier are examples of unholy Relics. The Omega Weapon, the Philosopher's Stone, and Pandora's Box are examples of neutral Relics. Relics are rare and scattered throughout the world. Those of us who pay attention to such things know where some of them are. The Omega Weapon, for example, is wielded by Omega, a young Hero who took his name from the Relic. Others are lost. The Philosopher's Stone, for instance, was being used by the Rogue Doctor Alchemy, but it seems to have disappeared now that he's been captured by the authorities.

"One such lost Relic is one of the most powerful of them all—the Spear of Destiny. It has had many names over the centuries: the Holy Lance, the Holy Spear, the Spear of Christ, the Spear of Longinus, and the Lance of Longinus. Regardless of what name you give it, it is the spear a Roman soldier named Longinus stabbed Jesus with as he hung on the cross to make sure he was dead. The Bible's Gospel of John talks about how blood and water came out of the puncture wound cause by the spear. Coming into contact with fluid from Jesus' body imbued the spear with wondrous powers. Those powers range from the ability to heal the sick on the benign side, to the ability to cut through any substance on the neutral side, to the ability to rule the world on the evil side. Whoever wields the Spear holds the destiny of the world in his hands, for good or for ill."

"That sounds like a fairytale," I scoffed.

"Is that a fairytale?" Daniel pointed at the wooden staff on my floor. "You've glimpsed the power this fragment of Noah's Ark possesses. The fragment is not even an offensive weapon, unlike the Spear of Destiny. Besides, if what I'm telling you is a fairytale, would Adolph Hitler have started World War Two over the Spear? Because that is exactly what happened. Obsessed with the occult and having heard of the powers of the Spear of Destiny, Hitler was convinced he would rule the world once he possessed the Spear. Since the Spear was in Vienna, Austria, Hitler's first land grab in the months before the outbreak of the world war was to annex Austria. Once the Spear was in Hitler's possession, Nazi Germany began the invasions that led to the formal declaration of war against Germany by France, Britain and others, most notably the invasion of Poland in 1938.

"Fortunately for the world, Hitler did not have the knowledge or the ability to unlock the Spear's full potential. Even so, things were touch and go there for a while. Had things gone slightly differently at certain key moments, the Axis powers would have won the war instead of the Allied powers, and the world would be a much darker place than it already is.

"But fortunately, the Allied powers did win the war. The Spear of Destiny was recaptured by U.S. General George S. Patton when he and his men advanced into Germany in 1945. Luckily, Patton retrieved the Spear before the Red Army did, which had seized Berlin." Daniel shuddered. "I hate to think of what would have happened if Joseph Stalin had gotten his hands on the Spear instead of the Americans. Stalin was as bad if not worse than Hitler, despite the Soviet Union having fought on the side of the Allies."

I suppressed a yawn. By this point I'd gotten sucked into what Daniel was saying, but it had been a very long day. "That's quite a history lesson. But what has any of it got to do with me?"

"I'm getting to that," Daniel said, waving away my impatience. "Patton supposedly returned the Spear of Destiny to Vienna after the war was over. The artifact Patton returned to Vienna is on display in the Hofburg Palace there. But Patton, being a Master Magician and a member of the Conclave, knew better than to risk a Relic so powerful falling into the wrong hands again. So—"

"Whoa, wait, hold up," I interrupted. "You're telling me General Patton was a magician?"

"Oh yes. Quite a powerful one. He concealed that fact, of course. The First Rule of Magic was in place then as much as it is now. However, if you check the history books, there are hints of Patton's magical nature. For example, he openly discussed how he had been reincarnated several times. Before the 1943 Allied invasion of Sicily, a British general told Patton that he would have made a great marshal for Napoleon had Patton lived in the nineteenth century. Patton's response was 'But, I did.'" Daniel laughed. "Patton got a visit from a representative of the Conclave shortly thereafter, who told Patton to keep his lip buttoned about his past lives. Many prominent figures, both historical and present day, are either Gifted humans or Otherkin passing as humans. Or Metahumans, but that's far more so the case historically than it is now since Metahumans are so tightly regulated by the Hero Act of 1945.

"Anyway, as I was saying, Patton did not take the real Spear of Destiny back to Vienna. Rather, the Spear that's on display there is a replica. In fact, the Vienna spear is not the only fake Spear of Destiny. A so-called Spear of Destiny is preserved under the dome of Saint Peter's Basilica in the Vatican. Another object carrying the name of the Spear of Destiny is in Vagharshapat, the religious capital of Armenia."

"First Armenia gives the world a fake celebrity like Kim Kardashian. Now, a fake relic," I joked lamely. I was exhausted, and this history lesson wasn't exactly a shot of espresso. My jokes were better when I was well-rested and hadn't just been kidnapped by Space Ghost.

"Indeed," Daniel said dryly. He was a tough crowd. "Patton shipped the real Spear of Destiny to friends of his here in the United States for safekeeping. High-level members of the Conclave. After all the horrors of World War Two, they concluded the Spear was too powerful for anyone to know where it was. Since they did not know how to destroy such a powerful Relic, they hid it. They were so committed to the idea that no one should ever discover the location of the Spear that they all committed suicide afterward. They hoped the location of the Spear would go to the grave with them.

"It's recently come to my attention that the Hero turned Rogue Millennium has been searching for the Spear of Destiny. Now that he's been exposed as a Rogue, he wants to conquer the world he once was sworn to protect. Millennium's hands were severed during his battle with the Hero who exposed Millennium's evil deeds. Since it is difficult to effectively perform magic without hands, Millennium hopes to restore his hands with the healing power of the Spear. With his hands, Millennium is the most powerful sorcerer in the world. With his hands intact and armed with the Spear of Destiny, no one would be able to stand against him." Daniel paused, and looked at me probingly. "Why do you have that look on your face?"

"It's a long story. The short version is that a Hero was asking me just a little while ago how to locate Millennium."

"It is indeed a small world. In any event, I cannot let a Relic as powerful as the Spear of Destiny fall into the hands of someone like Millennium."

"Why you? Why is that your responsibility? Tell some Heroes about it and let them handle it. This looks like a job for supermen."

Daniel stared at me in disbelief again. "I've told you that one of the most potent artifacts in history might fall into the hands of an unscrupulous sorcerer, and you're making jokes?"

"I do that sometimes when I'm skeptical. And boy, am I ever."

"I'm making it my responsibility for two reasons. One, because it's the right thing to do. Two, because if I foil Millennium's quest for the Spear, I'll earn my angel wings back. I'll be allowed back into Heaven."

"What did you do to get kicked out? Did you bore the heavenly host to death by talking too much? I see you haven't learned your lesson."

"I questioned divine policy. If you read the Bible, especially the Old Testament, you know that sort of thing is frowned upon. I was stripped of my wings and banished to Earth. I am compelled to roam from place to place, doing good deeds to try to earn my wings back. You were not wrong in thinking I am homeless because, by divine decree, I am very much so. I cannot stay in one place for very long."

"That sounds an awful lot like the premise to *Highway to Heaven*."

Daniel ignored my reference. Maybe he didn't understand it. Perhaps fallen angels weren't allowed to watch TV. That sounded like cruel and unusual punishment to me. Instead of complimenting my classic TV knowledge, Daniel said, "I've been roaming the world for over two thousand years now. Thwarting Millennium's attempt to acquire the Spear will be enough to finally allow me to ascend back to Heaven."

Exhaustion felt like a weight on the back of my neck. "It seems like it was a mere fifteen years ago when you said you were going to explain what this all has to do with me. I'm going to have to become immortal like you to live long enough to get a straight answer."

"I'm here in Washington because I have intelligence which indicates that the Spear of Destiny has been hidden in the city or in the surrounding area. Millennium has learned the same thing. I need to find the Spear before Millennium and before my divine compulsion forces me to move on. I believe I'll need several different forms of magic to find it before Millennium does. I therefore need the services of a sorcerer or sorceress. I want that person to be you."

I was glad I was sitting down for that one. "Me? Why me? There are far more powerful and accomplished magicians than me. Go talk to one of them."

"If I approached a really powerful magician with this, he might be tempted to keep the Spear and use it for his own selfish purposes. It was bad enough with the Spear of Destiny in the hands of a mundane like Hitler. But in the hands of an unscrupulous powerful Gifted?" Daniel shuddered at the thought. "It would be almost as bad as handing the Spear over to Millennium. I won't risk it. I've been watching you. You're a lot of things, some good, some bad. Power mad is not one of them. You've got a good heart. I'm more concerned in this situation about the content of a magician's character than I am about how powerful her magic is.

"Besides," Daniel added, "as I said, the Spear of Destiny is not the only Relic. There are others, some of which can augment your abilities. I know of one here in D.C., less than four miles from where we sit."

The issue of protecting the world aside, I had to admit the idea of having something to augment my abilities was appealing. With my magic augmented, maybe I could get certified as a Master Sorceress and become a voting member of the Conclave. That would mean the Conclave's punishment for my violation of the First Rule would not be as severe, assuming they punished me at all. Rank had its privileges.

Daniel might have sensed I was wavering because he added, "And you wouldn't be helping me simply out of the goodness of your heart. I'll pay you. How does a ten thousand dollar retainer sound? I'll give you another twenty-five thousand when the Spear of Destiny is in my possession."

I perked up like a plant getting watered for the first time in a while. Then I tamped down my sudden surge of interest, remembering that Daniel had been rooting around in garbage earlier today. "I don't think you have that kind of money," I said.

Daniel stood, went to the duffel bag, unzipped it, and pulled something out. He tossed it to me.

It was a bundle of hundred dollar bills. A currency strap, bankers called it. Assuming it was a traditional strap, I now had one hundred hundred dollar bills in my hand. I quickly riffled through the bundle. It was real, not Monopoly money.

Ten thousand dollars in cash. I had never held this much money at once in my entire life. The temptation to slip the bundle down my blouse, insist I'd grown a third boob, and say I had no idea where the money had gone was almost too much to resist. With thirty-five thousand, I could pay my rent, avoid eviction, and erase some of my debt.

I looked with amazement at the money, over at the other bricks of money peeking through the open duffel bag, then back up at Daniel. "How in the world did you get all this money?" I asked.

Daniel shrugged modestly. "I've been on Earth for over two millennia. I can't have a home, but there's no prohibition against me having money. Time and compound interest are a powerful combination."

Daniel smiled down at me with satisfaction, putting me in the mind of a fisherman who had hooked a fish.

"Let's go save the world," he said as he played with the coins in his pocket again. "What do you say?"

I thought about it. Thanks to Oscar's suspension, I had lots of free time. Why not fill it by doing something good for both the world and me, and kill two birds with one stone? Daniel's money would solve my financial issues. The nearby Relic Daniel described would maybe solve my Conclave issues. And, if I found out where Millennium was, I could tell Ghost and get that nosy Hero off my back.

Add all that up, and the answer was clear. How could I say no?

"No," I said. I gave the ten thousand dollars one last longing look, then tossed it back to Daniel. "Gimme back my forty-six dollars I gave you on the street. I need it more than you do."

CHAPTER TEN

I heard somewhere that if you wanted to turn your life around, instead of tackling everything all at once, you should take baby steps: first make your bed, organize your closet, fold your laundry, that sort of thing. In honor of that, when I padded sleepily into my tiny kitchen the morning after yesterday's craziness, I thought today was as good as any to turn over a new leaf and transform the hot mess that my life was right now.

I would start with breakfast. I'd blow the dust off the unopened canister of oats on the counter and make myself some heart-healthy oatmeal, perhaps with a side of vitamin-rich sliced grapefruit.

After further contemplating turning my life around one small change at a time, I threw the grapefruit away. I had let it sit uneaten for so long that it was collapsing in on itself like a dying star. Instead of making oatmeal, I nuked some bacon in the microwave and paired it with a side of the champagne donuts I had picked up from Georgetown Donuts a few days ago. *Breakfast is the most important meal of the day* was probably just oatmeal company propaganda, anyway. The donuts were made with actual champagne and were topped with edible gold leaf. The cost of just one would feed a Third World family for a while.

Oscar paid a good wage, yet I was always broke and behind on my bills. I knew part of my problem was I lived a *Sex in the City* lifestyle when I should have been living like *Roseanne*. I would not have been in the monetary fix I was in now if I spent less money on frivolities like gold leaf donuts and more money on necessities like rent. But that realization had come too late. I'd already bought the donuts, so what was I supposed to do with the decadent treats? Throw them away? Wasting food was a sin. Surely that was in the Bible somewhere. If I ever ran into Daniel again, I'd ask him to be sure.

I bit down on a donut. A donut had never given me an orgasm before, but this donut came close. My taste buds cheering me on drowned out the sound of my thighs cursing me.

I turned the oats canister around to face the wall when I got up for a third donut. The Quaker Oats guy had seemed to be staring at me reproachfully. Body-shaming bastard.

I thought about Daniel's visit while I ate. Daniel had an obsessive glint in his eye. I had seen that look in other people before, and it always spelled trouble. People with that look in their eye would do anything it took to achieve their aims, heedless of the danger they might expose others to. If I had seen Ghost's eyes, I suspected he would have had a similar look in them.

Taking Daniel up on his offer would solve most of my problems. That was another thing that troubled me about Daniel's offer. *Beware Greeks bearing gifts* was a cliché for a reason—if something seemed too good to be true, it probably was. Something about Daniel and how he had shown up at just the right time to solve my problems set off alarm bells in my head. If I went along with every single thing a smooth-talking man wanted me to do, I'd be a single mother with baby daddies of every color in the human rainbow.

Then again, maybe Daniel had been telling me the gospel truth and the world really was at risk in the face of a Spear of Destiny-toting Hero turned Rogue. If so, somebody else would have to deal with it. I had my own problems to worry about.

I hopped in the shower after breakfast and stood under water as hot as I could stand for as long as I could stand. Though I had soaked in the bath for a while after throwing Daniel out last night, I still felt dirty after tangling with the wererats and being abducted by Ghost.

In a fancy sports bra and matching panties I knew I had spent too much money on, I contemplated myself in my full-length bedroom mirror. This was the only mirror in the apartment, and I kept it covered with a heavy tarp when I wasn't using it. Too many nasties could use a mirror as a peephole, or even as a doorway.

The gargoyle-inflicted wounds on my back were healing nicely, the wererat claw wounds on my arm had already scabbed over, and my numerous bruises were fading. The magic that made me super strong and enhanced my speed and reflexes also helped my body heal at an accelerated rate. I did not yet feel one hundred percent, but I did not feel like lying down and dying either. Good enough.

I poked my tummy. I winced as it jiggled. If eating too many donuts gave you a belly, was it still called a muffin top? *Tomorrow*, I silently vowed to my donut top, *the Quaker and I will start trimming you down to size.*

As I turned away from the mirror my belly quivered, but not in terror. It had heard my vow before. Its convex contours silently mocked me.

Like the rest of my apartment, my bedroom looked like a bomb had been set off in it. I dug through a pile of laundry in the corner, eventually finding what I was looking for: a black t-shirt with the white image of a stylized mouse's head with huge ears. I put it on along with dark jeans and black sneakers. I'd picked the shirt up at a Deadmau5 concert a while ago. Deadmau5 was pronounced "dead mouse." It seemed an appropriate shirt to go wererat hunting in.

Of all the trouble I was in, the wererats were the issue I could do the most about immediately. I did not know what I was going to do for money while I was suspended, how to keep a certain nosy Hero from following me around like a creep in a bar who would not take no for an answer, or how to deal with the Conclave when they came knocking on my door (or, as was more likely, upside my head). I *could* do something about my rodent problem, though.

If I didn't do something about the wererats, they would surely do something about me. There was no way I had seen the last of them. They were a mercenary people the shadier elements of the magical world hired when they wanted to intimidate or kill someone. The wererats who attacked me had not been merely trying to scare me, though they had certainly done that. My lingering wounds were proof those wererats had been sent to kill me, and they would have succeeded in their mission had Ghost not intervened.

But they were not merely a mercenary people—they were a stubborn mercenary people. If wererats had been hired to kill me, they would not stop trying until they succeeded.

I had enough problems already without needing to look over my shoulder every two seconds for bared wererat fangs. So instead of waiting around to be attacked again, I would take the fight to the wererats. It was better to fight at a time of your own choosing than to fight at a time of the enemy's choosing. I think the military strategist Sun Tzu said that. Or maybe it was Optimus Prime. I couldn't remember.

I would confront the wererats and get them to tell me who had hired them. Then I would deal with whomever that was. If I had to put money on it, I would've bet

Willow had hired them, but I'd keep an open mind until I knew for sure.

Anyway, first things first.

I covered my mirror back up. I unsealed the plastic sandwich bag in which I had put the brown wererat fur that I had picked up from the alley yesterday. Fortunately, Ghost and his goons either had not gone through my pockets when I was unconscious, or they had and simply left the fur where it was in my pocket, perhaps not understanding what it was.

There was dried blood at the roots of the fur. A tick engorged with blood crawled around in the bag. I shuddered with revulsion. To think I had carried this filthy thing around naked in my pocket. What if it had latched onto me? I felt like getting a flea dip.

I upended the bag and flicked it until the tick fell out, on top of my dresser. It oriented itself, then started crawling toward me. I conjured up a bit of spellfire and burned the disgusting bug into oblivion, while being careful to not set the dresser on fire. Then I teased a long strand of fur free from the rest of the clump in the plastic bag. Uncoiled, the brown strand was maybe six inches long, and as coarse as pubic hair.

I shuddered. I really wished I had not thought of that pubic hair thing.

I sealed the sandwich bag again, suppressing the urge to set the whole thing on fire. I wound the long strand around my left wrist. I gathered my thoughts, drawing on dusty knowledge I barely remembered. As Oscar had said, elemental magic was my strength, but I had trained in other magical disciplines under my father before quitting my formal training when he died.

I focused my will, visualizing precisely what I wanted to do. I waved my right hand in the barely remembered pattern over the strand of wererat fur on my wrist, and I murmured the words of the spell: "Mus invenit." *Find the rat.*

Tiny green arcs of magic sparked around the strand of fur, making my wrist tingle, as if an electric current ran through it. The green arcs then ran up my wrist, right under my skin's surface, and into my palm. There the arcs spread out, molding themselves into the shape of a small green glowing arrow. The arrow rose off my skin, stopping when it hovered about a quarter of an inch above my palm. The arrow quickly spun around in a circle several times. Then it slowed, coming to a stop in what appeared to be a southeastern direction.

I slowly turned my body around. The green glowing arrow rotated as well, keeping its head pointed in the same direction. I had invented a wererat compass. Perhaps I should've patented it.

"Ready or not wererats, here I come," I announced. I grinned, delighted to see that not all the spells I had learned as a youth had trickled out of my brain over the years. Oscar had called me intellectually lazy. This proved he didn't know what in the heck he was talking about. Maybe, after I tracked down the wererats who had attacked me, I would go to Oscar's office and throw him through his window for calling me names.

I frowned at the thought. Who was I kidding? Oscar was half orc. Even with my magic, it was more likely he would throw me through his window than vice versa.

While part of me concentrated on maintaining the locator spell, I grabbed some cash I had hidden in my closet and stashed it and my cell phone in my pocket. I put the sandwich bag with the rest of the wererat fur in another pocket in case I needed more later, or in case I ran into someone I wanted to gross out. I thought about bringing Dad's revolver too, but decided against it. I shared the contempt most Gifteds had for mundane weapons. If you carried a gun, that implied you were insufficiently skilled in wielding magic that you needed one. Plus, the gun was the only thing of Dad's I had left, and I did not want to risk losing it.

I set my burglar alarm, went outside, locked all three locks on the front door, and set the wards. Maybe I should not have bothered. Daniel had no problem getting past all that yesterday thanks to the Ark fragment. Maybe what I needed was a magic guard dog. I wondered if Cerberus was available for rent.

I walked around to the front of the house. It was mid-morning, and the sky was bright and clear. The air was already hot and muggy. Ideal wererat hunting weather. I believed in the power of positive thinking.

Everyone on my block who worked was long gone, so Tobacco Place was mostly quiet and was empty of cars. Following the twisting green arrow on my hand led me to Georgia Avenue. Since I had no idea if the wererat I looked for was five minutes or five hours away, I hailed a cab.

"Where to, lady?" the black cab driver asked. He spoke with a heavy Caribbean accent. I deduced he was not originally from the District. The wererats did not stand a chance in the face of my awesome detecting abilities.

"Just drive. I'll tell you when to start turning."

The man shrugged, hit the gas, and we were off. My request had not fazed him in the slightest. As a cabdriver in D.C., he had probably seen everything before. I might have been his fifth Otherkin-hunting fare of the day.

I cupped my left hand so the cabbie would not see the glowing arrow. It shifted and spun as the cab made its way through the city, with me telling the driver to turn as the green arrow dictated.

The buildings and people around us slowly shifted, going from well-maintained and racially mixed to run-down and almost one hundred percent black. We were in Southeast now, the District's poorest quadrant.

By the time I told the cabbie to pull over, we were in Washington Highlands in Ward 8. The D.C. area was one of the wealthiest in the country. That wealth had not trickled down to Washington Highlands. The neighborhood was one of the poorest and most crime-ridden in the city.

The cab idled in front of a public housing project which looked like it was slowly collapsing in on itself. There was so much graffiti on its façade that you could not tell what color the building had started off as. Trash littered the sidewalk and the street. The cars parked on the street looked like they were a hairsbreadth away from the junkyard.

I stuck my right hand over the front seat to pay the fare. The cabbie twisted to look at me. "You sure you want me to let you out here? This place is not safe." The *for a white woman* was implied in his tone. I doubted even SEAL Team Six would be safe here for long if they lingered.

"I appreciate the concern, but I'll be fine," I said as he took the money. Understanding flickered over his dark face, followed by a look of barely concealed disdain. He thought I was here to buy drugs. Why else would someone who looked like me come here?

If he only knew.

As soon as I climbed out of the cab, the cabbie locked his doors and peeled away with a screech of burning rubber. He could not wait to get out of here and into a better neighborhood. I knew how he felt. There were a lot of people loitering, especially dangerous-looking young men. They looked like they had been here for a while and were not going anywhere anytime soon. I got looks from them ranging from apathetic, to curious, to predatory.

Still cupping my left hand to conceal the glow there, I hastened to follow the arrow's direction before someone accosted me. I could fight off a bunch of mundanes, of course, but why draw unneeded attention to myself?

Following the arrow led me through a weed-infested lot behind an abandoned single-family dwelling, which in turn was behind the housing project the cabbie had dropped me off at. When I got to a narrow street that ran behind the house, the arrow dipped down, pointing toward the ground. The arrow directed me to a storm drain in the middle of a partially torn-up, weed-overgrown street that clearly had not seen traffic in quite some time.

I was going to have to climb into the sewer? Ugh! Was I chasing after Master Splinter from *Teenage Mutant Ninja Turtles*? I supposed I should not have been surprised considering how the wererat and its friends had escaped me and Ghost by crawling through a sewer grate.

The idea of wandering around in D.C.'s sewer system made me pause, not only because the prospect was disgusting, but also because I would be on unfamiliar terrain. I had no idea what I would find down there, aside from disgusting muck. Maybe I should just turn back.

No! I said firmly to myself as soon as the thought crossed my mind. The magical community was a small one, and gossip spread like wildfire. I would never live it down if word got out a bunch of wererats got the best of me before a Hero intervened. Who would want to hire a bodyguard who was not even capable of protecting herself? I could not continue to do what I did if I ran scared every time something crawled out of the shadows and said *Boo!* to me. Plus, there was the not so small issue of me not wanting to grow eyes in the back of my head until the wererat issue was resolved.

Thinking of Ghost made me look around for him. I had been keeping a wary eye open for him since leaving my apartment. The only people around, though, were two old men who sat on the warped stairs of the abandoned house. They eyed me with curiosity.

"What you doin' over there, girl?" one of them called out to me. One of his eyes was cloudy and seemed to look out into forever.

"My wedding ring fell off earlier, and I think it fell into this storm drain," I said.

The man barked out a harsh laugh. "You better off letting the rats have that thing than foolin' around down there."

"You may be right," I said honestly, "but I'm going to do what I've got to do to find it."

I bent over and shoved my fingers through the grates of the storm drain cover. Such covers typically weighed over a hundred pounds to secure them as vehicles drove over them and to prevent people from removing them without the right tools. I tugged, flexed, and lifted, removing the heavy metal cover from the storm drain in one smooth movement. If the old guys staring at me realized an ordinary woman could not remove the cover so easily, they gave no sign.

I looked down the now exposed hole into darkness. The smell wafting up from it was like that of a landfill. Pee-yew! I really didn't want to go down there.

I glanced at the glowing arrow in my cupped hand. I said to it, "Are you *sure* Timmy fell down this well, Lassie?" The arrow did not bark, wag its tail, or do anything but continue to point downward insistently.

I sighed with resignation. I was procrastinating.

I got down and sat on the edge of the manhole with my lower legs dangling down. Gripping the edges of the hole, I lowered myself until the hole's darkness swallowed me.

"White people be crazy," I faintly heard Cloudy Eye say to his friend, who grunted in agreement. When it came to this particular white person, I could hardly argue with them.

The smell of the sewer tunnel hit me like a wall as I dangled above it. The stench would gag an elephant. It smelled like . . . well, a sewer. I held my breath and waited for my eyes to adjust to the darkness below me.

Finally, they adjusted, allowing me to see part of the sewer tunnel thanks to the sunlight canting through the hole I clung to. The ceiling of the tunnel was an arch made of old, discolored concrete. Each side of the arch ended at narrow stone walkways. Those walkways flanked a shallow channel at the bottom of the tunnel that was about three feet wide. The channel oozed with fetid, chunky water. The water was such a dark green, it was almost black.

Space yesterday, a sewer today. From heaven to hell in less than twenty-four hours. What was next, a trip to purgatory?

I pumped my legs, making my body swing back and forth like the pendulum of a grandfather clock. At the top of a forward swing, I released my hold on the manhole. I dropped like a gently tossed ball.

I landed on one of the walkways, bending at the knees to absorb the impact from the over twelve-foot fall. I gave myself a ten out of ten for sticking the landing.

I was forced to take a breath. The noxious fumes down here burned the inside of my nose. My stomach churned, and bile rose to my throat. I gave the smell a zero out of ten.

Sewer gas was a combination of hydrogen sulfide, carbon dioxide, carbon monoxide, ammonia, methane, sulfur dioxide, and a bunch of other stuff. Some toxic, some not. I bet the wererats I was after would have a hearty laugh at my expense if I suffocated or poisoned myself to death on the way to find them.

While still maintaining the locator spell, I marshalled my will, and visualized clean, fresh air entering my body instead of the soup of noxious fumes that surrounded me. I waved my right hand in a familiar pattern and said, "Aer."

The air around my head shimmered faintly, like my head was suddenly enclosed by an iridescent fishbowl. I took an experimental breath. Though the air still didn't smell like a bouquet of roses, it did not burn my nasal passages when I inhaled it anymore.

The bubble around my head was keeping the bad stuff out and only letting in breathable air, a mixture of mostly nitrogen and around twenty percent oxygen. Though it was a far more complicated spell than the locator one, casting it had not been hard at all. Like Oscar had said yesterday, elemental magic was kinda my jam.

The air situation taken care of, now I needed to take care of the light situation. It would be as dark as a cave down here once I moved away from the open manhole above me.

I paused, concentrating, getting the spell's exact effects firmly fixed in my mind. Though I knew this was a simple spell in the grand scheme of things, light magic was most definitely *not* my jam. Some of the gases in the air were not only toxic, but flammable. If I accidently caused a spark while casting the light spell, goodbye Sage Hawthorne and hello Sage Flambé. I was immune to my spellfire, but not to regular fire. Prick me, do I not bleed? Light me on fire, do I not burn to a crisp?

With part of my will still focused on maintaining the locator spell and the air spell, I made continuous small circular motions in the air with my right hand. I murmured "Lux" while I eased my will into the circle I drew in the air.

A pinprick of light blinked into existence in the center of the circle. It spread out as I eased my will into it. In seconds, the light became the size of a softball. Its illumination cast a soft light all around me. So the light was not shining directly in my eyes, I made the ball move to float slightly above me with a hand wave and an exertion of will.

I let out the breath I had been holding. I was not on fire, a sign I had cast the spell correctly. It had taken me months to master creating light when I had gone through my magical training. God had created light in less than a day. It was further evidence I wasn't Him.

I glanced at the glowing arrow above my hand. It pointed straight ahead into the pitch blackness in front of me. I walked forward, following the arrow's direction. I frowned in concentration as I walked. Maintaining three spells at once was an effort, like walking while juggling three balls.

The tunnel gently curved left, and slightly down. The narrow walkway I stepped on was slick and smooth. There were a couple of times I almost slipped and fell into the waste gurgling in the channel next to me. I wished I had worn my waterproof boots instead of these sneakers. And a hazmat suit.

After I had walked for a while, the tunnel came to an intersection. I could proceed straight or turn left or right. I went left after consulting the green arrow.

I made several more turns like that as I went deeper and deeper into the tunnels. The tunnels transitioned from concrete to being made from bricks that, even to my inexpert eye, looked hand-molded. I surmised I was in a much older part of the sewer system now.

I also realized I was thoroughly lost in this maze of pitch black, stinky tunnels. I would have a hard time retracing my steps. Next time I would have to leave a trail of bread crumbs.

I prayed to heaven there would never be a next time.

After a while, I got a vague itchy feeling between my shoulder blades, like someone who might stab me in the back was watching me. Though I did not see anyone, I did not discount the feeling. I had a similar feeling when Ghost had been watching me, and I had been right about that. I wished Ghost had shadowed me down here. As annoying as he was, Ghost would be an improvement over what probably lurked down here.

I started hearing scratching and squeaking. At first I thought I was finally approaching the wererat I stalked. Then the noise became too loud for it to come from just one creature. And, the louder the sound became, the more obvious it was the noise came from all around me.

The surface of the water in the channel began to ripple. Whatever caused it was closing in on me fast.

Fear crawled out of my belly and wrapped its icy claws around my throat. The impulse to run became almost irresistible. But where in the heck would I run to?

Suddenly, my light was reflecting off of dozens—no, hundreds—of beady red eyes.

Rats. So many, it was like a Biblical plague.

They crawled out of the darkness all around me. They were on the ceiling, in the muck of the channel, and on both walkways. They were everywhere.

They swarmed around me. They didn't crawl on me, thank goodness, but they got close enough to almost touch me. They carpeted everything for as far as my light let me see. The squirming, squealing, tangled, disgusting mass of small bodies was everywhere.

Two wererats in humanoid form stepped out of the shadows. One was on the walkway in front of me, the other on the other walkway. Their front incisors were terrifyingly long. *The better to eat you with, my dear*, popped into my head. I wished I had never heard of *Little Red Riding Hood*.

"Oh look," one wererat said to the other over the din of squealing rats. "It's lunch."

CHAPTER ELEVEN

Though I would not have sworn on a Bible about it, I was pretty sure neither of the wererats in front of me were the ones who had attacked me in the alley. The one on my walkway, the one who had spoken, was light brown, with a patch of darker brown on its long snout. The other one had dirty gray fur. Like the wererats who had attacked me in the alley, the only clothing they wore was soiled leather loincloths that covered their private parts.

In addition to the two wererats, I was surrounded by hundreds if not thousands of squealing rats that could rip me apart if they turned on me. Despite what my fluttering stomach urged me to do, fleeing was out of the question. I'd have to brazen my way out of this.

I said to the brown wererat on my walkway, "I'm looking for someone. And you're not him. Stand aside and let me pass. I have no quarrel with you." I said it with a confidence I most definitely did not feel. However, I knew from experience that the best way to get attacked was to show you were afraid of being attacked.

The wererats let out a noise that sounded like a hacksaw cutting through a nail. Laughter. I'd hate to hear the sound they'd make if I told them the only rat joke I knew. It was just as well. The punchline was too cheesy.

"You're in no position to make demands, witch," Brown Patch said. His voice was hard to understand, alternating between low guttural rumblings and high-pitched screeches that were almost whistles. "Nothing can stop us from killing you, drinking your blood, gnawing your flesh, and grinding your bones to powder and making them into bread. You're in our domain, not Aboveworld."

They clearly weren't afraid of me. Maybe they hadn't gotten a good look at my Deadmau5 t-shirt.

I ignored the witch slur and the threat. He was trying to provoke me to violence. "I said stand aside. My patience wears thin."

"And if we don't?" Dirty Gray said.

"All right, I was trying to do this the easy way, but have it your own way. I formally request safe passage and an audience with your leader under the terms of the Conclave Compact of 1500."

They laughed at me again. "Foolish witch," Brown Patch said. "The wererats are not a part of your Conclave, or your Compact."

"True, but almost all of the rest of the magical world is. Which means that if you don't honor my request, the Conclave will fall on you like a ton of bricks. Remember what happened to the vampires? They weren't signatories to the Compact either, so they thought they could violate its terms with impunity by attacking and turning Conclave members. And you know what happened to them? The Conclave has almost exterminated them as a species."

"Conclave, Conclave, Conclave," Dirty Gray repeated mockingly. "You wield the word like it's a sword. I don't see the Conclave here. I just see a foolish woman, alone and surrounded by my kin."

"Do you really think I would be stupid enough to come down here without telling others where I was going?" Unfortunately, I had been stupid enough to do just that, but I was not going to volunteer the information. Maybe Oscar had been right about me being impulsive. In my defense, I had no idea I was walking into what was apparently a nest of wererats. "If something happens to me, a bunch of Conclave Otherkin and magicians will come down here and kill every rat and wererat they can get their hands on. The Conclave is not to be trifled with." That last part was true. It was why I was so scared of them.

The wererats hesitated for a moment. Then, Brown Patch said to his companion, "Let's take our chances with the Conclave. They're not here, she is, and I'm hungry." He stepped toward me. His companion followed after a moment's hesitation. The swarming rats parted in front of them like the Red Sea.

"Stop right there," I said sharply. "Don't you know what I am? Look at this globe of light, the sphere around my head that lets me breathe down here, and the glowing arrow hovering over my hand. Add it all together, and it equals sorceress. And as a sorceress, it'll only take a split second for me to conjure up some spellfire. Here's another math problem: Add spellfire to the flammable gas swirling around down here, and what do you get? If you're thinking 'Kaboom!' then you're smarter than you look."

The wererats froze in their tracks.

"You're bluffing," Brown Patch said nervously. "If you set off an explosion, you'll kill yourself too."

"I die in an explosion, or I die while you're chugging my blood and tearing my flesh. Either way, I'm equally dead. And an explosion that kills me quickly is more appealing than what your teeth and claws would do to me." I shrugged. "You two have a choice: You can continue to stand in my way, threatening and annoying me. In that case I'll light the invisible powder keg surrounding us, and we'll blast off to that big mousetrap in the sky together. Then the Conclave will come down here and kill all your friends and relatives in retribution.

"Or option two, we can play nice with one another, and you can take me to your leader as I requested pursuant to the Compact. I know which option I'd take if I were in your loincloth, but maybe you've got a death wish."

The wererats just stared at me. Their beady eyes glittered malevolently in the light of my glowing orb. Then they broke eye contact with me and looked at each other. They screeched at one another in what must have been their native tongue. It sounded like a bagful of drowning cats.

"Follow," Brown Patch finally directed me grudgingly. He turned and retreated into the darkness. I hesitated for a beat, then cautiously followed him. The swarming rats moved out of the way as I walked, narrowly avoiding my footsteps.

Dirty Gray leaped from his walkway onto mine once I passed him. He trailed behind me as I followed his companion. I felt like the Pied Piper of Hamelin with Dirty Gray and all his disgusting rodent friends behind me. I did not like having Dirty Gray's claws and fangs where I couldn't see them. I wished I had eyes in the back of my head. I kept my fire spell at the ready, alert for the first sign of treachery. I had not been joking before—I would blow us all to kingdom come before I let myself become a wererat snack.

There were more twists and turns as I followed Brown Patch with Dirty Gray as my creepy shadow. On a positive note, my tracking spell indicated we were moving toward the wererat whose fur I carried.

On a negative and nauseating note, droppings from the rats crawling on the ceiling fell on my head and shoulders as we traveled. It was the most disgusting drizzle ever. I resisted the temptation to brush the rat dung off. I pretended to be unfazed, like I got pooped on by a swarm of rats every day of the week and twice on Sundays. I feared the wererats would see anything else as a sign of weakness and pounce on me.

Finally, the tunnel we were in widened dramatically, becoming a massive cavern that, thankfully, had no sewage running through it. I was even more twisted around now than I had been before the wererats showed up. If someone told me we had reached the center of the earth, I would not have been surprised.

I had hit the rodent mother lode. Rats and wererats dotted the cavern for as far as the eye could see. My heart, already pounding like a drum, skipped a beat and tried to take refuge in my throat. I fought to keep my anxiety off my face.

The rats who had escorted me here fanned out in the cavern, most of them getting lost in the gloom of the large space. Other than my magical floating sphere, the only sources of light in the vast space were luminescing objects mounted high on the curved walls of the cavern.

I realized with a jolt the glowing objects were skulls. They were mostly human and werewolf skulls, but there were several others I could not figure out the origin of.

Brown Patch paused until I was abreast of him; Dirty Gray came up and joined the two of us. Both of their nostrils flared. Wererats were said to have a very acute sense of smell. A look of disgust passed between them as if it were I, not they, who reeked.

With the two wererats on either side of me, they escorted me through the cavern. I only saw male wererats. I wondered where the females were. Maybe the regular-sized rats were all male too. I had no idea how to tell a male rat from a female one, and I had zero interest in learning.

The rats and wererats in the cavern stared at me as we passed by. Their hard looks did not say, *Oh goodie, a guest. Let's break out the good china.* It was more like, *Oh goodie, long pork. Let's break her bones and eat her on the good china.* I wished, for probably the hundredth time since encountering Brown Patch and Dirty Gray, that I had told someone where I was going before I descended into the sewer. If my skull wound up joining this wall of glowing skeletal fame, no one aboveground would be the wiser.

I relaxed my will, and let my light spell dissipate. Not only did the skulls glow enough so I could see without my spell, but I also wanted to have as much of my will available as possible if the rat poop hit the fan. I had no illusions about surviving if all these wererats attacked, but I would go down swinging. There was no way I would let myself become the star of a wererat gangbang and dinner party.

We came to a short line of wererats who were queued up in front of steps to a stone dais. The dais was pitch black, and it glittered dully like it was wet.

Thirteen grinning skulls shined down on a throne resting on the dais, bathing the massive chair in an otherworldly light. Initially, I thought the throne was made of a white wood. As I got closer to it, I realized it was not. It was made of bones of different body parts, species, and lengths, arranged so cunningly that it was as if the throne had been carved from a single block of wood rather than assembled out of hundreds of bones.

It had taken me a while to realize what the throne was made of because I had been too busy staring at who was on the throne. Or maybe *what* was on the throne was more accurate.

A three-headed wererat sat there. The eyes of each head glowed like they were radioactive—red on the left, white in the middle, and blue on the right. God bless America. The creature was bigger by far than any other wererat in the room; it was probably almost nine feet tall if it stood up. Its fur was slick, and black as soot. The oiliness of the fur reminded me of how a snake looks right after it sheds its skin—slick, wet, and evil.

That was not the only way the wererat reminded me of a snake. The wererat's fur rippled and spasmed like a molting snake's skin, as if small creatures were crawling around inside the wererat, right under its skin, trying to break out.

Each of the wererat's heads bore a crown, one platinum, one crystal, one gold. Unlike the other wererats I had seen, this wererat's loincloth was made of gold cloth, not leather. I wondered if the gold was real. The thought of getting close enough to touch it and find out gave me the heebie-jeebies.

On each side of the throne stood two strapping wererats, one white, one black. Each had a gold collar around its neck, and each was armed with halberds. The shaft of the weapon was wooden, while the ax and spear parts appeared to be silver. The edges of the axes gleamed with sharpness.

"Who's this, Cerberus' distant cousin?" I asked Dirty Gray about the three-headed wererat in a low voice. I tended to say silly things when I was nervous, and I was most definitely nervous now.

"This is the Rat King," Dirty Gray said, also in a low voice. Even with his heavily accented voice, I heard the surprise in it, as if I had just asked what the sun was. "Now hold your tongue before I bite it off." I didn't like being told to shut up, but being surrounded by dozens of Otherkin with sharp fangs and claws was not the best time to take offense.

I did not know how anybody could have heard my whispered question over all the noise in the room, anyway. The noise did not come from all the rats and wererats in the cavern. Rather, two wererats knelt on the dais in front of the Rat King, screeching at each other in their native language. It sounded like they were arguing. However, since I didn't understand wererat, for all I knew they were singing the praises of the city's cat spaying program.

The Rat King's red-eyed head said something. The kneeling wererats immediately fell silent, as if their vocal cords had been cut. The red-eyed head spoke again, and the white rat armed with a halberd stepped forward. The halberd descended like a silver scythe toward the head of one of the kneeling wererats. The wererat's alarmed squeal shut off like a light when his head was sliced off his neck. Like a dropped watermelon, his head hit the dais with a dull thud and a spray of red.

The other kneeling wererat stood up while his companion's headless body fell sideways, spurting blood from its neck like a geyser. The standing wererat picked the other's head up by its ears and held the still-bleeding head over his head like it was a trophy. He lifted his snout and drank the blood dripping down from the severed head. Screeches and squeals rose all around me. They were cheering the blood-drinking wererat. I deduced the two wererats had been arguing, and the Rat King had decided on the winner. To the winner, apparently, belonged the bloody spoils.

My mouth filled with saliva. My stomach churned, threatening to spew at the revolting sight. Conscious of Brown Patch's and Dirty Gray's malevolent eyes on me, I fought the internal eruption down by sheer force of will. I forced myself to look calm and disinterested, as if this was my fourth decapitation of the day. I sensed that, Compact or no Compact, the wererats would be on me like rabid dogs if I showed any sign of squeamishness or weakness.

While the cheering continued, I glanced down at the green arrow still hovering over my palm. It pointed to the left, blinking instead of being solid green as it had been while I followed its lead. That meant the wererat I sought was close.

I looked at where the arrow pointed. I spotted in the crowd an Otherkin who I thought was the brown wererat I had fought in the alley. Without the guidance of my locator spell, I would not have known it was him. For all I knew, the other wererats who had attacked me were in this cavern as well. Except for their differing coloration, one wererat looked much the same as another to my untrained eye. In fairness, they probably thought I looked like every other human female. Kate Upton would have been insulted.

Perhaps feeling the weight of my gaze, the brown wererat turned his head and looked at me. He did a quick double-take. He obviously recognized me.

I smiled broadly at him. I mimed shooting him with my forefinger, dropping the hammer that was my thumb. The wererat's bloodshot eyes just glittered at me, and he turned to face the dais again. My quivering insides gave lie to my surface self-assurance, but I believed in faking it until I made it. I had hoped to find the wererat alone, not find him surrounded by dozens of his closest friends. Beating answers out of the Otherkin about who had hired him and his friends to attack me was out of the question here.

The wererat who had drunk the decapitated head's blood stepped off the dais, still carrying the dripping head. Several wererats mounted the dais, picked up the headless body, and carried it away into the gloom. A shrill whistle from the black wererat with the halberd brought dozens of four-legged rats scurrying onto the dais. The rodents licked the black dais clean of blood. In seconds, the dais glittered again. My stomach gurgled anew at the sight.

The rats scattered off the dais. Three wererats in line ahead of us mounted the steps onto the dais. They knelt before their king. The center head said something to them, and they answered with a series of shrieks, screeches, and caterwauls. It was like listening to a violin concert performed by six-year-olds. It set my teeth on edge.

Eventually, the three kneeling wererats were dismissed, and left the stage. Two more in line ahead of us took their place on their knees on the dais. I started to think the wererats were bringing problems and disputes before their king for him to resolve them. It was like *The People's Court: Wererat Edition*. I hoped my turn on the dais was a lot less bloodthirsty than the first adjudication I witnessed.

Finally, Dirty Gray, Brown Patch, and I mounted the dais. Dirty Gray and Brown Patch knelt as the others had. I hesitated for a beat, then remained standing.

The king's right head, which had seemed bored and half-asleep through the rest of the proceedings, perked up. His glowing blue eyes looked down at me with interest. The king's other four eyes studied me as well, making me feel like I was pond scum examined under a microscope. The constant writhing under the Rat King's skin made it appear like he was always moving, though he sat still. It creeped me out.

"Kneel before the king, Aboveworlder," the white halberd wielder snarled. At least he had the decency to say it in English. The way he brandished his weapon threateningly needed no translation.

"No," I said loudly. My voice echoed through the cavern. "I kneel before no one." A stunned hush fell over the assembled wererats. I was still playing my show-no-weakness game. My bold words were betrayed by my mind recoiling from the sudden mental image it got of the halberd whistling through the air and biting into my neck.

Incensed, the white wererat stepped toward me. My thoughts might have become reality had the king's blue-eyed head not stopped the white wererat with a sharp whistle.

"Let her be," the right head said. "I am curious what has made this human bold enough to enter our domain."

"Why do you soil our presence with an Aboveworlder?" the white-eyed head asked of Dirty Gray and Brown Patch. His snout wrinkled, as if his big nose had just gotten a whiff of me and he did not like what he smelled.

"This creature is grotesquely ugly and it stinks. We should kill it before it reproduces," the red-eyed head said.

So far, old blue eyes was my favorite. I would have laid massive odds a few short hours ago I would not now be thinking things like *the right head is my favorite.*

127

"She claims safe passage and the right of entreaty under the Compact," Brown Patch said. Neither he nor Dirty Gray looked the Rat King in the eye. I knew how they felt. Looking the Rat King in the eye felt akin to a deer staring a tiger in the eye. I forced myself to do it anyway. If I didn't play this right, my head would do its best bloody basketball impersonation on the stone dais. I'd have to rely on my wits, not my magic. The wererats on the dais with me were too close. There was no way I'd be able to get a spell off before they were on me.

"I'm perfectly capable of speaking for myself," I proclaimed, putting a lot of haughtiness into my voice despite my flip-flopping stomach. I addressed the Rat King, saying, "My name is Sage Hawthorne. I am a sorceress. Four wererats attacked me without cause aboveground yesterday. I used my magic to track one of them here. I want to know why they attacked me and, if they were hired to do so, who hired them."

"The creature is immensely stupid to come here alone," the red-eyed head said. "We should kill it before it reproduces."

"My brother king has a point," the blue-eyed head said to me. "You are either very powerful, very brave, or very foolish."

"All of the above," I said. The blue-eyed head laughed out loud. Even the homicidal red-eyed head chuckled slightly. A ripple of laughter ran through the rest of the cavern. Apparently, when the king laughed, everyone did. Rat see, rat do. Perhaps wererats and humans were not so different after all.

Only the white-eyed Rat King head didn't laugh. Glowering down at me, he said, "We know nothing of such an attack."

"Maybe you don't, but he does." I pointed at the wererat in the assembled throng whose fur was wrapped around my wrist. "He is one of the ones who attacked me yesterday, and the one my magic led me to today."

When it became obvious whom I pointed at, the wererats around the brown wererat shied away from him. The fearful way they did it, I got the feeling a wererat attacking someone without the king's knowledge was a definite no-no. Assuming, that is, the king wasn't lying about not knowing of the attack.

After hesitating for a moment, the brown wererat I pointed at said, "I have no idea what this human is talking about." He said *human* the way Loopy had said it yesterday, like it was an insult. "I've never seen her before today. But if she comes over here and bends over, I'll introduce myself to her." The wererat thrust his pelvis back and forth suggestively. All three heads of the Rat King laughed, followed a beat later by everyone else in the cavern. The laughter was not good-natured. More like gleefully mocking.

I waited for the laughter to die down.

"He's lying," I said. I held my left palm up so the Rat King could see the glowing arrow hovering above it. "See? My locator spell points directly at him."

"The creature foolishly tries to trick us. We should kill it before it reproduces," the red-eyed head said. I had never seen a broken record in rat form before.

"Any Gifted fool can produce a lightshow in an attempt to dupe us," the white-eyed Rat King head agreed. "I knew an illusionist who could make his manhood appear as long as his leg. I bit his leg off, making his leg and his manhood equally long in reality." The throng laughed again. When you were a king, the whole world laughed with you.

"Several of our brethren can vouch for my whereabouts here in the sewers all day yesterday," the brown wererat said. *The others who attacked me, no doubt,* I thought. "I have not been Aboveworld in days. The human lies, not me."

The white-eyed Rat King head impaled me with his gaze. "The protection the Compact affords you is nullified if you abuse its provisions by deceiving your host." The red-eyed head whistled, and the wererats armed with halberds instantly lowered their weapons, pointing their silver tips at me. Under different circumstances, I might have admired how on the ball they were.

"If I'm lying and that wererat has never seen me before, then how do I have a clump of his fur?" Moving slowly so as to not provoke the wererats with the halberds, I pulled the sandwich bag containing the fur out of my pocket. I unsealed the bag and pulled the fur out. I kept my disgust off my face as I held the fur out toward the Rat King. "I retrieved his fur from the alley he attacked me in."

The blue-eyed head looked at me with interest, with things still writhing right under the skin of its body. A part of whatever the squirming things were rose into the blue-eyed head's throat. It looked like a giant, wriggling Adam's apple.

As I watched with disguised disgust and horror, the blue-eyed head opened his mouth. The bulge at his throat slid upward. Two big rats crawled out of his mouth, one after the other, like noxious gas bubbling out of a swamp. Both rats were black and slick with film, like they had just crawled out of an oil spill. They landed on the Rat King's lap with wet plops. Their tiny eyes glowed blue, just like the head they had come out of.

In a flash of revolting insight, I realized the things crawling around inside of the Rat King were rats. There must have been dozens of the rodents inside his big body.

The two rats hopped from the monarch's lap to the dais. They shook themselves dry like wet dogs. I thanked my lucky stars I was far enough away I didn't get splattered by the droplets. No amount of bathing could cleanse me of that grossness.

One rat scampered off the dais toward the brown wererat. The other scurried over to me. As I suppressed shudders of disgust, the black rat crawled up my leg, past my stomach, and perched on my breast. Its twitching whiskers were so long, they grazed my chin. It took a superhuman effort of will to remain still and not slap the thing off me.

From my chest the rat bounded onto my outstretched arm, scampering across it to where I held the fur of the wererat who had attacked me. Its small claws dug into my wrist as it sniffed the wererat fur. I looked over and saw the other rat which had come out of the Rat King's mouth doing the same thing to the brown wererat. The rat sniffed the brown Otherkin like a bloodhound catching a scent.

The blue-eyed head turned sharply to stare at the brown wererat. His blue eyes blazed, like a fire splashed with gasoline. "The sorceress speaks truly," he hissed balefully. "It is your fur. You dare lie to your king?" The wererats near the brown wererat shrank even farther away from him, obviously not wanting to be near someone who had incurred the wrath of the Rat King.

The brown wererat cursed. He snapped his long tail around like a whip. It smacked the sniffing black rat. The rat's body split open like an overripe cantaloupe. Blood went flying like spray from a sprinkler. The ruptured rat's keening died stillborn.

The brown wererat looked at me with hate in his bloodshot eyes. His hand disappeared under his loincloth. It reappeared holding a curved silver dagger.

The wererat's legs coiled and sprang. They propelled him into the air, over the heads of the throng. He shot toward the dais.

The brandished dagger glinted evilly under the skulls' glow as the wererat hurtled toward us.

CHAPTER TWELVE

I reacted without thinking. I released my hold on the locator spell. "Terra!" I cried, waving my hand in the necessary pattern at the dais and exerting my will as Dirty Gray and Brown Patch scrambled out of the way. The blue-eyed black rat fell off my gesticulating arm with a squeal.

The brown wererat was about to land on the dais near me. The small part of me that wasn't focused on casting my spell realized the dagger-wielding brown wererat hurtling through the air wasn't aiming for me. He was aiming for the Rat King.

The wererat was going to land on the dais between me and the Rat King. Knowing what was going to happen, I dove to the right, out of the way.

The brown wererat's feet touched down on the dais. The stone under him exploded like he had stepped on a land mine thanks to the earth-based spell I had cast.

The wererat was blasted backward. He fell heavily. The force of the blast made him roll like a ball. He tumbled back off the dais.

The wererats armed with the halberds rushed forward in pursuit of the brown wererat. The Rat King stayed them with a whistle.

The Rat King rose from his throne. He had been terrifyingly large seated. Standing, he was the stuff horror movies were based on.

Moving faster than I would've expected a creature his size being able to, the Rat King snatched the halberd out of the hands of one of his guards. With his skin still rippling with all the rats inside his body, he stepped off the dais toward the brown wererat.

The brown wererat was back on his feet. He staggered slightly due to being blasted off the dais, and he bled from a gash on his snout. He still held the curved silver dagger. He waved it in front of himself at the Rat King in silent invitation.

The Rat King and the smaller wererat circled each other, brandishing their weapons, like wary gladiators in an arena. The wererats and rats near them quickly got out of the way. Everyone else in the cavern just stood and watched. I might have intervened had I known which side to intervene on. After all, the brown wererat had tried to kill me, and two of the three of the Rat King's heads wanted to kill me as well. Maybe I should have been cheering, "I hope you both die!" but even someone as undiplomatic as I knew that probably wasn't the right move.

The cavern was so quiet, you could've heard a pin drop. The only sounds were the shifting of the dueling wererats' feet and the brown wererat's labored breathing. I had really walloped him with my spell. The fact he was still moving was a testament to how tough he was.

The Rat King made the first move. He lunged forward, thrusting the spiked tip of the long halberd at his opponent. The brown wererat sidestepped the thrust, and rushed forward, slashing with the dagger.

The brown wererat had made a big mistake. The Rat King's thrust had merely been a feint. The Rat King spun out of the way of the flashing knife, and simultaneously yanked the halberd back. The sharp axe edge of the weapon sliced through the back of the brown wererat's leg.

Blood flooded from the wound. The brown wererat shrieked. He staggered and fell to a knee, his injured leg rendered useless.

The Rat King kicked the downed wererat hard. Like a toppled domino, the wererat fell on his back with a thud. The halberd became a blur in the Rat King's hands as the weapon spun, reversing direction. The Rat King slammed the weapon down. Its blunt butt hit the supine wererat square in his chest. There was the loud crack of breaking bones. The wererat's scream abruptly died to a whimper. The dagger fell out of his hand. The Rat King kicked it away.

The Rat King flipped the halberd around again. He stood over the brown wererat with the axe edge of the weapon pressed against the downed creature's throat. The brown wererat's limbs twitched, but he otherwise appeared to be incapacitated.

The center head of the Rat King screeched at the supine wererat in the creatures' native tongue. The brown wererat responded in a weak voice.

The two went back and forth like that for a while, with the rest of the cavern completely quiet as the two spoke. Maybe they were talking about what they would have for dinner post-fight, but I doubted it.

I was right. Once the two finished talking, the Rat King took a step back. He raised the halberd over his three heads like he was about to chop wood. The halberd descended. The axe part of the halberd cleanly chopped off the brown wererat's head like his neck was made of butter. The brown wererat's head went rolling. His decapitated body gushed blood.

The cavern erupted into squeals, squeaks and cheers so loud I wanted to cover my ears. I wanted to, but did not. I was still doing my tough as nails impersonation, despite the fact I wanted to turn away from the revolting sight and throw up everything I had ever eaten in my life.

The Rat King dropped the halberd. He stepped over to where the head had stopped rolling. Picking the head up by its ears, the Rat King drank blood from the dripping head just as the wererat on the dais had done earlier. Clearly this was not the place to lose an argument or fight. The cheering got even louder as the three Rat King heads took turns drinking the dead wererat's blood. Wererats stomped their feet; rats jumped up and down in glee. I felt the vibration of the pandemonium in my teeth. It was as if I stood in the home stadium of a football team who had just scored the winning touchdown.

The Rat King dropped the head like it was an empty milk carton. With his faces' mouths slick with blood, he mounted the dais again. He went right by me on his way back to the bone throne. I got a whiff of blood as he passed, strong and sickly sweet. My stomach rumbled threateningly again. I really regretted those rich champagne donuts I had for breakfast.

The Rat King sat on his throne again. He raised a single clawed finger. The screeches and cheering died off into nothingness as if a dimmer switch had been twisted to an off position. The king's white guard hopped off the dais to retrieve the halberd the Rat King had taken from him. Other wererats in the crowd hustled forward to pick up the brown wererat's decapitated body and his head. They disappeared deep into the crowd with him. Four-legged rats scurried forward to lick the blood off the cavern floor.

The rat that had crawled up me to sniff the brown wererat's fur bounded back over to the Rat King. It crawled up the monarch's seated body and began to lick the blood off the muzzle of the blue-eyed head. The other two heads vomited up rats of their own, and those rats licked the muzzles they had been disgorged from.

All three sets of the Rat King's eyes stared at me as the heads were groomed. Incredibly, the heads' crowns had not fallen off. Because I didn't know what else to say, I said, "I guess it's true what they say: If you attack a king, you'd best kill him. I'm glad that did not happen here. I was rooting for you."

"It was your moral support that sustained me in my hour of need," the blue-eyed head said. The other two heads laughed, which set off a chain reaction of laughter which rippled throughout the cavern. Now I knew what my life was missing: A sea of sycophants who would laugh and cheer me on command.

I decided to not mention that if it hadn't been for me and my spell, the brown wererat might have been the one to survive the fight with the Rat King. Diplomacy. If I ever lost my job permanently with Capstone, I could become the ambassador to the wererat underworld. It would be the worst job ever.

"I'm happy about what happened, but I must admit I don't entirely understand it," I said. "Why did that wererat attack you and not me?"

The rats that had been grooming the Rat King were finished, and they crawled back into the Rat King's throats. Once his rat's tail disappeared down his throat, the blue-eyed head said, "In our society, all mercenary work must be approved by me. Further, I receive a percentage of all the proceeds. Since that wererat attacked you without my approval and without tendering my kickback, he violated wererat law. Rather than submit to punishment, he chose to challenge me. Had he succeeded, he would have assumed my mantle and become the new king."

"Before he died, did he tell you who hired him and his companions?" I asked.

"He did," the blue-eyed head said. "He made a full confession after I defeated him, as is our way."

"Good. Then if you'll tell me who hired him and his friends, I'll be on my way." I couldn't get out of here soon enough. I didn't know if there was water hot enough or soap strong enough to wash the stench of this place off me.

"No," all three Rat King heads said at once.

"No?"

"No," they repeated firmly.

"It is not our way," the white-eyed head said.

"This creature is more valuable dead than alive. We should kill it before it reproduces," the red-eyed head said.

"My brother speaks truly," the blue-eyed head said to me. "We must assume the obligation of the contract on your head. You indeed are far more valuable to us dead than alive." So much for him being my favorite head.

I was suddenly hyperconscious of the fact that the white guard was back on the dais, having retrieved his halberd. I didn't want either guard to use their weapons on me. I had gotten used to my head being right where it was. "But I saved your life," I protested. Diplomacy could go to Hades. My diplomacy ended where my life began.

"We hardly needed your help to fend off one wererat," the white-eyed head scoffed. "And even if you did assist in some small, insignificant way, it is of no matter. You should not expect gratitude. Gratitude is a human emotion, not a wererat one. As we wererats say, a contract is a contract is a contract. If we do not do the job we are hired to do, soon people will stop hiring us."

"Under our laws, the only way to nullify the contract on your life is if you buy it out," the blue-eyed head added.

My heart sank to my stomach, and they both took up residence in my feet. I couldn't even pay my rent. How was I supposed to pay for my life? But what choice did I have? If Ghost hadn't intervened, I wouldn't have survived the first wererat attack. There was no way I'd survive swarms of them coming after me.

"How much to buy out the contract?" I asked. I dreaded the answer.

"The contract itself is ninety-three gold talents," the blue-eyed head said. Gold talents were the universal currency of the magical world. "Add to that the twenty percent buy-out surcharge, for a total of one hundred and twelve gold talents."

I did a rough conversion to dollars in my head. My stomach twisted at the answer: over forty thousand dollars. It was both too much and too little. Too little because my life was apparently only worth that. Too much because I didn't have forty thousand dollars. When you were almost flat broke like I was, forty thousand dollars might as well be forty billion. There was no way I could pay that amount.

"I'll give you twenty-eight," I countered. Twenty-eight gold talents equaled a little over ten thousand dollars. I did not have ten thousand lying around, but it was better than trying to raise forty.

"This is not a negotiation," the white-eyed head snarled. The Rat King's fist thumped the throne's armrest in irritation. "Our rate is our rate. Take it or leave it."

I felt the eyes of all the rodents in the cavern on me. With a word from their Rat King, it could just as easily be their teeth and claws on me.

Again, what choice did I have?

"I'll take it," I said.

* * *

I paced the floor of my tiny living room. My hair was wet. I only had on my robe. I had just finished showering after returning from the sewers. The stench of the sewers seemed to be baked into my clothes. I would just throw them away instead of trying to wash the filth and smell out of them. Besides, the fewer the reminders of my idiocy, the better.

I took a swig of Elven wine. The fact it did not make me feel better showed just how massive a mess I was in. I was worse off now than I had been before I had gone down into the sewers. Before, only four wererats had been trying to kill me. Now, the entire wererat community would try to kill me if I did not come up with forty thousand dollars. The Rat King had given me two and a half weeks to produce the money. If I didn't, my life would turn into *The Fugitive*, with me playing the role of Harrison Ford, and every wererat in the world chasing me.

Dumb, dumb, dumb, dumb, dumb. I wished I had never heard of a sewer, much less ventured into one. I was like a reverse King Midas—everything I touched turned into complete crap. First the Institute of Peace, now this. I shouldn't even venture outside. I was a hazard to myself. I should lock myself into this apartment and throw away the key.

The problem with that plan was that first Mrs. Leverette and her sons would come knocking, and shortly thereafter, a hit squad of wererats would then knock to knock me off. And that was assuming the Conclave didn't get to me first for my First Rule violations.

I took another swig of wine. What to do, what to do, what to do? Coming up with forty thousand dollars was problematic. Even if I sold everything I owned, I would not come even close to that amount. Ghost had been right when he said I had no assets to speak of.

Could I borrow the money? The only person I knew who had that kind of money at his fingertips and who might be inclined to help me was Oscar.

Ugh! The thought of crawling back to the office and begging him for a loan after what he said about me and after he suspended me turned my stomach. I'd be like a dog returning to her vomit to lap it up.

No. Going to Oscar would be the last resort. There had to be another way.

I could attack the wererat problem at its source and go after the person who put out the contract on my life. I could persuade them to cancel their contract with the wererats. By "persuade them," I meant beat them to a bloody pulp. My fists could be quite persuasive when I needed them to be. And oh boy, if there was a time I needed them to be, that time was now.

The problem was I did not have a better idea now of who hired the wererats than I did before I ventured into the sewers. However, I still thought the leading candidate was Willow Wilde. The fact the wererats attacked me just a couple of days after I punched Willow was too big of a coincidence to ignore. Despite all the other enemies I had made over the years, surely this wererat-hiring enemy had to be her.

But what if it wasn't? If I beat the tar out of Willow and it turned out she had not hired the wererats, there would be consequences. The wererats would still come after me, Oscar would probably fire me, the Conclave would punish me even more severely than they already would, and I'd be in trouble with the mundane authorities if Willow called the cops. I'd be even more in the soup than I already was. I'd be jumping from the frying pan into the fire.

What the heck was the deal with all my cooking metaphors? Maybe it was a side effect of Elven wine mixed with panic.

I shook my head at myself. The idea of beating up someone who might in fact be innocent didn't appeal to me. I was no bully. I was stupid sometimes, but not a bully.

No, strong-arming Willow without evidence she was connected to the wererats was out.

More wine disappeared into me. Its disappearance inspired me, which further proved Elven wine had never let me down:

I could disappear. I could go hide somewhere the wererats and the Conclave couldn't find me.

I thought more about running away as I paced. The problem was, running required money which I didn't have. Plus, I was not sure a place where I couldn't be found existed. And even if it did, the idea of spending the rest of my life looking over my shoulder for the wererats and for Conclave enforcement officials didn't appeal to me. My life wasn't much, but it was mine. I didn't want to walk away from it because I was afraid.

The thought of running away like a scared girl was repugnant to me. If I was going to get stabbed to death, I'd rather get stabbed in the chest while fighting back than get stabbed in the back while running.

Running was out, borrowing money was out, and smacking Willow around was out. That left me with one option, the one I had been trying to avoid because of all the misgivings I had.

I put down the wine and picked up the slip of paper Daniel had left me. It had his cell phone number on it.

I stared at the piece of paper for a while.

Finally, I picked up my cell phone and tapped out a text message to Daniel. It took me longer than it should have. The wine had made my fingers clumsy.

Make it $60,000 total and I'm in, the text read.

CHAPTER THIRTEEN

I was sweating, both from nerves and from the District's relentless summer humidity, even at this time of the day. I glanced at my watch. It was just a few minutes before 3 a.m. Almost the witching hour. How appropriate.

I looked around, making sure nobody was nearby. The coast was clear.

I pulled a ski mask over my head. The black mask matched the color of my pants, socks, and long-sleeved shirt. Then, to avoid leaving fingerprints, I tugged on the $600 leather black gloves I picked up at Neiman Marcus last year. Stylish and thin, the gloves were almost as good as not having anything at all on my hands. Sorceress turned cat burglar chic.

"I've been involved in some cockamamie schemes in my time," I whispered to Daniel, "but this one takes the cake. This is a terrible idea."

"You might have mentioned that a time or twenty already," he whispered back. "Cool your jets. I wouldn't have pegged you as a worrywart." Also dressed in dark clothes, Daniel had the Ark fragment tucked between his legs as he slipped on his own ski mask and gloves. A thick coil of black nylon rope was wound diagonally around his torso.

The red, white, and blue of a D.C. Metropolitan Police car approached on Independence Avenue. Despite the bright moon overhead and the numerous nearby street lights, we were shrouded in the shadows of the museum we stood next to and probably couldn't be spotted from the road. Even so, I held my breath and thought invisible thoughts until the cop car passed.

"I worry because there's reason to worry," I said once the cop's taillights faded from view. "I can't believe you talked me into stealing this Cloak of Wisdom thingamajig. What if we get caught? I've already got a record. The judge will throw the book at me."

"It's not a thingamajig. It's a Relic of great power. One of the neutral ones. Show some respect. It can augment your magic to help us find the Spear of Destiny. And, we're not stealing it." Daniel saw me roll my eyes. "Okay technically, under mundane law, we are stealing it. But under magical law, the Cloak belongs to whomever has the wit to find and wield it."

"If we get caught, it'll be a mundane judge we're dragged in front of, not a magical one."

"We're not going to get caught. And even if we did, it's for a just cause."

I snorted. In the still hours of the early morning, the sound was louder than I meant it to be. "Yeah, I can see me in court now: 'You should just let me go, your Honor. The fallen angel I broke into the Smithsonian with so we could steal a magic cape assured me we did it for a just cause, namely to help us find a spear that's also magic and that can be used to conquer the world.' I imagine that defense will go over like a lead balloon, assuming the judge stops laughing long enough to hear it."

"Stop being such a nervous Nellie."

"And you stop being such a . . ." I groped for an appropriate alliteration.

"Definite Daniel? Decided Daniel? Dauntless Daniel?" he supplied.

"No one likes a know-it-all. Especially not an overly confident one."

We stood next to the Arthur M. Sackler Gallery, a squat, rectangular pink and gray granite building on the District's National Mall, the huge area which stretched between the United States Capitol building and the Lincoln Memorial. The one-story granite structure was the only part of the gallery that was aboveground; the other three stories were underground.

I had been to the Sackler Gallery many times, but never in the wee hours of the morning when it was closed. It was part of the Smithsonian's Quadrangle Complex, which also included the National Museum of African Art and the S. Dillon Ripley Center. The African museum with its domed roof was directly ahead of where Daniel and I stood. Independence Avenue ran by us on the right. The four-acre Enid A. Haupt Garden was to the left. The towered Smithsonian Institution Building was on the other side of the garden, and the rest of the Mall beyond that.

The Smithsonian Institution Building loomed over us. That building was more commonly called the Castle because that was what it looked like—a red sandstone, Gothic castle. Urban legend said the Castle was haunted. A necromancer at Capstone Security had assured me a while ago the legend was true. I wondered if some of those ghosts were staring down at me now from the Castle's towers, wondering what in the world I was doing here in the middle of the night. I wondered the same thing.

Ghosts looking at me would be far better than the Hero Ghost looking at me. I scanned the air for him but did not see anything but the night sky. Now would be a terrible time for the meddling Hero to show up, right when I was about to commit several felonies.

"Okay, let's get this party started," Daniel said. He looked at me expectantly.

I took one more wary look around. I still did not see anyone, but it was what I could not see that I was worried about. "Are you sure we're not being electronically surveilled? A major tourist destination like the Mall must have hidden cameras all over the place."

"There are cameras everywhere, but not here. The tiny area we're standing in is a dead zone the cameras don't cover." Daniel shook his head impatiently. "We've been over this. Just like we've been over how the gallery's alarms don't cover the roof. Just like we've been over how there are cameras inside, but no one monitors them in real-time, so if we keep our masks on, no one will be able to identify us later. Just like we've been over how there are no security guards in this particular gallery from 2:00 a.m. until 5 a.m. Thanks to budget cuts, only certain museums get round-the-clock protection, like the National Museum of Natural History where the Hope Diamond and other priceless gems are on display. The lack of round-the-clock guards at certain museums is not common knowledge, so keep it under your hat."

"I still can't believe a homeless guy is on the Smithsonian's board of directors."

"It's called the Board of Regents. The fact I'm not allowed to keep a permanent residence doesn't mean I don't keep my fingers in a bunch of pies. How am I supposed to do enough good to earn my wings back if I don't know what's going on in the world? My connection with the Smithsonian is how I got this piece of the Ark. In the 1960s, the Smithsonian secretly excavated where Noah's Ark landed on Mount Ararat in Turkey. You can accumulate a lot of money, power, and intel in a couple thousand years. Now would you hurry up and get us to the roof before another thousand years passes me by? You're procrastinating. The longer we linger, the greater the chance somebody will wander by and spot us."

"Stop jogging my elbow. Add Demanding Daniel to the list of names. All right. Hold still." Trying to swallow my fears and doubts, I summoned my will, visualized what I wanted to do, waved my hands in the necessary pattern, and said, "Ventus."

The moist air, still up until now, stirred. The gentle breeze became a gust of wind, which in turn became a powerful mass of air that swirled around me and Daniel, picking up dust and small debris from the surrounding area. The whirlwind lifted us into the air like an invisible elevator.

The whirlwind deposited us on top of the Sackler building. I relaxed my will and allowed the whirlwind to dissipate. Daniel immediately crouched down between two of the six pyramids that adorned the roof, hiding from the view of someone who might be passing by. I also crouched down.

"This way," Daniel murmured, still crouching down as he led me toward the center of the roof. A trapdoor was there, secured by a large padlock that would make a picklock gnash his teeth in frustration. Daniel touched the tip of his staff to the lock. The dark wood shimmered rainbow colors for a moment, and the lock snapped open. First my place, now this gallery. No supposedly secure location was safe from this guy.

"Why does the staff always shimmer like that when you draw on its power?" I asked.

"Like a rainbow? It's because of God's promise to man."

"What promise? What are you talking about?"

"It's in the Bible. Genesis. Don't you read the Bible?" When I hesitated, he said, "Don't you read anything?"

"Sure. My horoscope. The *National Inquiry*. Twitter. I read lots of things."

"You're quite the scholar," Daniel said wryly. "Since you're such a big reader, perhaps we should go after the Philosopher's Stone instead of the Cloak of Wisdom. The Philosopher's Stone is a book, you know."

"Of course I know." I did not.

"Back to rainbows and the Bible. After God destroyed the world with a massive flood, the one He had Noah build an ark to escape from, He promised Noah He would never destroy the world again by flooding it. Rainbows are a reminder of that promise. As long as this fragment remains intact, the rainbow and God's promise remain intact."

Daniel flipped the trapdoor open. He then took the rope from around his body and tied one end of it to a thick metal pipe that jutted from the roof. After tugging hard on the rope a few times to make sure it was secure, he tossed the other end of the rope into the open trapdoor. The rope disappeared into the void below.

On our hands and knees, Daniel and I peered into the dark gallery below us. Other than the first few feet of rope, nothing was visible. I was reluctant to climb down. The last time I descended into a dark and scary place—namely the sewers—it had not worked out so well for Team Sage.

"Ladies first," Daniel urged me.

"Me?" I said, balking. "Why don't you go first? Whatever happened to chivalry? Or does that concept not exist in Heaven?"

"My chivalry ends where your employment begins."

"I'm not your employee. I'm an independent contractor."

"You're also procrastinating." Daniel motioned with his head. "Down you go."

Daniel was right. I was procrastinating, and I had been since we'd gotten here. I knew that me going into the building was like Julius Caesar crossing the Rubicon— once I did it, there would be no going back. I would have fully committed myself to this insane enterprise.

I sighed. After a bit of haggling, Daniel and I had finally settled on a total of fifty thousand instead of my initial demand of sixty. He had already paid me a fifteen thousand dollar retainer, and the rest would be paid if I located and obtained the Spear of Destiny for him. I had already used some of Daniel's retainer to get current on my rent. I would need the rest of the money Daniel promised to pay off the wererats and get them to cancel the contract on my life. There was no turning back now.

I reached for the rope. "If I wind up getting arrested, I'm telling the cops you coerced me into this. If I give them my wide-eyed innocent look and squeeze out a few tears, they'll believe me. Men are such chumps. Hopefully they'll curb stomp you and accidentally shoot you a few times while taking you into custody. It'll give you some lovely new scars."

"If your yammering could find the Spear of Destiny, I'd have it already." Daniel's eyes twinkled in the moonlight.

The only reply that sprang to mind was *Oh yeah?*, and I was too ashamed of its lameness to say it aloud. Since I didn't have a wittier retort handy, I instead replied by lowering myself down the rope into the darkness of the gallery.

Soon my feet touched the museum's floor. I froze, straining to hear the slightest noise. Despite Daniel's assurance about the absence of guards, I halfway expected to hear footsteps on the gallery's stone floor.

I heard nothing. No footfalls, no alarms, no swarming police yelling I was under arrest. The place was as silent as a tomb. Unlike outside, the air in here was dry and cool, no doubt to preserve all the exhibits on display. Other than the faint moonlight which trickled in from the skylights on the roof, it was as dark in here as the inside of a whale.

I cast a light spell like the one I had used in the sewers. I made the light dim so it would not draw the attention of someone who might pass by outside and see the light through the windows on this floor. Even on low, my magic globe's glow gave me plenty of light to see by.

I stood in the gallery's atrium, near the building's grand staircase which led to the underground floors. I waved to Daniel. He tossed down his staff, which I caught before it hit the floor. I did not like touching something that had blasted me across a room, but Daniel had assured me the staff was harmless unless I was trying to do violence to its bearer.

The plan was for Daniel to lead us to the Cloak of Wisdom on the lower levels, we'd grab it, and return here. I'd climb back up the rope to the roof, use my super strength to pull Daniel up, and we'd then beat a hasty retreat before the guards returned to their patrols. Simple plans were the best plans.

Even so, I was on pins and needles. I expected Murphy's Law to exert itself at any moment. Things had not exactly been breaking my way lately.

As Daniel shimmied down the rope with the coins in his pocket tinkling faintly, I realized the nylon rope was not the only thing hanging from the ceiling. A suspended sculpture hung from the roof's skylight and disappeared into a hole the grand staircase was built around. The sculpture hung all the way down to the third underground floor, almost touching the reflecting pool there.

I knew from prior visits the sculpture was called *Monkeys Grasp for the Moon*. It was composed of twenty-one laminated pieces of dark wood, with each piece fashioned to look like a stylized monkey. Each piece was a rendering of the word *monkey* in a different language, including Chinese, Japanese, Thai, English, and Braille. *Monkeys Grasp for the Moon* was based on a Chinese folktale in which monkeys in trees were intrigued by the moon's reflection in a pool of water. Linking tails and forming a monkey chain, they hung down from one the trees, with the last monkey in the chain trying to scoop up the moon's reflection. The moon's reflection disappeared as soon as the monkey disturbed the water by touching it. The moral of the story was that the thing you work to achieve might prove to be an illusion.

I stared at the sculpture, reflecting on its moral. *The thing you work to achieve might prove to be an illusion.* Huh. If the universe was sending me a message about finding the Spear of Destiny, it was not being terribly subtle about it.

Daniel touched down on the stone floor next to me, jarring me from my reverie.

"Where to next?" I whispered. The whisper turned into a surprised shriek when I caught sight of a hulking figure sitting in a chair against the wall. I nearly jumped out of my skin. "What the—"

"It's all right," Daniel said as he grabbed my arm. He probably didn't know if I had been about to run or blast the shadowy figure with spellfire. I didn't know either. I rarely knew what I was going to do up until I did it. "It's just a sculpture."

I stepped toward the seated figure, bringing my magic light closer. Now that I could see it better, I saw Daniel was right. The figure was a very rough sculpture of a naked man sitting on a stone chair. Whoever the sculptor was had taken a page from action figures because the nude figure was not anatomically correct. The fact that I looked probably meant it had been far too long since I had gotten laid. The man was made of what appeared to be clay. The clay was such a dark red, it was almost black. Even seated, the sculpture was almost as tall as I, and it was much wider than I was. It had hollow eyes which were set deeply in a rough-hewn face that only a mother could love.

"What in the world is this thing?" I asked. "It wasn't here the last time I visited the museum."

"Ichiro Kato, the last magician to wear the Cloak of Wisdom, willed the Cloak to the Sackler Gallery upon his death, along with a slew of priceless Japanese artifacts. The bequest stipulated that this statue and several others like it be housed in the same facility as the Cloak."

"Why?"

"I'm an angel, not a medium. Who knows what a dead man was thinking?"

There were yellow letters engraved on the forehead of the statue. "I wonder what that says," I said, pointing. "It doesn't look like Japanese."

"It's not. It's Hebrew. In English, the letters spell out emet. Emet is the Hebrew word for truth."

"You understand Hebrew?"

"I understand all languages. I'm an angel, remember?" Daniel shook his head impatiently. "C'mon, you're wasting time again."

I eyed the back of Daniel's head wistfully as he led us down the grand staircase, with my globe of light traveling overhead with us. Maybe when all this was over, I'd smack him upside the head for repeatedly talking to me like that. I didn't know if assaulting a fallen angel was a sin, but I'd be willing to risk it.

While going down the stairs, we spotted on the first underground level a couple of the same sort of rough clay sculptures as the one we had seen on the ground floor. I wondered how many of the statues were in the building.

We got off the staircase on the second underground level. Now that windows were not a concern, I made my magic light brighter. Daniel walked confidently, leading the way, since he knew where the Cloak was on display.

Despite our soft-soled shoes, our footsteps echoed off the laminated wood floors in the otherwise total silence. Dark shadows shifted as my floating overhead light passed by various objects, making it appear as though we walked amid living things.

We passed through exhibits that would make the heart of an Asian art enthusiast go pit-a-pat. I spotted Chinese jades and bronzes, Indian tapestries, Japanese ceramics, and more pieces of sculpture from various cultures than you could shake a Noah's Ark stick at. Also, the ugly red clay sculptures were everywhere. They dotted this level like acne on a teenager's face.

Even to my unsophisticated eye, it was obvious a bunch of the items on display were valuable. Even so, a lot of the items were not in security cases and were simply out in the open. With no security guards to stop me, it would be all too easy to fill my arms with stuff. If I were a criminal, I could make out like a bandit.

Then I remembered why I was here. *If I were a criminal.* Ha! More like *if I were a greedier criminal.* Fresh anxiety surged through me. I had not enjoyed prison and was not anxious to go back. The sooner we grabbed the cloak and got the heck out of here, the better.

"This is the room we want," Daniel said. Through a doorless entrance, we went into a large, square room. Another rough red clay sculpture sat in a stone chair near the entrance. A second doorless entrance was in the wall on the left. A massive, ancient tapestry depicting armored samurai warriors fighting each other took up the far wall ahead of us. The other walls were bare and white. Objects of various sizes were on display atop white pedestals, some enclosed in clear display cases, others not.

"Everything in this room was gifted to the Sackler Gallery by Kato, but this is what we're looking for," Daniel said as he stopped in the center of the room in front of a thick, transparent glass case.

A headless mannequin was inside the case. Around the mannequin's neck was a thick cloak. The cloak was the color of blood and was secured around the mannequin's neck with a gold clasp. The clasp was shaped like an eagle with its wings spread wide. The clasp was so artfully wrought that it almost looked alive.

Except for the clasp, the Cloak reminded me a little of the red cape Avatar used to wear. Avatar had been the world's greatest Hero until he was murdered a few years ago.

The Cloak of Wisdom, circa 1400, read the plaque mounted on a stand next to the case. *Acquired by wealthy businessman and occult enthusiast Ichiro Kato in 1971, Kato believed he could make the Cloak become a part of his body, and the*

Cloak then imparted to him knowledge and wisdom Kato used in the pursuit of his supernatural studies.

Next to these words on the plaque was a drawing of two hands with their palms out, wrists crossed, and the thumbs twisted around one another. Behind and slightly above the hands was the shadow of a bird, as if a light was shining at an upward angle on the entwined hands and throwing a bird shadow puppet on a wall behind them. I concluded it was supposed to be an eagle like the eagle on the clasp, but I still thought it was weird the drawing was there.

"Occult enthusiast? Supernatural studies?" I said. "Whatever happened to keeping the secret magical world a secret? Though I'm one to talk. That might not be a First Rule violation, but it's awfully close."

"I'm told everything on the plaque was taken verbatim from Kato's will," Daniel said. "Knowing someone else might need the Cloak one day, I suppose he thought he would hide it in plain sight à la *The Purloined Letter.*"

"The what kind of letter?"

Daniel sighed. The sound echoed off the walls of the enclosed space. "Promise me you'll spend some of the money I'm paying you on books. A sorceress who doesn't read is like a rusty sword: You can still use it, but it doesn't work as well."

Smacking Daniel upside the head when this nonsense was over looked like a better and better idea with each passing moment.

But this nonsense was not yet over. The first step toward finding the Spear of Destiny and getting this know-it-all out of my life was to grab the Cloak of Wisdom and get the heck out of dodge. The longer I stayed here, the greater the chance I'd get caught here.

I raised my hand, about to probe the case the Cloak was in to see how strong it was.

Daniel pushed my hand away. "Let's look before we leap," he said. "Maybe there's an alarm or some other sort of protection in place." He raised his wooden staff. He held it in front of the transparent case. He closed his eyes, concentrating. The dark wood began to shimmer with rainbow colors.

Increasingly impatient to get the cloak and get out of here, I glanced around for something to break the case with once Daniel gave me the go-ahead.

A few steps away was a dark metal rod resting on a waist-high display case. I went over to it. Up close, it reminded me of a metal baseball bat, only the rod was over five feet long. Also, the rod had wicked-looking metal spikes on its top half. According to the plaque next to the rod, it was a kanobō, which translated into *metal stick* in English. The plaque said it was a two-handed war club used by the samurai in feudal Japan.

If it was good enough for the samurai, it was good enough for me. I picked the two-handed club up with one hand because, unlike the samurai, I had super strength. Score one for feminism.

I took it back over to the Cloak of Wisdom. Daniel still stood before the case, with his eyes closed and the Ark fragment shimmering.

My toe tapped impatiently as I waited. To say I was antsy would be a massive understatement. My fears of going back to prison had me convinced an armed guard was going to stroll in here any minute now on an unscheduled patrol.

Finally, I couldn't stand waiting any longer. "You detect any alarms on the case?" I asked.

"No," Daniel said, frowning slightly with his eyes still closed. "But—"

"Then what the heck are we waiting for?" My patience was at the end of its rope. "Stop pussyfooting around."

I stepped forward. I swung the metal club at the case like I was trying to hit a homer at Nationals Park.

There was a huge crash, like that of a car driving into a streetlight. The impact of the kanobō on the case reverberated up my arm painfully. The case cracked like a dropped hard-boiled egg, with ever-expanding fissures racing all throughout it. Daniel's eyes flew open. He jumped back, startled.

The case shuddered for a moment, as if an earthquake had hit it. Then, all at once, the case collapsed loudly into a multitude of pieces on the wood floor.

I looked with satisfaction at my handiwork. Sometimes a situation called for a hammer instead of a scalpel. Now nothing stood between us and the Cloak of Wisdom. All I had to do was reach out and take it. Easy peasy lemon squeazy.

I saw movement out of the corner of my eye. I turned to see the red clay sculpture rising out of its chair as if it had been napping and the racket had awakened it. The Hebrew letters on its head and its sunken eyes glowed red, as if a LED was in its skull.

The glowing red eyes looked straight at me and Daniel. The sculpture grabbed the solid stone chair it had been sitting on and picked it up with one arm. The chair must have weighed several hundred pounds.

The sculpture whipped the chair at me and Daniel.

I dove to my left, plowing into Daniel with my shoulder. We fell to the hard floor as the stone chair rocketed through the space we had occupied an instant before. The chair slammed into the far wall with a crash that might have awakened the First Family over a mile away as the crow flies in the White House.

"I was saying the Ark fragment detected some sort of magical trigger in the case," Daniel yelled in my ear, "and that we shouldn't act until I figured out how to disarm it."

"Oh," I said.

The big statue lumbered toward us. The floor shook ominously with each of its steps.

CHAPTER FOURTEEN

I scrambled to my feet. I grabbed the kanobō I had dropped when I'd tackled Daniel. I brandished it at the statue like it was a sword.

"Grab the cloak and stay behind me," I snapped at Daniel. I eyed the approaching red clay statue. "I'll take care of this thing." Since Daniel was the immortal one, I probably should have been the one to stay behind him. You could take the girl out of the bodyguarding gig, but not the bodyguarding gig out of the girl.

I swung the kanobō at the statue, expecting the statue to shatter like the case around the Cloak of Wisdom had.

Moving faster than I expected, the statue lifted its hand and grabbed the end of the kanobō racing toward it. The statue pulled. I was yanked off my feet. The statue was much stronger than I, and I was no weakling.

I had been the swinger, now I was the swung. The room became a blur as the statue pulled its arm holding the kanobō back, then flicked it forward, like someone casting with a rod and reel.

I was not sure if the statue let go of the kanobō, or if I did. Maybe the kanobō let go of me, figuring I wasn't safe to be around. Regardless, I went flying.

I slammed into the tapestry-covered wall with a bone-rattling thump. It felt like a few of my internal organs got rearranged.

I fell to the floor, ripping the tapestry down with me. It fell on top of me like a giant rough blanket. The opaque artwork blinded me. I pawed feverishly at the tapestry, trying to get it off me before the statue came over and stomped me like a bug trapped under a rug.

No good. It was like one of those Chinese finger puzzles—the more I struggled, the more entangled I became.

New plan. Hoping this wasn't a one of a kind irreplaceable work of art, I grabbed two handfuls of the tapestry. I yanked hard. With a rending sound, the tapestry ripped apart, freeing me.

I stood, blinking bits of fabric out of my eyes. Daniel came hurtling through the air toward me, with something red fluttering behind him like a streamer. I halfway caught him, halfway served as a human airbag. Daniel's collision with me slammed my back into the wall again. We both went sprawling.

Daniel had the Ark fragment in one hand, and the Cloak of Wisdom clutched in the other. The fact the Ark fragment had not protected Daniel from the statue's attack the way it had protected him from me in my apartment did not bode well.

Pushing Daniel out of the way, I scrambled to my feet again. I summoned a ball of spellfire. I flung it at the approaching statue.

Bullseye. The fireball hit the statue square in the chest. The statue's whole body caught fire with a whoosh, like a lit match had been put to a pile of charcoal drenched in lighter fluid.

The fire stopped the statue's advance. But before I could dislocate my shoulder patting myself on the back, the statue's body sucked up the spellfire like a thirsty sponge. The statue vibrated, growing visibly bigger off the magical energy I had flung at it.

The fire now extinguished and the statue bigger than ever, it continued its thunderous advance toward us.

I hastily tried an earth-based spell, hoping that since the statue appeared to be made of clay, I could break it apart.

No go. Trying to latch onto the statue with the spell was like grabbing a fistful of air. Something about the statue made it impossible for me to get a magical grip on it.

Brute force had been a bust, as had magic. Time for Plan C.

"Run!" I cried. I headed for the exit furthest from the statue, with Daniel hard on my heels. My globe of light zoomed over our heads like a drone. I was grateful I had not lost hold of my light spell despite having been flung around like a rag doll. A small—very small—victory.

With the statue lumbering after us, we darted out of the room. I turned left, toward the stairs leading back up.

We left the statue behind. Fortunately, as fast as the statue had been in an enclosed space, it did not seem capable of running. Plodding was more its speed.

I skidded to a stop when I turned a corner. Daniel almost slammed into me. Another statue, its eyes glowing red malevolently, was in the middle of the corridor between us and the stairs. It advanced toward us.

With a sinking feeling in the pit of my stomach, I wondered if me breaking the case had brought every single red clay statue in this joint to life. Me and my impulsiveness. Would I ever learn?

"Another way out?" I panted.

"The elevator," Daniel said, turning and running before the words were out of his mouth.

I trailed after him. We left the second statue in our dust. If those things could run, we'd be dead already. Or at least I would be. Daniel would likely be twisted up into a pretzel. He wouldn't die, but certain types of pain were worse than death.

I turned a corner. Daniel was already halfway down the hall, past the entrance to another exhibit room. As I hurtled down the hall, a red clay statue stepped out of the exhibit room, bent at the waist to fit through the entryway. It straightened up once clear of the doorway. It blocked the corridor between me and Daniel, standing facing me with its legs wide.

I silently cursed. I didn't want to get separated from Daniel. So instead of stopping, I increased my running speed. Adrenaline and fear gave my feet wings.

The statue grabbed for me as I approached. My glowing orb skimmed the ceiling, over the head of the clay monster.

I dropped, sliding feetfirst, like I was a batter sliding into second base. My butt burned from the friction with the wood floor. For the first time ever, I was happy to have all that extra padding down there.

"Ventus!" I cried breathlessly. I made the necessary hand motions as I skidded toward the statue grasping for me.

A sudden gust of magically induced wind sent me shooting between the statue's legs like a wet watermelon seed flicked across a tabletop.

The statue's hands clutched for me but came up empty. I was already through its legs and behind it. I stumbled to my feet. My right thigh burned, as did my derrière. Better burning buttocks than a mangled everything.

I took off running again toward Daniel. He looked at me like I had scored the winning run of the World Series. I didn't let it go to my head. We weren't out of the woods, not by a long shot.

The statue whose legs I slid through turned and pursued us, but Daniel and I quickly left it behind. The problem was we could hear the thud of multiple statues approaching, from all sides.

When we got to the corridor the elevator was at the end of, two statues were already there, blocking our access to the elevator. We were forced to retreat.

"C'mon, this way," Daniel shouted over his shoulder as he led me deeper into the gallery. I was glad he knew where everything was because I was completely lost.

Daniel stopped in front of a closed door. "In here," he said. He touched the Ark fragment to the doorknob. The knob and staff glowed for an instant, and the door swung open. I shot inside, followed by him. Daniel slammed and locked the door. Not that a locked door was going to do any good against statues that were stronger than I was.

I looked around. There were rows of metal shelving which groaned under the weight of various boxes and artifacts. Some sort of storage area for the gallery, obviously. There was no exit other than the door we had come through.

"We're trapped," I exclaimed. "Let's get out of here before the statues come."

Daniel blocked the door. "I know." He panted, and his nose bled. The blood made the bottom of his ski mask glisten under my magic light. "Running is doing us no good. They're tightening the noose around us, cutting off our avenues of escape. We need to make a stand."

"You mean like General Custer did? That worked out great for him. What are we supposed to do when they bust down the door?" I felt the vibration of their distant approach through the floor. The shelf closest to me began to shake. Pretty soon we would be standing in the middle of a red clay statue jamboree. "I hope you've got a brilliant idea, because I'm fresh out."

Daniel flung the Cloak of Wisdom at me. "Put the Cloak on. It can help us."

"That seems like more of a Hail Mary pass than a brilliant idea," I said, but hastened to put the cloak on anyway. My fingers fumbled with the eagle clasp.

Finally, I got the cloak on. I fastened the clasp around my neck. The fabric was heavy on my shoulders. It felt like I wore a Halloween costume. I was Wonder If I Am About To Die Woman.

I waited expectantly for several seconds that felt like hours. Nothing happened. Other than feeling like I was getting hot flashes because of all my running and the fact I had a heavy piece of fabric draped over me, I did not feel any different. If the cloak was making my magic powers level up like a character in a video game, I couldn't tell.

"Am I supposed to say 'Shazam' or something?" I demanded of Daniel.

"How the hell am I supposed to know? You're the sorceress. It's why I hired you. Make it work." Daniel turned away from me and faced the door. The sound of the approaching statues was noticeably louder. His jaw clenched, and his grip tightened on his staff. "And do it fast. I may be able to secure the door for a while with the Ark, but I can't do it forever. Those things can absorb magic."

No pressure. I've always sucked at tests, especially ones with a literal deadline.

I took a deep breath and let it out, trying to force my panicking brain to slow down and reason us out of this situation.

The Cloak of Wisdom was a magical Relic. Magic usually required a spell to activate it. So, maybe I needed a spell to use the cloak. But what was that spell?

Okay, a spell was triggered using the Word, the Will, and the Wave. That was Magic 101, the first thing every Gifted learned when she trained in the use of her inherent magical capacity. What could the Word, the Will, and the Wave be in this case?

I remembered what was on the plaque next to the case I had smashed. Daniel said the former owner of the cloak had mandated what appeared there. There was an image of two hands intertwined in the shape of a bird. Maybe that was the Wave. And the plaque had said Kato believed the cloak became a part of his body, and then it imparted to him occult knowledge. Maybe that was the Will part—I had to will the cloak to become a part of my body.

If I was right, that only left the Word. What could the Word be? The only thing that immediately sprang to mind was *abracadabra*. I suspected that wasn't it.

The Word did not have to be a single word. It could be a phrase, or a sentence. Heck, with really complicated spells, ones that were beyond my capacity, the Word could be pages and pages of text. It was why most Master Magicians kept spellbooks, so they wouldn't mess up complex spells.

The sound of the approaching statues got even louder. My mind frantically groped for the Word that might activate the cloak.

It came up empty, at least as far as the Word was concerned. Instead I got a mental image of the statues squeezing the life out of me.

Wait a minute! The statues! Obviously, they were magically programmed to be guardians of the clock. Kato had mandated they be on display wherever the cloak was. And they all had the same Hebrew word on their foreheads: Emet. Truth.

What was the word for truth in Latin? Crap! I couldn't remember. I cursed myself for not hitting the books after Dad's death. If only that Roman centurion who had stabbed Daniel was handy.

Wait. Daniel had said he knew all human languages. "Quick, what's the word for 'truth' in Latin?"

"Veritas," Daniel supplied immediately, still staring at the door. A rainbow shimmered over its contours, just like the shimmering wood in Daniel's hand. I assumed he was trying to fortify the door to make it harder for the statues to get in.

I remembered now. *Veritas*. Yes!

Feeling a bit like a clown at a children's party, I put my hands together in the bird shape I had seen on the plaque. "Veritas," I said, willing the cloak on my shoulders to become a part of me and impart the magical wisdom it possessed.

The eagle clasp got warm, enough so that I felt it through my shirt. The cape's fabric around my neck shifted like something alive, moving so that it touched my bare skin.

Once it did, I felt a strange sensation, like my mind was being sped up. Everything I had seen and done whizzed by in my head, almost like my life was flashing before my eyes the way people said it did as you were dying.

I gasped when the strange sensation stopped as abruptly as it had begun. Moving on its own, the cloak enfolded my body. It tightened around me like a boa constrictor.

Finally! A girl! said a male voice. I did not hear the voice with my ears. I heard it inside my skull. The cloak got even tighter around my breasts and buttocks. *And what a girl! Yowzah!*

CHAPTER FIFTEEN

Startled and confused, it took me a moment to react. I had been sexually harassed before, but never by an inanimate object.

"Stop that," I said aloud, spreading my arms with effort to move the cloak away from my body. The cloak struggled against me. It was like wrestling an octopus.

Aw, come on baby, the voice in my head said. The voice was young, like that of a teenager. *Don't be like that. Me love you long time.*

"I said stop it!" I exclaimed sharply. I was arguing with a piece of laundry. Just when I thought my life could not get any crazier, it had. "I'm in trouble and need help."

I need help too, the cloak said. A tendril of fabric caressed my butt. *Help you're just the type to provide. I like my girls on the healthy side. More cushion for the pushin', if you know what I mean.*

Dry cleaning had just implied I was fat. Now I'd heard everything. I felt insulted, and I felt even sillier for feeling insulted.

I gathered the groping folds of fabric into a bundle, and held the squirming mass away from my body, with the warm clasp still around my neck. "Stop trying to touch me, you creep. This is serious. Creatures are trying to kill us."

The vibrations from the stomping statues were so loud now, I felt them in my teeth. Loud pounding on the door started.

I'm a creep, am I? The voice in my head was indignant. *How rude. I'd hoped we'd be friends, but we won't be if you're gonna call me names. Way to win friends and influence people. If someone's trying to kill you, I wish them Godspeed. You're on your own.*

Daniel, still holding the shimmering Ark fragment, peered over his shoulder at me. He looked concerned about the statues pounding on the door, but not at all puzzled about why I had suddenly started talking to myself. I realized he knew I was talking to the Cloak of Wisdom. The rascal had known this would happen when I activated the cloak. If I could travel back in time, I would go ahead and slap him upside the head the way I had daydreamed of.

Who's the third wheel? I assumed the cloak meant Daniel. Apparently, it could see. *Your boyfriend?*

"He's definitely not my boyfriend. He's the reason we're in this mess. But he's not important right now. Animated statues that are super strong and immune to magic are trying to kill us. You're the Cloak of Wisdom, so drop some wisdom on me. How do we escape?"

The cloak sniffed contemptuously. *What about "you're on your own" did you not understand? I'm a spirit bound to a magic cloak. Conventional means can't destroy me. So, whatever's after you is not my problem. Not my circus, and not my monkeys. Be a doll and try not to bleed on me too much when you die. Blood is a beast to get out.*

There was so much pounding on the door now, the sound was like jackhammers. Sweat poured off Daniel's brow as he concentrated on keeping the door shut with the Ark fragment.

"You've got to help us," I insisted. "We're going to get slaughtered."

My advice? Stick your head between your legs and kiss your ass goodbye. Next time, dig your well before you're thirsty by being nice to the person who can help you instead of insulting him. Not that there'll be a next time if what you say is true.

The pounding had spread from just the door to the walls surrounding the door. Cracks began to appear on the walls. With Daniel visibly straining, the rainbow colors shimmering on the door spread to encompass the walls.

Out of curiosity, what's trying to get in here? the cloak asked. *Whatever it is, it sure has a hard-on for you.*

"Like I said, they're statues that have become animated. Tall, big, blocky, and made of red clay."

Wait a minute. These statues don't by any chance have a Hebrew word carved into their foreheads, do they?

"They do."

Glowing red eyes? The voice sounded worried now.

"Yeah. You know what they are?"

The cloak cursed. *Golems,* the voice said bitterly. *I told Ichiro they were too single-minded and stupid to serve as protectors. But noooooo, Captain Know-It-All goes right ahead and uses them as guard dogs anyway. A Japanese sorcerer fooling around with Jewish animated beings was bound to end in disaster. A clear case of cultural appropriation.* For the first time, the cloak sounded panicked. *Take me off right now!*

"Why?"

Because when the golems rip you apart, they'll do the same to me. Now he was talking so fast, his words tumbled over each other. *Like I said, they're stupid. If I'm linked with you, they'll perceive me as the enemy also even though I'm the one they're supposed to protect. And since they can absorb magic, they're one of the few things that can kill me. Take me off right this instant. Toss me in a corner somewhere, out of harm's way. There's no sense in both of us going to that big golem heap in the sky.*

"I won't take you off until you help me figure a way out of this."

The cloak was silent for a moment. *Fine. But I'm only telling you this because my own neck is on the line.* The cloak sighed in resignation, like a kid whose parents were forcing him to eat his brussels sprouts. *You can't defeat the golems with magic. Retreat is the only option. The magic that animates them will dissipate once I'm sufficiently far from them.*

"We can't retreat. That door is the only exit. We're trapped."

Whose genius idea was it to seek refuge in a spot with no exits? The cloak's tone was incredulous. *No, don't tell me. I can already guess. Somebody rude and hippy. Not terribly bright, are you? All body, no brains. No matter. That's all water under the burning bridge now. Just open a portal and whisk us right out of here.*

I was confused. "Open a what?"

A portal. A magical doorway from one place to another. Chop, chop, hurry it up. That wall's cracking like a teenager's voice. It's not going to last much longer.

The cloak was right. The wall and door were as cracked now as a dry riverbed. Daniel was barely holding them together with the Ark fragment.

"I don't know how to open a portal," I said. "That kind of magic is way over my head."

Wait, hold up. With all the magical capacity I sense in you, you don't know how to open a portal? I was opening portals when I was 12-years-old. What are you, stupid?

"Don't call me stupid."

Stupid is as stupid does.

"That doesn't even make any sense."

You don't make any sense.

I wanted to rip the cloak off and set it on fire. "You know, I've had just about enough of you."

"Sage!" Daniel yelled. "Focus on getting us out of here. I can't hold these things off much longer."

The third wheel's right. First we need to get out of here, then we can talk more about how dumb you are. I'll give you a crash course in portal opening. Hmmm, where to begin? I got a sudden image in my head of a pipe-smoking college professor writing on a chalkboard. *To open a portal, you must cast a spell. To cast a spell, you need the Word, the Will, and the Wave.*

"I know about the three Ws," I snapped. "I'm not an idiot."

Could've fooled me, the voice muttered. *Alright, if you already have a grasp of the fundamentals, we'll jump ahead. We'll start with the Word, which is the simplest part of this particular spell. Repeat after me: Nulla tenaci invia est via.*

I repeated it several times, until the cloak was satisfied I had the pronunciation right. It didn't take long; having homicidal golems literally beating down the door to get to you concentrated the mind. *It will never do for you to say the words even slightly wrong,* the cloak said. *If you're not precise, you might open a portal to the bottom of the Arctic Ocean. Or worse.*

Okay, now let's tackle the Will. When you open a portal, it can only be to a place you've been to before. You'll be using magic to open a wormhole from here to that other place. Visualize it like two funnels, rotated so the bottoms of each are facing and connected by a tube. Like this. I got a mental image of what the cloak described. Later—if there was a later—I'd have to ask it how it projected those images into my mind. *You'll be focusing your magical will to push us from this side of the funnel, through the tube, and out of the other side of the funnel. Don't lose focus on what you're doing, or else we won't wind up where you want us to wind up.*

"Got it," I said.

I hope so. He did not sound like he was drowning in optimism. *Finally, the hardest part of this spell. The Wave. First, take off those idiotic gloves. Are you driving Miss Daisy? You can't cast a complex spell wearing gloves. You need nimble fingers. Better. Okay, pay close attention.*

A picture appeared in my mind of two disembodied hands. They moved in a complex pattern, so quickly I couldn't follow. It was like watching someone speak in sign language at high speed.

"Wait! You're going too fast," I said. The hands stopped and started over from the beginning, more slowly this time. I mimicked the movements, my sweaty hands feeling clumsy performing the unfamiliar motions.

"Hurry!" Daniel urged. His face was red, and his arm holding the Ark fragment shook. Some of the cracks in the door and wall were now holes. It was obvious that only the Ark's power held the golems back, but the rainbow colors shimmering on the surface of the wall got visibly dimmer with each blow from the golems.

Okay, those are all the components of the portal spell, the cloak said once I finally finished mimicking the motions of the hands in my mind. *Just put them all together, and we'll blow this popsicle stand.*

I gathered my will, visualizing what I wanted to happen as the cloak had instructed. I started the motions of the Wave and said, "Nulla tenaci invia es via."

Stop! It's "est," not "es." Merlin's beard! What are you trying to do, blow us to kingdom come? Start over.

Despite being able to see the golems through all the holes in the wall now, I tried to calm myself. I started again.

Nope, nope, nope, the cloak said, stopping me in the middle of the Wave. *Are you an old crone? Do you have arthritis? Why are your fingers curled like that? Straighten them out. Are you trying to commit seppuku and save the golems the trouble? Begin again. Hurry!*

I started from scratch for the third time. Sweat dripped into my eyes, but I didn't dare take time to wipe it away. The golems were almost through the wall.

Daniel cried out and staggered backward. The rainbow sheen on the door and wall disappeared. Two golems burst through the damaged wall like the Kool-Aid Man. Others followed. Plaster and sheetrock went flying. A piece of debris hit my temple. I ignored the starburst of pain that expanded in my head, keeping my focus on trying to open a portal back to my apartment in Columbia Heights.

Daniel backed hastily away from the approaching golems, to where I stood my ground. "Whatever you're going to do, do it now," he yelled.

I'm only 635 and three-quarters years-old. I'm too young to die! the cloak wailed.

The golems were almost on top of us. The air crackled with building magical power as I neared the end of the Wave, praying I was doing it right.

The shambling golems reached for us like Frankenstein monsters run amok. The rumble of their steps made my teeth chatter. Running, or even moving out of the way, was not an option. I was too deep into the process of casting this spell. There was no time to start over. The third time *had* to be the charm.

My stomach gurgled as I began the final motion of the Wave. I wondered if what I had for dinner last night had been my last meal. I wished I had gone out for chili dogs instead.

One of the golems reared back, its fists over its head, about to smash us to a pulp, right as I spread my arms wide, completing the Wave, willing a portal to open so we could step through it into my apartment.

The air crackled like a powerful electric current ran through it. With a ripping sound that was like dozens of thick books being simultaneously torn apart, a swirling blue and black mass that looked like a mini-thunderstorm spread out on the floor under my and Daniel's feet.

We fell into it like a trapdoor had swung open under us.

We tumbled, end over end, falling as a kaleidoscope of endless shades of blue and black danced around us. Nauseous, I wanted to throw up. I fought the impulse. It felt as though if I succumbed, every fiber of my body would fly apart like an exploding grenade. I had never taken psychedelics, but this was what I imagined a bad LSD trip was like.

In a fraction of a second that felt like minutes, we fell out of the bad acid trip into near darkness. The swirling blue and black mass boiled above us before winking out of existence, revealing the night sky.

This was not my apartment. The portal had deposited us into mid-air, like we were passengers on a plane that had abruptly disappeared.

Spinning wildly, Daniel and I fell like dropped rocks. The Cloak of Wisdom fluttered around me like a broken glider. The air whistled around us. The cloak was screaming. Daniel was screaming. I was screaming. All God's chillun were screaming.

I slammed into something hard. My breath whooshed out of me. Daniel followed a split second later. We tumbled down a hard and jagged slope. The world spun around us.

I snatched a glimpse of emptiness below. I flung an arm out, grabbing with my hand. I caught hold of a hard protuberance right as the rest of me tumbled off the edge of whatever it was we had fallen on.

My shoulder shrieked with pain as my body jolted to a halt. I dangled off the edge of something. Daniel tumbled past me, clutching the Ark fragment. The tip of the staff smacked my head, making my ears ring.

I shot my free arm out. My shoulder shrieked again when I caught Daniel, preventing him from hitting the ground below.

Daniel and I swung like a pendulum. Panting, I held on to both Daniel and the outcropping for dear life.

I looked around. I clutched a stone on the edge of a roof. We had obviously fallen out of the sky, hit this sloped roof, then tumbled off it. I had barely stopped us from slamming into a sidewalk nearly two stories below us.

I'm guessing this is not where you wanted to wind up, the cloak said. *I give you a five out of ten for execution. I deducted three points for showing up at the wrong place, and another two points for not sticking the landing.* Now that we seemed out of danger and he wasn't screaming like a little girl in my head, the cloak sounded like he was having the time of his life. *All in all, not a bad first effort. I'll admit you had me worried for a second or two there. It could've gone worse.*

The mortar under the stone I clutched suddenly shifted and crumbled. The stone fell away from the roof. Daniel and I tumbled again.

We bounced off an awning. Daniel hit the sidewalk first. I fell on top of him with the Cloak of Wisdom flipped over my head. The cloak covered both of us like a shroud.

Daniel groaned in pain under me. Falling on Daniel didn't hurt as badly as hitting the concrete sidewalk directly would have, but it didn't feel great either. I felt bad about landing on Daniel. I also kinda didn't. This was all his fault.

Ow! the cloak complained, as if the fall had hurt him too. *"It could've gone worse," I foolishly said. Me and my big mouth. I should know better than to tempt Fate. She's probably still pissed about what I said about her centuries ago. She has the memory of an elephant.*

I rolled off of Daniel. I sat up. Everything ached. I felt like an old woman. If this was what being an elderly woman was like, I didn't want to become one. Then again, the way things had been going, something would kill me soon and I wouldn't have to worry about growing old and decrepit. Every dark cloud had a silver lining.

I tugged the cloak from around my face. A bright yellow light shined in my eyes. I blinked, letting my eyes adjust.

We were on the sidewalk in front of a building painted a garish yellow, red, and white. I knew this place all too well. It was the iconic Ben's Chili Bowl on U Street, about a thirty-minute walk from my apartment. Ben's was famous for its chili dogs and chili half-smokes. A half-smoke was a half-beef, half-pork, all-delicious smoked sausage popular in the District and the surrounding area. I had eaten at Ben's many times and had a few dimples on my thighs to show for it.

Obviously, thinking about chili dogs when I'd been trying to open a portal to my apartment had been a mistake.

Though it was the wee hours of the morning, Ben's was still open. A racially mixed group of men stood on the sidewalk near us with hot dogs and sodas in their hands. They stared at me and Daniel with open-mouthed surprise. They must have never seen a sorceress, an angel, and a haunted cloak fall out of the sky before. If they started hanging out with me, stuff like this would soon be old hat to them.

Eyes roved over me, taking in my all-black outfit, mask, and red cloak that looked like a Hero's cape.

"Yo lady," one of the men said. "You some kind of superhero?"

She most definitely is not, the cloak said firmly in my head.

CHAPTER SIXTEEN

"Why in the world didn't you tell me the Cloak of Wisdom was inhabited by a horny, adolescent, smart-mouthed ghost?" I demanded of Daniel angrily.

Unfazed by my anger, Daniel puffed placidly on a cigar. He leaned on the large sweetgum tree in the small backyard of the Leverettes' house. The Ark fragment rested against the base of the tree.

It was mid-morning, just hours after we had escaped the art gallery. Birds chirped and fluttered in the branches above us. They seemed carefree. For them, it was just another day. Unlike me, they must've had the good sense to not get involved in a bunch of shenanigans.

It was hot, even in the shade of the tree. The sticky heat exacerbated the aches and pains I suffered in the wake of stealing the cloak. I had changed into shorts and a t-shirt. My arms and legs were bruised from last night's craziness. I looked like a battered spouse.

The Cloak of Wisdom was inside my apartment, draped over the back of my couch. I had been tempted to stuff the mouthy thing into the garbage instead.

Daniel blew a smoke ring. He watched it expand as it wafted heavenward, perhaps thinking he would be joining it soon. Daniel responded, "I believe he was eighteen when his spirit was bound to the cloak. He was an adult, not an adolescent."

"Don't bandy words with me. That is not the point, and you know it. The point is you lied to me."

"I didn't lie. I just failed to disclose certain facts."

"You're as slippery as a politician. You should run for Congress."

"I already did. I served in the Second Continental Congress for almost a year after the Declaration of Independence." Daniel shook his head at the memory, then winced in pain at the movement. He was even more banged up than I was. He had a big bruise on the side of his face that looked like a giant inkblot. "Politics wasn't to my liking. Too much talking, not enough doing. Much like now. Shouldn't you be inside, working with the cloak to figure out how to find the Spear of Destiny? For all we know, Millennium is closing in on the Relic as we speak."

"If the Spear's been hidden all these years, it can stay hidden a few minutes longer. I'm still waiting to hear why you didn't tell me everything you knew about the cloak."

"If I had told you, would you have put it on?" Daniel asked.

"No."

Daniel shrugged, and winced again. "That's why I didn't tell you."

I stepped closer and got in Daniel's face. "You listen to me, and you listen good. When I'm in the field, what I don't know could get me killed. I need to know everything you know if we're going to continue to work together. It's too dangerous otherwise."

"If memory serves, it was you flying off the handle and smashing the case which activated the golems, not me not gossiping like a school girl about the cloak."

He certainly had me there, but I was in no mood to admit it. "I'm not going to tell you again: No more lying or not disclosing information." I poked Daniel in the chest with each word for emphasis. I took sadistic pleasure from the fact he winced as I did so.

Daniel brushed my hand away. He looked irritated. "There's far more at stake here than the fact your tender feelings are hurt because I withheld information and because the Cloak of Wisdom did not speak nicely to you. Stop being childish. The end goal here is to find and secure the Spear of Destiny before Millennium does. The Cloak of Wisdom can help us do that. It's already proved its utility by helping us escape from the golems." He jiggled the coins in his pocket. "The divine compulsion for me to move on is getting stronger. I'll have to leave the city soon. Who knows when I'll be able to return? Millennium will have the Spear long before then. So how about you stop wasting time, go inside, play nice with our new friend, and use him to figure out how to get the Spear? I'm paying for results, not your griping."

I wanted to slam Daniel's head against the tree so badly, it was almost a physical ache. "No more lies or omissions," I insisted. "Promise me right now, or so help me, I'll quit. You can find your precious Spear all by your lonesome. I don't need your money that badly." I did need it that badly, but I wasn't about to tell him that.

"Very well. No more omissions. Everything I know, you'll know. You have my word." He grinned, then made a motion on his chest. "Cross my heart and hope to die."

I felt like I was being mocked. The indulgent smile on Daniel's face was more than just a little patronizing. I yearned to wipe it away with a tree branch.

"When this is all over, you and I are going to have a long talk," I vowed. "And there's not going to be a lot of talking."

Still smiling, Daniel blew another smoke ring. The threat did not seem to concern him. "Looking forward to it."

Unsatisfied with the exchange but not wanting to beat a dead horse, I turned away from Daniel and started back toward my apartment. If Daniel was an angel, angels were more disappointing in reality than they were in theory. Then again, who wasn't more disappointing in reality than in theory? My father was the only person who had never disappointed me.

On the way to the stairs to my apartment door, I noticed movement between the slightly cracked curtains on one of the Leverettes' second-floor windows. Since Mr. Leverette still worked part-time and therefore wasn't home, I guessed it was Mrs. Leverette, spying on me. Using Daniel's retainer to get up to date on my rent clearly had not also bought me privacy. Mrs. Leverette likely thought she was watching me and Daniel post-booty call. With all the bruises on our bodies, she probably thought we were real freaks. We were, just not the kind of freaks she thought.

I waved and blew a kiss at the window. The curtains flicked closed. *The real-life soap opera is over*, I thought to Mrs. Leverette. *Go back to watching your TV ones.*

Correction: The soap opera was over for Mrs. Leverette. Not for me.

I went into my apartment. I was vaguely disappointed the Cloak of Wisdom was still on my couch, right where I had left it. Nobody had broken in and stolen it. People broke into my place when I didn't want them to, and they didn't break in when I did want them to. Perverse.

I sighed in resignation. I didn't want a snarky and condescending voice in my head again, but I did want to hurry up and find the Spear of Destiny so I could pay off the wererats and get back to a normal life. Well, as normal as my life ever really got.

Feeling like a superhero cosplayer getting ready for Comic-Con, I draped the cloak over my shoulders, closed the eagle clasp, and cast the spell to activate it.

Oh, it's you again, were the first words out of the cloak's invisible mouth. The tone was that of someone who had slammed his front door on Jehovah's Witnesses, only to open it again to find them still there. *Where are we? This place is a dump.*

It was going to be a long day.

"This is my apartment in Washington, D.C.," I said, keeping my voice calm and level. I was not going to be baited into arguing with a piece of clothing again.

You should hire a maid, the cloak sniffed. *Better yet, a team of maids. Or rent a flamethrower and start over from scratch.*

I bit back a caustic response. I was going to be the adult in the room if it killed me. It might since I wasn't used to it.

"I feel as though we got off to the wrong foot before," I said diplomatically, in disbelief I was sucking up to an article of clothing. Next, I'd be assuring my panties I loved them just the way they were and that they were so much prettier than their Size Small cousins. "I'm sorry about that. It was my fault. Let's start from scratch. First, thank you for your help in us getting away from the golems. My name is Sage Hawthorne. What's yours?"

The cloak hesitated for a beat, then said dramatically, *You may call me The Caped Crusader.* I got a vivid mental image of the cloak standing on top of a skyscraper with the wind rustling the folds of its fabric, somehow managing to look heroic as the sun's rays glinted off it.

I swallowed a snort. "I'm not calling you The Caped Crusader. What's your name? Your real name."

You're the biggest wet blanket I've ever met. And that's saying something because I've been around for a while. His voice was surly. *Fine, have it your way. My name is Puck. Like the sprite in Shakespeare's* A Midsummer Night's Dream. *That character is named after me, you know. Will never did give me a penny of the royalties the way he promised he would. Writers can't be trusted. They're almost as bad as lawyers.*

"You're some kind of sprite?"

Of course not. He sounded offended. *I'm a spirit imprinted on a cloak. Do I look like a fucking sprite?*

"No cursing."

Why?

"Why?" My patience was slipping. "Because I said so, that's why. You're in my head, not the other way around. I make the rules."

You can take your "I said so"s, fold them up until they're all sharp corners, and shove them up your prissy ass. You're not the boss of me. I don't take orders from somebody who can't even cast a simple portal spell without her hand being held.

My resolve to be the bigger person crumbled. My fingers fumbled at the clasp around my neck. "I don't have to put up with this. I tried being nice to you, and this is the thanks I get. Goodbye, and good riddance." I'd just have to find the Spear of Destiny without this smart aleck's help.

Wait! Hold on. Don't take me off. I'll be good, I promise.

The fear and panic in Puck's voice made me hesitate, staying my hands. "Why? What happens when I take you off?"

When I'm not bonded to anyone, it's like I'm in a dark, cold room. Like solitary confinement, but worse. No light, no sound, no anything. It's been years since anyone's worn me, and I think I'll go crazy if I have to go back there. Please don't make me. He sounded like a little kid now, both scared and powerless. Maybe I was the world's softest touch, but I felt sorry for him.

"All right, I won't take you off right now. But if you're going to be in my head, we both must make an effort to get along. The first step is no cursing. I don't want that kind of language in my head. How does that work anyway, you being in my head? Can you read my mind?"

Nah, it doesn't work like that. When you cast the spell that bonded us for the first time, I downloaded a bunch of information from the Wernicke and Broca areas of your brain—cultural references you understand, colloquialisms, that sort of thing—so you and I can communicate effectively. The fact I can project images into your mind helps with that. But it's not like I have access to your thoughts or memories or anything like that. The same thing happened with my last host, Ichiro. I couldn't speak a lick of Japanese until I bonded with him for the first time.

"The Wernicke and Broca areas of my brain," I repeated slowly, stumbling over the unfamiliar terms. "I don't know what those are."

Oh wow, someone who doesn't know how to open a portal and who lives in a sty a pig would be ashamed of isn't an expert on brain anatomy? Imagine my surprise.

"Sarcasm? I thought we were going to be nicer to one another."

You're right. My bad. It's hard for me to communicate with lesser minds without sounding condescending. I'm a genius, you know. He didn't say it boastfully. It was more like him saying "The sun is hot." He said it matter-of-factly, like he was stating a fact that should be obvious to everyone. *Not only is my IQ off the charts, but I have an eidetic and photographic memory. Even at the tender age of eighteen, when my consciousness became bonded to this cloak, I was the most gifted magician of my generation. Over the centuries I've bonded with dozens of magicians of various disciplines. Since they wore me to help them create and cast spells and do magical research, thanks to my perfect memory, I know just about everything they knew. I'm the closest thing the magical world has to a Library of Alexandria.*

I didn't know what the Library of Alexandria was either, but not wanting to be ignorance-shamed again, I kept my lack of knowledge to myself. "How did your spirit get bound to the cloak?"

It's a long story, Puck said in a tone that made it clear he was not interested in telling it. He changed the subject. *While you're wearing me, I hear what you hear, see what you see, feel what you feel.* He hesitated. *Speaking of feeling things, are you by any chance a lesbian?* His voice was hopeful.

"No."

A shame. I wouldn't mind having a front row seat to some girl-on-girl action. Bi?

"No."

Bi-curious?

"No. And even if I were, I wouldn't satisfy any such curiosity while wearing a cloak."

Ooooh, I'm intrigued. What would you be wearing instead? Speak slowly, and don't leave out any details.

"Um, no." I shook my head. If someone had told me two weeks ago I'd be discussing my sexuality with an article of clothing that had the brainpower of a mystical supercomputer and the maturity of a horny 16-year-old boy, I would have said a meteor must've hit them in the head. "Daniel and I didn't take you out of the Sackler Gallery to discuss the intimate details of my life."

And by "take," you mean steal. Not that I'm complaining. Even though this is a dump—no offense—it's still light-years better than being draped over some dumb mannequin's shoulders and trying to stave off going crazy by replaying past experiences repeatedly in my mind. Puck chortled. *The Conclave's Magic Suppression Division must be tearing its hair out trying to explain away camera footage of a bunch of statues coming to life.*

"Yeah," I said, suddenly more uncomfortable than I already was at the mention of the Conclave. The faster I found the Spear of Destiny, the faster I could do something about the Conclave investigation into my First Rule violation. Well, the violation they knew about. Thank God I'd been smart enough to wear a mask to the Sackler Gallery.

I told Puck about our quest to locate the Spear of Destiny before Millennium did. And, since presumably Puck would not be bonding with anyone else anytime soon, I went ahead and completely spilled the beans about the madhouse that my life had been lately, starting with the gargoyle attack at the Institute of Peace and everything that followed thereafter. I figured the more he knew, the more he could help me.

It was the first time I had told anyone everything that had happened to me lately. Honestly, I found getting it all off my chest was a bit of a relief. Maybe that old cliché was true: maybe a problem shared really was a problem halved.

Puck whistled when I finished my tale of woe. *Well, you've been quite the busy beaver.* He giggled lewdly, tickled about the vulgar double-meaning of the word. *I'm not gonna lie—part of the reason you're in this mess is you've got some deep-seated anger and impulse issues that need to be addressed.*

"I don't have anger and impulse issues," I protested. It was one thing for me to sometimes think I did; it was quite another for an uppity cloak to tell me I did.

Sure you don't, cupcake. That's why your hands aren't balled up in anger right now. I looked down, and realized my fists were clenched so tightly that my nails dug into my palms. Feeling foolish, I unclenched them. *Then again, what do I know? I'm a cloak, not a counselor. At any rate, you've got problems more pressing than the need to get your head shrunk.*

Lemme recap those problems to make sure I'm not missing any: For Daniel to get his angel wings back and for you to not become a wererat entrée, you need to find the Spear of Destiny, one of the most sought-after holy Relics in world history. And despite the fact some people have fruitlessly spent their entire lives searching for it, you—an uncertified, half-trained sorceress—need to find it sometime between yesterday and right this second, before Daniel is compelled to ease on down the road and before the most powerful sorcerer in the world gets his grubby hands on the Spear and goes on a rampage with it.

After that, you need to deal with whomever hired the wererats to come after you in the first place. You also need to somehow get your Master Magician certification after years of neglecting your magical studies to try to stave off the Conclave imprisoning you—or worse— for flouting the First Rule of magic. All while looking over your shoulder for this Ghost character so you won't further expose the magical world to a mundane.

Whew! What a clusterfu—um, I mean, nightmare. Did I miss anything? Perhaps one of the lesser gods having a vendetta against you?

Feeling overwhelmed by the odds against me, I sat down heavily on the couch. I was careful to not sit on Puck. He hadn't said anything sexual in a while, and I wanted to keep the platonic streak alive. "When you put it like that, it sounds impossible."

Difficult, yes. Impossible? No. The difficult I can do immediately. The impossible takes a little longer. The U.S. Army Corps of Engineers stole that adage from me. First Shakespeare and my name, then those sappers and my awesome expressions. Good engineers copy; great engineers apparently steal.

Despite everything, I found myself smiling. When he wasn't being insulting or lecherous, Puck's irrepressible energy was almost charming. "I don't think you're telling the truth about that one."

Maybe, he said breezily. *Only the unimaginative tell the truth all the time.*

"Does your allegedly stolen can-do saying mean you're going to help me with the Spear and with the Conclave?"

Sure. Why not? I haven't had a challenge worthy of my abilities since I formulated the theory of relativity for Einstein. Besides, you're not quite as bad as I first thought. You're growing on me. You're not as knowledgeable, composed, wise, thoughtful, or as disciplined as a sorceress really ought to be, but you're plucky.

"Wow. All this flattery is going right to my head."

CHAPTER SEVENTEEN

My eyes were so bleary and watery that the words of the dense book I read seemed to come alive and dance on the pages.

I blinked. The words still swam on the pages. Not that I understood half of what they said, anyway. The fact the seer stone Puck had taught me to create days ago translated this book's ancient Greek to English did not change the fact that the import of the words was still Greek to me. Daniel playing with the coins in his pocket more than usual did not help my concentration.

Irritated, I slammed the book shut. *The Soul: Theory and Practice* were the words etched in Greek on the cover of the ancient, thick, leather-bound book. What someone like me needed was *The Idiot's Guide to the Soul.*

What was the point? I would never figure this stuff out. I had hit the wall.

I hadn't slept in four days. Red anger and dark frustration cut through my exhaustion. Though Puck had warned me more volatile than normal emotions were a side effect of the no doze spell he had taught me, that did not make the emotions feel less real.

I flung the fist-sized seer stone. It whistled away from me with such force that it embedded itself into the wall of my apartment. I swept the book I'd been reading off my storage chest that did double duty as a living room table. It thumped onto the floor, knocking over a stack of equally obscure and abstruse books there. Puck had taught me the word *abstruse*. At least I had learned something these past few days.

Daniel was reading an epic fantasy novel, sitting with his feet propped up. He played with those infernal coins in his pocket like they were a talisman. He looked up at my outburst. His eyes flicked from the seer stone in the wall, to the scattered books, then to me.

"Well, that's certainly productive," he said.

"Shut up," I snapped irritably. I flung myself back on the sofa and stared at the popcorn ceiling. Though I was weary due to lack of sleep, I was simultaneously wide awake thanks to the no doze spell, like I had mainlined gallons of coffee. "This is stupid. Why do I have to read all this stuff, anyway? While I'm sitting here cramming, Millennium could be putting his hands on the Spear of Destiny."

We've been over this, Puck said. I had not taken him off in days. Though I did not always like what he had to say, I was getting used to having his voice in my head. *I think the best way to find the Spear is to teach you to astrally project so you can search the city for it. Unless you want to just search door-to-door, which was the boneheaded suggestion you had yesterday.*

"I'd rather do that than sit here going blind poring over ancient texts which are as clear as mud. Why can't you just teach me the blasted astral projection spell without putting me through this idiotic remedial education course?"

We've been over this too. It's like asking why NASA can't just teach you which buttons to push in the space shuttle instead of making you go through astronaut training. To be able to astrally project safely, you must understand the theory and the methodology behind it. It's not as simple as saying a word, waving your hand, and conjuring up a ball of spellfire. It's really high-level magic. Some of the highest, actually. I only know of one Master Magician who can do it safely, and he's a soul manipulation specialist. I doubt even Millennium can do it. If you don't have a solid foundation in the theory, you're liable to get yourself killed. Or worse yet, me.

"Well why don't you give Soul Man a jingle and get him to find the Spear? I'm sick of sitting here, sick of reading stuff I barely understand, and sick of forcing myself to stay awake. Plus, I can't shake the feeling something terrible is going to happen if I go through with this."

The man I'm thinking of is a black guy from the Democratic Republic of the Congo, so I wouldn't call him Soul Man to his face if I were you. Racist. I get that you're tired, but you've made a lot of progress. We're compressing years of study into just a few days, after all.

Feeling stubborn, I said, "I don't care. I'm through wrestling with high-level magic. I'm no good at it. Quick and dirty stuff is more my speed. The last time I did high-level magic, I got somebody I cared about killed." I started tearing up at the memory. I blinked hard, embarrassed, hoping neither Puck nor Daniel noticed. My exhaustion had made my emotions volatile and had made me reveal more than I normally did. I willed myself to not start crying. "Never again. We're going to have to find another way. I'm tapping out."

Daniel put his feet down and spun in his chair to face me. "Stop being such a baby."

"Excuse me?" I said, startled.

"You heard me. Stop being such a whiny baby. Ever since I brought you all these books after scrounging for them in obscure occult bookstores armed with the Cloak of Wisdom's reading list, it's been one complaint after another." His voice became high-pitched and mocking. "'I'm tired.' 'This stuff's too hard.' 'I don't want to do this anymore.' 'Ooooh, I'm scared of what might happen.' 'Me, me, me, me, me.'" Daniel looked at me contemptuously. "I for one am sick of your belly-aching. The world does not revolve around you. Everybody's got their own problems. I don't know what happened in your past or who died because of you. And frankly, I don't care. What I do care about is finding the Spear of Destiny before it falls into the wrong hands. We went to a lot of trouble to acquire the Cloak of Wisdom. If it says you need to hit the books before you attempt astral projection, then that's what you're going to do."

Hey! Puck said, sounding outraged. *I have a name, you know. Tell him to stop calling me an "it."*

Daniel of course couldn't hear Puck. Daniel continued, saying, "I'm paying you a lot of money to do a job, and I expect results. So shut up, man up, get your head out of your ass, and put it back in those books."

I got off the sofa and stepped over to Daniel. I stood over him. I was so mad, I was shaking.

I stopped myself with a herculean effort from reaching down and throttling Daniel. "Get out of here right now," I said, my teeth clenched, "or so help me I'm going to pick you up by the scruff of your neck and kick you back up to Heaven."

Daniel stared up at me, holding my gaze in challenge. Finally, he stood.

"I'll go," he said, reaching for the Ark fragment. "But once I'm gone, get back to work. I'm not paying you to whine."

It took every ounce of will to not fling one of the heavy books I had been studying and cave the back of Daniel's skull in as he walked out the door.

Once the door was closed, I punched the wall as hard as I could. My fist punctured the drywall. My arm sank into the wall up to my elbow. In my anger, I barely felt the impact.

Wow, Puck said. *It's not often that I'm the level-headed one in the room. What did that poor wall ever do to you?*

"You looking to get thrown out too?" I snarled.

Nope. Just making conversation.

"Well don't."

I yanked my arm out of the wall, raking my skin on the jagged hole's edges. My arm bled, and my fist throbbed. Stupid, stupid, stupid. Now I'd have to pay to get the hole patched. And what if I had broken my hand, hindering my ability to cast spells? I gingerly clenched and unclenched my aching hand. Fortunately, it didn't feel like I had broken anything.

Though you're hardly Miss Calm, Cool and Collected yourself, Daniel's gotten increasingly antsy the past few days, Puck said thoughtfully as I went to the kitchen sink and washed the blood and drywall dust off my arm.

"He has to move on from D.C. soon. He says it's his divine compulsion."

Don't you think that's a little weird?

I laughed bitterly. "There's nothing about this whole situation that's not weird."

After gingerly patting my bleeding arm dry with paper towels, I pulled the last of the Elven wine I had left out of the cabinet. I uncorked the flask and took a long swallow. Almost immediately I felt the drink's effects. It washed away the pain of my arm and most of my anger, leaving only numb sorrow.

Hey, go easy on that stuff, Puck said. *The no sleep spell you're under has already weakened your ability to control your emotions. Mixing Elven wine with it will just make it worse. No one enjoys being alone with a pie-eyed girl who's liable to make bad decisions more than I do, but now's not the best time to get a snootful. We've got too much work to do.*

"I don't care." It was a lie. I did care. Despite how much of a jerk Daniel sometimes was, he had paid me to do a job. When you were paid to do something, you should do it to the best of your ability. Dad had taught me that. I didn't have much—no family, few friends, and the kind of personality which made it likely that would not change—but I did have the pride I took in doing what I said I was going to do. And I said I would try to find the

Spear of Destiny. But, what Puck was trying to teach me to do was hard. Beyond my capacity to learn, maybe. I was afraid I wouldn't be able to pull it off.

And, I was equally afraid I *would* pull it off. The last time I had fooled around with high-level magic, it had ended disastrously.

Miserable, I drank more wine. The wine's warm glow spread from the pit of my stomach all throughout my body. Elven wine wasn't the solution to my problems, but it did an awesome job of masking them.

Are you going to tell me what's wrong with you, or am I gonna have to guess? Puck asked.

"Nothing's wrong with me. Besides, what could be wrong when you've got a bellyful of Elven wine?" I hiccupped, burped, then giggled. Nobody ever complained about Elven wine not being fast-acting.

Oh sure, everything's clearly just dandy, Puck said sarcastically. *We're racing to see who can find the Spear of Destiny the fastest, yet you're flying off the handle, punching walls, and getting drunk off your ass in the middle of the day when you ought to be studying.*

"No cursing," I said automatically.

Oops. Force of habit. Ichiro used to curse like a whore stuck at a celibacy convention. I've been meaning to ask, what've you got against cursing, anyway? I thought cursing and badass chicks went together like peanut butter and jelly. Thunder and lightning. Sturm and drang. Strippers and daddy issues. Black guys and—

"My father," I quickly interjected, afraid of what was coming next. "I don't curse in honor of my father." I had never told anyone that before. The lack of sleep, the no doze spell, and the wine must have conspired to loosen my lips.

Does he live around here?

"No. He's dead." Hot tears formed and started dripping down my cheeks. "I killed him."

There was stunned silence in my head for a moment. Then Puck said, *I haven't known you very long, but I find that hard to believe.*

"No, I killed him all right. Just as sure as if I had pulled the trigger myself." I was bawling now. I felt my face contort as I wept. Mortified about being so vulnerable in front of Puck, I tried to stop, but couldn't. Exhaustion, frustration, anger, and Elven wine obviously were not a good mix.

I flung the wine flask away before I drank more and further embarrassed myself. The open flask bounced off the wall and landed on the floor. Its contents gurgled out, forming a pool of red on the linoleum. It reminded me of the pool of blood I sat in ten years ago as I held Dad's lifeless body after he shot himself.

The remembrance made me cry even harder, long racking sobs that made it hard to breathe. I sank down onto the floor.

Puck was uncharacteristically quiet as I cried. My back was against the wall, and my legs were sprawled out in front of me. My sobbing rebounded off the walls of my tiny kitchen.

After a long while, when I finally quieted down some, Puck spoke gently, so much so that I thought at first his words were my imagination. *Tell me what happened to your father,* he said.

I blew my nose on a paper towel. It was rough against my nose. I angrily wiped my cheeks dry with the back of my hand. Daniel had been right—I was a baby. The world's oldest. If the world needed someone like me to protect it by locating the Spear of Destiny, the world was in serious trouble.

"I don't want to talk about it."

You may not want to talk about it, but it seems to me that you need to.

I opened my mouth, about to tell Puck no again. Salty snot dribbled onto my tongue. I spat it out, disgusted.

While Millennium was honing in on the Spear, I was eating my own mucus. I was a mess.

Maybe Puck was right. Maybe I did need to talk about it. How was I going to continue the search for the Spear like this?

"As is often the case with Gifted people, being Gifted runs in my family," I began after blowing my nose again. It was a good thing Puck was a cloak; most guys would run away screaming in terror when a woman cried the way I had. "My parents were both Master Sorcerers. My mother abandoned me and my Dad when I was a baby. Dad's name was Anwell. He raised me by himself. He was a good man. The best I've ever known. He never had an unkind word to say about anybody, always helped people when he could, and lived a good life. He was one of those guys you think is too good to be true when you meet them, that there's got to be something dark and disturbing under all that surface virtue. That wasn't the case with Dad. With him, what you saw was what you got. Everyone who knew him adored him. But nobody adored him more than I did. How he ever got hooked up with someone like my mother is to this day a mystery to me.

"In addition to taking care of me, Dad also trained me in the use of my magic when my abilities manifested. I absorbed his lessons like a sponge. Both because I loved magic, and because I loved pleasing him. When I was little, he had to make me go outside and play instead of me spending every second poring over books, studying magical theory, and learning new spells. Soon, I was casting spells magicians years older than me couldn't tackle. Dad often said I had the most magical potential of anyone he had ever known. And that was saying something because Dad knew some of the leading magicians of his time.

"Though Dad permitted me a lot of freedom in my magical studies, there was one area he declared off-limits: black magic. 'Black magic perverts its practitioner, often without her ever even realizing it,' he said. He made me promise I would stay away from it. Being a dutiful daughter, I promised. But, like telling a Catholic girl to stay away from sex until marriage, Dad telling me to stay away from black magic made it even more alluring.

"I managed to get my hands on some books on the subject. In the circle of young Gifteds I ran in, books on black magic were passed around the way mundane boys used to pass around copies of *Playboy*.

"After secretly devouring those books, I was convinced I could perform the feats of black magic they described. After all, as Dad had told me, I had the most magical potential of anyone he had ever known. I knew there was nothing I couldn't do.

"When I was sixteen I got everything ready one evening when Dad was supposed to be gone most of the night. First, I moved the furniture in the living room out of the way. I scrubbed down a part of the wood floor with the unholy water I'd bartered with a warlock for. Then I sprinkled holy water in a circle around that. The holy water smoked where it came into contact with the unholy water, searing a dark circle into the wood. I drew a large pentagram in fresh animal's blood on the part of the floor I had rendered profane with the unholy water. Then I positioned black tallow candles on each point of the pentagram and lit them with matches fashioned from a rotting oak tree.

"With the physical preparations complete, I executed the Word, the Will, and the Wave of the demon summoning spell I had decided on. I had practiced the components of the spell for a week, making sure I had everything right."

I paused. I felt sick to my stomach, like the wine wasn't agreeing with me. The wine wasn't to blame. It was the sickeningly vivid memory of what I called up from the pits of Hell that turned my stomach.

"It was the hardest spell I had ever cast, but I did it. I summoned a demon. It rose up from the pentagram like a fine red mist that hardened into flesh and bone once I completed the words of the spell. It looked like the bastard child of a ram and a spider, with huge curved horns and an exoskeleton dripping mucus that bubbled and popped when it hit the floor." I shuddered at the thought of the thing. I had a sudden sense memory of the way the demon smelled: of skunk, brimstone, decay, rot, and eternal grasping evil made flesh.

"The demon struggled against my Will, trying mightily to free itself. Its attempts to get free were like ocean waves smashing against the levees of my mind. But, my Will and the pentagram held.

"I had done it. I had summoned a demon, something I was sure no one my age had ever done before. At the rate I was going, I just knew I would become the youngest Master Sorceress in the history of the Conclave.

"If I hadn't been so busy congratulating myself, maybe I would have realized the demon and I were no longer alone. Dad had come home earlier than expected, and he had walked into the living room without me noticing.

"'Sage, what have you done?' was what he said. Simple words, yet I'll never forget them.

"Startled by Dad's unexpected appearance, my Will imprisoning the demon in the confines of the pentagram faltered for an instant. An instant was all the fiend needed. It sprang out of the pentagram and circle of holy water like a rabid dog that had broken its chain.

"It didn't leap at me, though. I wish it had. It leaped for my father. The demon's body merged into my father's like a raindrop hitting a bucket of water, disappearing as if it had been a figment of my imagination.

"Dad turned to me. I had never seen such hate on his face before. He flicked his wrist at me. I flew backward into the air like I had been thrown by an invisible giant. I slammed into the wall behind me and was held there by some powerful unseen force, unable to move a muscle. I dangled on the wall like a painting, with an immense weight pressing against my chest.

"My father stepped toward me, looking up at me with a twisted face I barely recognized. I'll never forget his words: 'Foolish girl, playing at magic you can't begin to understand, much less control,' he said in a voice that was his yet, somehow, not his. 'I could squash you like the bug you are, but this body's memories give me a better idea.'

"My father, obviously under the demon's control, climbed the stairs. He returned a few minutes later holding a knife in one hand, and the Smith and Wesson Dad kept in his nightstand in his other hand. It's the same gun I keep in the end table in the living room.

"Brandishing the gun at me, my father explained that he would carve me up like a veal cutlet, yet be careful to leave me alive. Only then, when I was begging to be put out of my misery, would he shoot and kill me. He would call the police and report that he had tortured and shot his own daughter. When the police arrived, the demon would vacate my father's body, leaving him to be arrested and imprisoned for murdering his only daughter.

"I would die, the demon said through my father, knowing that not only had my stupidity gotten myself killed, but it had ruined my father's life as well.

"I literally could not move a muscle as I hung on the wall. The demon's dark magic was too powerful. I couldn't even blink. I could hardly see through my tears by that point. The demon was right. Dad had warned me about fooling around with black magic. My arrogance and stupidity were about to get me killed and ruin Dad's life. Not only would Dad go to prison for something he was not responsible for, but he would have to live the rest of his life with the memory of cutting into and shooting me.

"Laughing maniacally like an escapee from an insane asylum, my father put the gun down on the table, about to get started on carrying out the demon's plan. But, Dad's hand hesitated when he tried to remove his hand from the gun. His arm started to shake, like when you've been working out a body part too hard and it gets tremors."

My blubbering, which had mostly subsided, started up again. "Dad picked the gun back up. He slowly lifted it. His arm shook like moving the gun took a superhuman effort. He pressed the barrel against his temple.

"'No! Stop! What are you doing? I command you to stop!' my father screeched, his voice almost inhuman. I'll never forget them, the last words Dad ever spoke. His last words, but not his last message.

"Dad was facing me. His face was still twisted and feral as his shaking hand pressed the gun against his head. But, for one brief instant, his face cleared, becoming normal, becoming the face I loved again. His lips flashed a brief, sad smile. He winked at me.

"Dad pulled the trigger, blowing his own brains out. His body toppled over. The magic holding me immobile against the wall dissipated. I collapsed into a heap on the floor, my legs so stiff they couldn't hold me up.

"I crawled over to where my father had fallen. I held him as his blood pooled around us, expanding like a dilating red eye."

I coughed, clearing my throat. "Dad loved me so much he was able to overpower the demon's control over him. When he killed himself, he also destroyed the demon which was bonded with him. He sacrificed himself to save me. He died because of me. I killed him just as surely as if I had pulled the trigger myself."

It took a little while for me to compose myself again. Puck was uncharacteristically silent, but I felt his presence, like a warm comforting blanket around me.

Eventually I said, "It was two days before someone found us on the floor of the living room. One of Dad's co-workers got worried because he hadn't shown up for work and wouldn't answer his phone, which wasn't like him. The police had to literally pry me from Dad's stiff body.

Though I remember them doing it, I remember it like it's a scene from a movie. You know, like it was happening to someone else. Shock, I suppose.

"A big part of me died along with Dad. I stopped studying magic altogether. To this day, everything I know how to do is a variant on what Dad taught me. It's why I don't have my Master's status. After Dad died, it was a long while before I cast another spell. It was years before I returned to some semblance of normal. During that time, just looking at me the wrong way would set me off. I was mad at the world, but especially mad at myself. I got into fights constantly. It's why I have a record. I had serious anger issues." I thought of me punching Willow and how I had wanted to cave Daniel's skull in. I shook my head. "Some things never change, maybe."

You ending your magical training at sixteen is why you aren't as skilled a sorceress as you could be? Puck asked.

I nodded, wiping my nose again with the paper towel balled up in my hand.

And that's why training for astral projection is so hard for you? Because you're afraid of what might happen if you practice high-level magic again?

I nodded again. "I am terrified of what might happen if I continue to pursue high-level magic. I clearly don't have the good judgment to handle it. Look at what I did to Dad."

You were a child then. Children do childish things. Now you're a woman. You must learn to trust yourself more.

"Yeah, and me trusting myself worked out so well for my father, didn't it?" I asked tartly. "Besides, 'trust yourself' is easy for you to say. You're a centuries-old magical genius."

Puck laughed bitterly. *Yeah, I'm a genius. But being a genius doesn't mean I'm wise. I've made my fair share of mistakes. Like how I got stuck in this cloak. That mistake was a humdinger.*

"Why don't you tell me about it?"

Nah. We're talking about you, not me.

"Believe me, I'm sick of talking about me." I again wiped my cheeks dry with the back of my hands. "You must think I'm the world's biggest crybaby."

Nope. Abraham Lincoln was hands-down the biggest crybaby. You should've seen the way he bawled his eyes out when he was engaged to somebody he didn't want to be engaged to, but was too much of a pus—uh, a scaredy-cat to break it off. I dictated a letter for him to send to her that subtly suggested how awful her life would be if she married him. And that was the end of that. He never heard from her again. Abe was so grateful, he later almost named his firstborn Puck, but Mary Todd put her foot down. If a guy with no backbone like him could win the Civil War, imagine what you can do.

"Sometimes I wonder how much of what you say is true, and how much is your way of distracting me."

Telling the truth, the whole truth, and nothing but the truth all the time is boring. The truth is for those who lack creativity. That reminds me of the time I gave my penis a nickname. Back when I had one, that is. I called it The Truth because it was so big, no one could handle it. Except for this Halfling named Big Bertha. She was half human, half giant, and all woman. Her vagina was so big, when she shaved it, the Environmental Protection Agency arrested her for deforestation. You could shove a—

"Okay, okay, stop." I shook my head. "I know what you're doing. You're trying to take my mind off my father, away from how you got trapped in the cloak, and onto whatever tall tale you were about to spin. I appreciate the effort, but it's not working. I want to know how you got trapped in the cloak. You're the first person I've ever told about my father. I shared a deep, dark secret, so now it's your turn."

Oh, all right, Puck said. *But only because you already spilled the beans about yourself.*

Like I told you before, I'm a genius. I knew it even at an early age. I made sure everyone else knew it, too. And as you know, people just love somebody telling them how much smarter he is than they are. Ha! Sike! Suffice it to say, before I got trapped in this thing, I didn't have many friends. I certainly didn't have any girlfriends. The only way I would've gotten girls to pay attention to me was if I had dosed them with a love potion. And believe me, I considered it. Never did it, though. It seemed a little too rapey, even though I was desperate for female companionship.

My lack of friends didn't bother me. Well, it didn't bother me much. I told myself everyone was just jealous of how smart I was. In hindsight, I might've been a little on the obnoxious side.

"I find that hard to believe."

Sarcasm is so unbecoming of a sorceress. Anyhoo, I thought that if I did something really spectacular, everyone would have to finally recognize my genius. They would finally be forced to like me. It wasn't until years later I realized that the words "forced" and "friendship" don't really go together.

But before I came to that realization, I strove to prove myself, to show the world how awesome I was. I wanted to achieve something big, something that would make the world sit up and really take notice.

After careful study, I became convinced it was possible to magically transfer human consciousness to an inanimate object. Think of how it would revolutionize human society if I pulled that feat off! Dying would be a thing of the past. People discounting me, ignoring me, not wanting to be my friend would be a thing of the past too. Or so I thought.

I concocted a spell I was sure would work. It took months to plan and work the kinks out of, and days to cast. Obviously, I pulled it off. The spell removed my consciousness from my body and transferred it to this cloak. The spell was supposed to wear off after a few hours and return my consciousness to my body. Unfortunately, it didn't. The spell's been going strong for centuries now. My body's long dead, obviously. I was only eighteen at the time of the transfer, and my body lived on in a coma for less than a year. I hadn't even lost my virginity.

That last admission confirmed a suspicion I had about Puck. People with a lot of sexual experience didn't talk about it incessantly like Puck did.

My parents and my sister Carmela are as dead as my biological body, of course. My sister had a few descendants, but they all died out, so I'm the only branch remaining of my family tree.

I never did figure out what went wrong with the spell, and I've literally spent decades trying to puzzle it out. Some of the other magicians who have donned me have tried to free me from the cloak, to no avail. Frankly, I've given up trying. I'm trapped here, probably forever. I'm eighteen going on infinity. Puck sounded bitter. *So, I understand when you said you were arrogant by summoning that demon. I'm the god-king of arrogance. Unfortunately, the title doesn't come with randy female worshippers. Just dry cleaning bills.*

Puck fell quiet. I let what he had told me sink in for a while.

"We're quite a pair, aren't we?" I asked. "We're both a hot mess. We've really screwed ourselves over."

I disagree. Despite the fact I sometimes feel sorry for myself, my life's not all bad. Thanks to my association with a string of magicians, I know more about magic than I would if I had lived conventionally. There's something to be said for knowledge for the sake of knowledge. Also, some of the magicians I've bonded with have been pretty good eggs. Don't get me wrong—I wish I hadn't gotten stuck in this cape. But it is what it is. There's no use in moaning and gnashing my teeth about it.

As for you and your situation, I'm not gonna lie: You shouldn't have been fooling around with black magic. Your dad was right about that. You made a mistake. A big one. But frankly, so what? Everyone makes mistakes. Unless you've got a time machine you haven't told me about, the past is the past. All you can do now is make sure your past mistakes intelligently inform your future decisions.

I'm buried alive in a coffin of my own making. You're not. You can move on with your life. I didn't know your father, but I suspect he'd say the same if he were here. He sacrificed his own life so that you could live. You should honor his memory by doing just that— living your life to its fullest. And for someone like you with your magical potential, that means embracing that potential, not being afraid of and running from it.

I mulled Puck's words over for a long while. Ten years had passed since Dad died, yet I was in many ways the same 16-year-old girl who had cradled his lifeless form in her arms. My magic hadn't advanced since then. I was impulsive and impetuous. Anger always boiled right under the surface of my psyche. I had flings like that one with Bigfoot instead of serious relationships. I lived for today with no thought of tomorrow, which was how I had gotten into so much debt and was always behind on my bills.

I was a fly stuck in amber of my own making, trapped in the mistakes of my past as much as Puck was literally trapped in his.

I was a grieving and fearful 16-year-old in a 26-year-old's body. As much as I hated to admit it, Daniel was right about me being childish.

Maybe it was time to grow up.

I stood up, stretched, and washed my face in the kitchen sink. I used cold water. A baptism of sorts. I was still tired, and I hoped the coldness of the water would give me a much-needed pick-me-up. I still had a lot of studying to do if I was going to attempt astral projection.

The water didn't do much. Maybe a baptism needed to be performed by a minister for it to work correctly. Preferably a hot one. Oh well. Nobody ever said turning over a new leaf and becoming a new woman was easy.

"You're pretty smart for an 18-year-old," I said to Puck as I dried my face.

You ain't just whistling Dixie. I am a genius after all.

"There's one thing you were wrong about, though. You said you didn't have any family. Well, now you've got me. I think we're going to wind up being pretty good friends."

Friends with benefits? Puck suggested eagerly.

"Definitely not. Besides, you're trapped in a cloak. How would that even work?"

I've given it lots of thought, he said with excitement. *We could—*

"No."

But—

"No," I repeated firmly.

Killjoy.

CHAPTER EIGHTEEN

*F*or *the love of all that's holy,* Puck exclaimed irritably, *there's a gap in that line in the upper right corner. Are you really that desperate to have the jikininki make a meal of your guts while we're gone?*

I looked closely where Puck had indicated. He was right. I was learning he usually was.

I shuddered at the thought of what might have happened had Puck not caught my mistake. Jikininki were ghosts with mouths filled with piranha-like teeth who ate human corpses and other bodies whose souls had vacated them. The jikininki were but one of the many dangers that could waylay the unwary astral projector. I had learned about them and things even more terrifying over the past week and a half during my crash course in astral projection.

I had drawn a complex symbol in the middle of my living room floor with ash wood charcoal. While I was doing my spiritual walkabout, the symbol was supposed to keep away from my body all the invisible nasties who flocked to soulless bodies like vampire moths to a flame.

I grabbed the charcoal and filled in the gap Puck had pointed out. Then, careful to not smudge any of the other carefully drawn lines, I reviewed the protective symbol, painstakingly going over it inch by inch.

The symbol was a giant circle with a large square inside it. Each corner of the square touched the circle. The square was big enough for me to sit in its middle without smudging it. In the four spaces formed between the square and the curve of the circle were various glyphs from my recent studies. I had carefully drawn them under Puck's sharp-eyed and even sharper-tongued supervision. Despite the heart-to-heart moment we shared several days ago, he still sometimes treated me like a child who couldn't be trusted with blunt-tipped kid scissors unsupervised.

"Well it certainly looks impressive," Daniel said once I stepped away from the circle after my final review. "But will it work?"

Daniel and I hadn't spoken about our blowup from days before. Since then, Daniel acted as though nothing untoward had happened. I was still angry about what he had said to me, though. The anger simmered right under the surface of my consciousness, like a pot threatening to boil over. It wasn't often that someone called me a whiny baby and I let them get away with it. Even if they were right.

In fact, I was so pissed at Daniel that I was starting to wonder if I had developed feelings for him. Otherwise, his comments would have slid off me like water off a duck's back by now. Daniel was an immortal angel who couldn't stay long in one spot. In other words, he was an unavailable older man with power and authority. A man like my father. Could I be more of a Freudian cliché?

I pushed the thought and my irritation with Daniel to the side. I had to focus.

"It should work," I answered him.

"Should" being the operative word, Puck said. *The Titanic was marketed as an unsinkable ship. It should not have sunk. Yet it did.*

"Well, aren't you a ray of sunshine?" I was already nervous enough without Puck pissing in my Cheerios. "You missed your calling as a motivational coach."

Sorry. I thought you were looking for objectivity, not a cheerleader. How about this? Puck's voice became sing-song. *Sage, Sage, she's our gal. If she can't do it, nobody shall. Better?*

"Very inspirational."

"From my perspective," Daniel said, with amusement in his eyes at my exchange with Puck, "you look like a crazy person who's talking to herself."

"You've got the crazy part right." I was still amazed I was about to attempt something only one other person in the world could do safely. I was the chick who had done little more than elemental magic for the past decade. It was like going overnight from only having your learner's permit to racing in the Indy 500.

I gave one last look around the small room. My tiny amount of furniture had been moved into the corner of the room, out of the way. It reminded me of how I had moved things out of the way to draw a pentagram on the wood floor of Dad's and my house ten years ago. I prayed this excursion into higher levels of magic did not also result in disaster.

I let out a breath and tried to push out my doubts along with it. I pointed at the intricate pattern I had painstakingly drawn on the linoleum. "This will keep out any spiritual threats to my body while my soul is out of it during the astral projection," I said to Daniel with more confidence than I felt. Fake it until you make it. If faking it worked here, maybe I'd start padding my bra too. "Your job is to keep out any physical threats by watching over my body while my consciousness is out of it."

"If any vampires or door-to-door salesmen come a-knocking, I'll send them packing," Daniel said. He patted the Ark fragment. "You're safe in my hands. I'm not going anywhere. At least not right away." He started playing with the coins in his pocket again. He'd gotten antsier and antsier with each passing day. He would have to leave the D.C. area soon.

I drank the cup of blue lotus tea I had left cooling. Daniel had bought the lotus flowers I had brewed into a tea, just as he had bought all the other preparatory material that dotted the room. My research indicated the tea would help calm me—and sister, did I ever need that!—heighten my awareness, and help me separate my soul from my mortal body.

I went around the room, lighting frankincense and myrrh incense. I breathed in the smell deeply. Between the tea and the incense, I was starting to feel unusual. Not bad, but definitely strange. Calm. I was a lot of things, but calm was usually not one of them.

I stepped into the charcoal pattern on the floor, careful to not smudge or break any of its lines. I sat crisscross applesauce in the middle of the square at the pattern's center. I carefully arranged Puck around me. I was going to do this with him because two heads were better than one, especially when one of those heads was centuries old.

"Are you ready?" I asked Puck.

Road trip! he exclaimed. *I call shotgun.*

I took that as a yes.

I executed the Wave and said the Word of the spell designed to protect my body from spiritual threats while my spirit was out of it, and I Willed the symbol I sat in to form a protective barrier.

The charcoal symbol flashed brightly, glowing like a white-hot ember, but with no heat. The glowing stopped just as quickly as it had begun, leaving the black symbol as I had originally drawn it. It felt different though, as if I was now surrounded by an invisible barrier. It was like being inside a perfectly transparent glass tube—I couldn't see the barrier, yet I still sensed it was there.

You've completed the first step. Well done, Puck murmured encouragingly.

"Shhh!" I was trying to focus my mind on the next spell, the most complex one I had ever attempted. I didn't need any distractions.

Puck grumbled something about how it must be my time of the month, then thankfully shut up. I had a quick but gratifying daydream about setting him ablaze with spellfire before I shunted the thought to the side. I'd deal with him later.

I closed my eyes. I did my best to shut out the world. Focusing on my breathing, I tried to stop thinking about anything but my body and the spirit that inhabited it.

Eventually, everything fell away. The weight of the Cloak of Wisdom on my shoulders, my awareness of Daniel's presence, the creaks and groans of the Leverettes' old house which always served as subtle background music . . . everything disappeared. There was only me and Puck. He was attached to my consciousness like a suckerfish to a shark.

I was ready. With my eyes still closed, my arms began to move. I flicked my fingers as my arms performed the intricate pattern of the Wave for this spell. I began to speak the Word. The memorized spell was so complicated, it would take several minutes to complete. As I spoke the Word and performed the Wave, I Willed myself to separate from my body. I envisioned it like I was magically removing the core of an apple, leaving the apple's flesh and skin completely intact.

The Wave complete, my arms slowly dropped to rest on my knees. They felt like leaves falling off a tree. My lips fell silent once the last syllable of the Word was out.

I opened my eyes. I blinked hard, disoriented for a moment. Everything was suddenly deathly quiet, like I was wearing noise-canceling headphones which were one hundred percent effective.

I stood up. "It didn't work," I said. My voice was especially loud in the eerie quiet which had fallen over my apartment. Even the kitchen sink, which normally dripped every few seconds like a metronome, was quiet. The quiet didn't much register on me, though; I was too busy being bitterly disappointed after all the work and studying I had done. What if I had to start over from scratch? I didn't even know what it was I had done wrong.

Daniel didn't respond to my statement. As if I hadn't said anything, he just stared at the spot I had risen from.

It didn't work? Puck sounded amused. *Look down.*

I did. I was startled to see I still sat with my legs crossed and eyes closed, wearing the same blue jeans and loose cotton t-shirt. Yet the seated me wasn't this me, the standing me who now realized the astral projection spell had worked after all and who felt like she had entered the Twilight Zone. That me stood in the middle of my seated body, with my legs rising through her shoulders.

I lifted a foot and eased it forward. My foot poked through the chest of my seated body, as if some kid had put Mrs. Potato Head together incorrectly. It was as though the standing, thinking me was a hologram, capable of moving, but possessing no physical substance. If I touched my spirit self, I seemed solid; I passed through everything else like a phantom. And, I obviously was invisible since Daniel did not react to me at all. The astral me, that is.

It was disconcerting to say the least to see myself in two places at once. Especially because this version of me was now sinking into the floor like it was quicksand.

I couldn't step out or push out because my hands and legs passed through everything. In seconds, I had sunk into the floor up to my waist. What would stop me from sinking to the center of the earth, if not farther, I wondered. Fear nibbled at me, threatening to grow into full-scale panic. "Uh, Puck? A little help?"

First you shush me, now you want my help? You're giving me whiplash. Make up your mind, will ya?

"Help first, berate later." My arms windmilled like those of a gymnast about to fall off a balance beam. Not that it did me any good. I was still sinking into the floor. At this rate, I'd wind up on the other side of the earth before I knew it.

Fine, Puck huffed. *The first thing you need to do is stop freaking out. You were doing so well until now. Your spirit—your soul, if you will—has separated from your body. You're on the astral plane. The laws of physics don't apply here. At least the laws of physics you are used to don't. When you want to move in a certain direction, don't move your body. Just think yourself there.*

Dubious, but anxious to do something before I wound up in China, I did what Puck suggested. I thought about not sinking.

I stopped on a dime.

Encouraged, I willed myself to rise.

I rose out of the floor like a zombie from the grave. My feet dangled several feet off the floor before I willed myself to stop.

I grinned. "This is kind of cool," I said to Puck.

Yeah, you're a real unsinkable Molly Brown.

"I don't know who that is."

Imagine my surprise.

Daniel scratched himself with one hand and played with the coins in his pocket with the other. I could not hear them or him. I couldn't hear anything. It was as if I had hit the mute button on the world.

I glanced around the room from a perspective I did not normally have. From up here near the ceiling, the dusty cobwebs in the upper corners of the room were even more obvious than usual. When this craziness with the Spear of Destiny was over, I desperately needed to clean.

The fact I was floating in the air like a balloon suddenly filled me with childlike glee. I grinned, and I spun around in the air like a top. The room became a blur around me. There was no sound or sensation of rushing air, no dust kicked up, no indication that anything I did affected the physical world in the slightest.

I slowed to a stop. I wasn't dizzy. I was a spirit—I didn't have an inner ear to make me dizzy. I also wasn't winded. In fact, I wasn't breathing at all. I wondered how Puck could hear me when I spoke. It probably had to do with the fact we'd been magically bonded together when I cast the spell that activated him.

Your Linda Carter spinning and turning into Wonder Woman rendition is cool and all, Puck said, interrupting my conjecture, *but doing superhero impressions is not why we're here.*

Puck was right. It was time to get down to business.

I opened my Third Eye. The room abruptly became as bright as the sun. The Ark fragment was the source of the harsh light. The light stabbed me like it was thousands of razor-sharp daggers. I winced in pain, and nearly fell through the floor again before I caught myself.

I hastily closed my Third Eye. The room returned to normal. Looking at the Ark fragment with my Third Eye when my spirit had been in my body had been overwhelming, like staring into the sun. In my astral form, looking at the fragment with my Third Eye wasn't merely like staring into the sun. More like traveling too close to the sun.

Ow! Puck moaned in pain. *I hope you got the license plate of the 18-wheeler that just hit us. I'd predicted your astral form would be more sensitive to the magic that radiates from holy and unholy Relics, but I wasn't expecting it to feel like that. Maybe you should slip back into your body, take me off, and go searching for the Spear on your own. Think of it Tonto! Your very own adventure. You're welcome. The Lone Ranger will sit this one out.*

I tried to shake off the lingering pain of looking at the Ark fragment with my Third Eye. "First of all, if anybody here is the Lone Ranger, it's me. You're the sidekick, not the hero. Second of all, casting the spell that got us to this point took a lot out of me. I'm not going through it again just because you're scared."

Tonto, every individual is the hero of his own life story, Puck said pretentiously. *And I ain't scared. Just cautious. I haven't survived this long by leaping before looking. You could learn a lot from my example.*

"Yeah, I could learn how to be a fraidy-cat. Come on, let's start our search. Bickering isn't helping us find the Spear."

As I had learned to do in my studies, I locked onto my physical body so I could return to it later. Magicians' souls becoming unmoored from their bodies was the main reason why few attempted to astrally project.

Then, I willed my astral form to float upward, through the ceiling of my apartment into the Leverettes' house above. I passed through everything like I was a ghost. I went through the Leverettes' kitchen. Its tidiness was in stark contrast to mine. Mrs. Leverette was there, appearing to be whistling merrily as she washed dinner dishes. It was yet another reason to be wary of her. A person who was happy about doing dishes was not a person to be trusted.

I went through the roof of the Leverettes' house, into the night air. Something other than me floated above the house.

No, not something. Someone.

"Speaking of ghosts," I murmured, though there was no need to keep my voice down since the figure hovering over the house couldn't hear me.

Who's this guy? Puck asked. *Friend of yours? He's mighty big to be dressed up for Halloween. Wrong time of year too.*

"No, he's definitely not a friend. This is that Hero named Ghost I told you about." The so-called Hero hovered over the Leverettes' house like a superpowered stalker. He wore the same full-body, off-white costume I had last seen him in. His lips were moving under the fabric of his mask. Though I couldn't hear him, he clearly was talking to someone. Since no one was nearby, I surmised he had some sort of communications gear built into his cowl. "He's probably here to check up on me like he threatened to when I refused to help him find Millennium."

The married couple who lived farther up the block walked by, arm-in-arm. A neighborhood kid pedaled his bike down the sidewalk on the other side of the street. None of them looked up at Ghost.

"Why do you suppose nobody's staring at Ghost?" I asked. "He's a big man wearing a white costume floating over a two-story house. You'd think that would catch somebody's eye."

Maybe he's invisible, Puck suggested. *Maybe that's one of his superpowers. You said he had followed you when you were on K Street without you spotting him. Maybe you can only see him now because you're in your astral form.*

"That would certainly explain it," I agreed. "I wonder how often he's spied on me without me realizing it."

I floated over to Ghost. I lifted my hand until it was inches from his face. I flipped him the bird. He could not see it, of course, but it made me feel better. Me dipping my toes back into the waters of advanced magic had obviously not advanced my maturity level.

My inner child satisfied, I ignored Ghost and rose higher into the air, until the Leverette house was just one of many geometric shapes below me. Once I was sufficiently far from my apartment, I cautiously opened my Third Eye.

The whirling colors of the magical world exposed themselves again. The Leverettes' house, thanks to the Ark fragment it contained, was lit up like a Christmas tree, standing out like a beacon amongst the mundane households.

Sweet! Puck said. *Now all we have to do is perform a sweep of the city, find another spot like this one that looks like it's sending out a mystical Bat-Signal, and bingo bango, that'll likely be the Spear of Destiny. We'll be back in time to catch* Dancing with the Stars.

"Bingo bango? Really?"

It's a very advanced and sophisticated magical term of art, Puck said loftily. *Beyond your years, no doubt. I wouldn't expect a young pup like you to understand it.*

Since I was already in Northwest, I started my search here, the largest of the District's four quadrants. I flew so high up in the sky that the city looked like a giant Lite-Brite. I searched for anything like the kind of mystical energy the Ark fragment emitted.

The whole time, part of me kept a lock on my physical body in my apartment. As per my crash course in astral projection, I visualized my link to my body as a massive ball of unwinding string which connected the spiritual me to the physical me. If I allowed the mystical filament to break, I would never be able to reenter my body. My body would wither away, and my spirit would be a ghost forever. I already had a name picked out if, God forbid, that happened: Sage the Pissed-Off and Very Unfriendly Ghost.

I doubted they would make a kid's cartoon about me.

CHAPTER NINETEEN

arly in my astral search for the Spear of Destiny, I flew over McMillan Reservoir, a body of water within walking distance of my place which supplied most of the city's drinking water. On the other side of it was Howard University, one of the country's most prestigious historically black colleges and one of the top colleges in the country, period. I did not see anything on the sprawling, 250-plus acre campus that made me think the Spear of Destiny was hidden there, but I did see something that made me pause.

I closed my Third Eye and dropped down to get a closer look.

One of the university's dorm buildings was on fire. The fire had already engulfed the bottom four stories of the tall rectangular building, and the blaze was rapidly spreading. Students were at some of the windows, screaming for help. People were clustered around the base of the building, staying a safe distance away. The thin crowd was composed mostly of black people with a sprinkling of other races, which was not surprising considering Howard was a HBU. A few in the crowd had their phones out, filming the inferno. Helpful. The people trapped in the building would burn to death, but at least they could take comfort in knowing their mass cremation would be immortalized forever on the Internet.

A few of the people around the building were in sooty nightclothes. I guessed they had managed to escape the mounting inferno. The way the fire was spreading, the people who remained in the building would not be so lucky.

I again rose high enough in the sky so I could see far down the roads leading to the campus. The flashing lights of fire trucks were nowhere to be seen.

"Puck, we've got to do something," I said. "A bunch of people are about to die."

There's nothing we can do. You can't perform magic in your spirit form, remember?

"I'll go back and get my body."

No. You need to stay focused on your mission. Our job is to find the Spear before Millennium does, not go around playing Smokey the Bear.

I was shocked by Puck's callousness. "How can you say that? Those are students in that building. They're practically kids."

If they were newborn babies I'd say the same thing. A lot more people than those few in that building will get hurt if Millennium gets his hands on the Spear. I've seen generations of people live and die. It gives you perspective, makes you realize no individual or group of individuals is all that important in the grand scheme of things. We need to do the most good for the most people, which means we should focus all our attention on the Spear. We gotta keep our eyes on the prize.

I thought about Puck's words. This was like the incident with the gargoyles all over again. Fighting those gargoyles had exposed my magic and landed me in the soup. Maybe I should just mind my own business this time.

It only took me a moment to decide. I took careful note of a spot near the burning dormitory that didn't have bystanders close by. I started racing back toward my apartment to retrieve my body. Right was right, and wrong was wrong. Dad had taught me that. I would not dishonor his memory even if doing the right thing wound up screwing me in the long run.

This is a mistake, Puck warned. *You're being impulsive again.*

"There's a difference between being impulsive and giving a flip about others," I said as I zoomed toward my apartment, careful to not lose my mystical tether to my body in my haste. I traveled so fast that the buildings below were a blur. "You say your long life has given you perspective. No offense, but maybe it's warped your perspective instead. A lot of the magical world is cavalier about the welfare of mundanes, but you're taking it to a whole new level."

What about the First Rule? You're in enough trouble with the Conclave as it is. And what if Millennium finds the Spear while you're roasting chestnuts on an open fire?

"Then he finds it," I said grimly. "I won't sacrifice humans to save humanity. If we become the kinds of people who'll let others burn to death, then we don't deserve saving."

Since it's your body, not mine, you get to call the shots. But I'll go ahead and say "I told you so" now in case I forget when this misadventure goes sideways.

"Thanks for the support."

I dropped into my apartment through the walls of the Leverette house. My body and Daniel were where I had left them. I sank into my body. I released my hold on the astral projection spell. Like a key sliding into the lock it fit, my spirit reincorporated into my body.

My body's eyes flew open. I nullified the protective spell that surrounded my body. I stood hastily. My legs were stiff from being in the same position for a while.

Daniel stood too, obviously excited. "You found the Spear?" he asked eagerly.

"Working on it." I dashed into my bedroom with Daniel dogging my heels. I neither had time to explain what I was doing, nor did I want to give Daniel a chance to tag-team me with Puck and try to talk me out of helping the Howard students.

With Daniel standing in my bedroom doorway asking questions I ignored, I raced around the room. Lives were at stake, and here I was scrounging around my disaster of a room, looking for something I had Daniel buy a few days ago. Darn my messiness!

I found it on top of a pile of laundry, under a pair of underwear.

If your panties were smaller, maybe you'd have found it sooner, Puck suggested. I didn't dignify that with a response, though the notion of throwing him into the building fire looked more and more appealing.

What I had found was my mask. More specifically, it was a Colombina mask, one of those ornate half-masks some women hid their faces with at the annual Carnival of Venice in Italy. This one was a glossy tan and black. I had Daniel get it for me while I was busy studying so I would have something to hide my face with other than a ski mask if I needed to use my magic in public to get the Spear of Destiny. Wearing this kind of mask made me look like I was going to a costume party; wearing the ski mask had made me look and feel like a criminal.

I secured the mask to my face with the ribbons attached to its end.

Now you really do look like the Lone Ranger, Puck said. *Except subtract the big horse and add small boobs.* He was being super helpful. I was learning Puck got snarkier than usual when I dared to ignore his sage advice.

I glanced at the digital clock on my dresser. Not even a minute had passed since I'd come here to get the mask, but it felt like an eternity. I needed to get back to the fire before it was too late.

I began the Wave for the portal spell I had learned from Puck.

"Where are you going?" Daniel demanded.

"I'll explain later," I said, then shut his protests out of my mind as I completed the Wave, said the Word, and Willed a portal to open. The magical doorway, roiling with black and blue colors, opened directly in front of me. I mentally high-fived myself. It was a vast improvement over the magical trapdoor I'd opened for us at the Sackler Gallery.

I stepped into the portal. The disaster area that was my room disappeared, replaced by the disaster area that the fire was causing at Howard University.

I closed the portal behind me. I had exited the portal at the spot near the dorm I had made note of before I'd flown back to get my body. I was behind most of the people around the building. No one seemed to notice that a masked woman in a red cloak had stepped out of a glowing hole in the time-space continuum. Even if I hadn't materialized behind everyone, they were too busy staring at the ever-growing fire.

Since I could hear and smell now that I wasn't in astral form, the scene seemed vastly different than it had before. Even this distance from it, I felt the heat of the fire. It crackled like something from the pits of Hell. The screams of people trapped in the building mingled with the crackling. The smoke was choking, and it smelled of burning plastic and chemicals. I heard the wail of police cars and fire trucks, but it was obvious they were still far off in the distance. They would be too late to save many of the students in the building.

Puck let out a loud, long-suffering sigh. *I still think it's a stupid waste of valuable time, but since you insist on doing this, there's a spell that should put out the fire. Hopefully you can learn it in time. The first thing you'll need to do is—*

"Take it easy with the capesplaining," I said, cutting him off. "I've got this."

"Those stupid Metas wear capes. I'm a cloak," Puck protested, sounding offended.

I ignored him, my mind focused on extinguishing the fire. Truth be told, I was not certain I'd been right about having the situation under control, but there was no time to learn a brand-new spell. Besides, successfully tackling astral projection had boosted my confidence. Perhaps disaster did not have to inevitably follow me engaging in high-level magic.

I didn't think I could use magic to extinguish the fire directly. The fire was too big, and fire I did not create was much harder to control than fire I generated. On top of that, I was tired after maintaining the powerful astral projection spell. Now was not the time to rest, though.

The first thing I needed to do was get the gawkers farther away from the building. I envisioned what I wanted to happen, planting it firmly in my mind. Then I executed the Wave, said "Ignis," and unleashed my Will.

With a loud whoosh that could be heard over the roar of the dorm fire, a ring of orange and red spellfire erupted into existence around the building, between it and the onlookers. They cried out in surprise and alarm.

Gritting my teeth with the effort of maintaining the biggest batch of spellfire I had ever conjured in my life, I willed it to expand. It got closer to the bystanders. They stumbled over themselves in their haste to run away from the encroaching fire.

There! The bystanders were far enough away from the building now. Unfortunately, in retreating from the spellfire, a few had gotten close enough to me to notice me. They nudged each other, pointing at me. With me wearing a mask and what looked like a cape, they probably thought I was a Hero. Either that or they thought I was a Rogue, maybe one who had set fire to the building in the first place. Oh well. I was more concerned about being identified as a sorceress than about being misidentified as a Metahuman.

I relaxed my Will, and the ring of spellfire winked out of existence. I switched mental gears, again envisioning what I wanted to happen now that the bystanders were out of the way.

"Ventus!" I cried, and unleashed my Will as I finished the Wave by extending my hands toward the building.

Winds kicked up around the base of the building, picking up debris as they circled the structure, faster and faster. It looked like a Metahuman speedster was running around it. I drew in magic from all around and poured it back out of me, channeling it into the burgeoning windstorm around the building.

While still maintaining the ever-expanding whirlwind, I moved my hands to the Wave of a different spell. "Terra!" I exclaimed, channeling magic into the building itself.

In seconds, a raging tornado surrounded the inflamed building, though there wasn't a single storm cloud in the sky. The tornado raged with the building in its eye. The wide end of the tornado's funnel reached far into the heavens, drowning out the sound of the fire and sucking in debris from all around us. People screamed, some ducking and covering to protect themselves from the debris that whipped through the air and into the magically created tornado.

So much magic poured out of me, it made me gasp. I was getting cold, like I had just fallen through ice and into a frigid lake. I knew I was draining too much of my magic and life force in maintaining the massive spells I had cast, the biggest forms of elemental magic I had ever attempted. But I also knew I had to hold on a little longer.

The fire inside the tornado dimmed, as if a giant jar had been placed over the building and the fire was running out of oxygen to consume.

Then, abruptly, the fire went out.

I maintained the tornado for a few seconds more to make sure the fire was out. When darkness started closing in from the edges of my vision like a closing camera shutter, I relaxed my Will and my hold on the wind and earth spells before I passed out.

With desultory swirls of air, the tornado dissipated, then disappeared altogether. Small pieces of debris pattered the ground like hail. The building still smoked, but the fire was out. The air was noticeably colder. People's breaths condensed in the night air when they exhaled.

I stumbled and fell to my knees. I panted, my lungs burning, with my head hanging between my shoulders. I felt like an orange with all the juice squeezed out of it.

Sweet baby Odin! Puck exclaimed. *Tornadoes create freezing conditions and a lack of oxygen in their eyes, like the death zone conditions high up on mountain peaks. You used that phenomenon to extinguish the fire. You simultaneously used an earth spell on the organic material in the building to help hold the structure together while the tornado whipped around it.* His voice was full of wonder, like he had just seen Willow Wilde and Marilyn Monroe making out while naked and standing atop a galloping unicorn.

I nodded yes. Talking right now was out of the question. I was too busy remembering how to breathe.

Holy magical mojo, Batman! Puck exulted. *I was wrong when I said at Ben's Chili Bowl that you're no superhero. You* are *a superhero. Not too many people could pull off what you just did. If I had a penis, I would be so hard right now.*

Through the haze that shrouded my sluggish brain, I became vaguely aware of people staring at me. I looked up.

Many of the bystanders who had been gawking at the fire were now gawking at me. Multiple phones were trained on me. I got a flashback of when I had been videoed at the Institute of Peace. Déjà vu all over again.

This was no place to linger. Cops and firefighters would be here soon, and they would have uncomfortable questions to ask, questions a certain conspicuously masked and caped sorceress who was already in trouble with the Conclave did not want to answer. Plus, I vaguely remembered something about how the Hero Act made it illegal to dress like a Hero unless you were licensed as one.

Though I didn't want to, I staggered to my feet. I lifted my arms. They felt like lead weights. Though people were looking at me, I was going to open a portal in front of everyone anyway.

Crap! I lowered my hands before I barely began the Wave. There was no way I had the energy to open a portal right now. And if by some miracle I did open one, I was so exhausted and unfocused, it might deposit me at the gates to Hell. However, to be honest, I was so cold from draining my magic that the warmth of Hell did not seem like a bad idea right about now.

Oh well. I'd just have to return home using conventional means. Once I got away from all these gawkers, I'd simply grab a cab home.

Then I remembered.

Double crap! I didn't have any money or my phone. My pockets were as empty as my magical reserves were. The next time I took a stroll down astral lane, I needed to make sure I had an emergency twenty in my pants pocket.

I had no choice. I started walking away from the smoking building and the increasing crowd of spectators. Once I was away from everyone, I'd pull Puck and the mask off so drivers and pedestrians wouldn't stare at me like I was a freak as I trudged the streets toward home.

Applause trailed me, picking up in volume as I walked through the bystanders. I lifted Puck, shielding my masked face from the people who were recording me with their phones. I felt like a celebrity trying to escape paparazzi.

Dude, this is embarrassing, Puck said. *You're making my imaginary woody go limp.*

"Shut up," I whispered. I tried to say it without moving my lips. It would never do to be filmed talking to myself. The only thing worse than people thinking I was a superhero was them thinking I was a crazy superhero.

CHAPTER TWENTY

The night after the fire at Howard University, I again flew over the city in my astral form with my Third Eye open, looking for any sign of the Spear of Destiny.

It was dark, with clouds covering the moon and most of the stars. Just like yesterday, the world was as quiet as a mute. It had taken me over eleven hours of sleep to recover from my first astral projection and extinguishing the fire at Howard.

Daniel sure was pissed at you, Puck said. Daniel had pitched a fit when I returned to my apartment after extinguishing the Howard fire and I told him I would have to put off looking for the Spear until I rested up some. He had taken the same position that Puck had, namely that it was more important to find the Spear than it was to save the lives of college students. Only Daniel had been more adamant about it and more colorful in his language than Puck had been. I wound up having to throw him out of my apartment again. He was back now, however, watching over my body as I did my ghost impersonation throughout the city.

"Daniel will get over it," I told Puck. "Or he won't. I don't care, frankly."

The name's Puck. Don't call me Frankly.

I groaned. "That's a terrible joke."

They can't all be good. With all the pitches I swing at, I'm bound to strike out from time to time. It's the law of averages.

"How about making just some of them good? You know, as a change of pace."

Now you're just being hurtful. You put out one fire, and suddenly you're an expert on everything, including humor. It was a mistake letting you people vote and wear pants. It's made you uppity.

"You people," I repeated. "Has anyone ever told you you're sexist?"

Of course I'm not sexist. Sexism is wrong, and only you broads can be wrong.

I laughed despite myself. The way Puck spoke to me had changed subtly since yesterday. Though he still had no problem teasing me, now it was the good-natured teasing of one colleague to another. Like we were equals. Before the Howard fire, much of the time Puck spoke to me like I was a mentally challenged child struggling through a remedial class. I must have impressed him at Howard.

The fact that an article of clothing being impressed with me gave me a warm glow of accomplishment made me wonder when my sanity had jumped the shark.

We had searched the city for a few hours. We were flying over the National Mall now. As cynical as I sometimes was about how the country was run, seeing symbols of our democracy like the Capitol building, the World War Two Memorial, the Lincoln Memorial, and the Washington Monument made my heart swell with pride and patriotism. I probably would have hummed *The Star-Spangled Banner* if I hadn't known Puck would tease me mercilessly.

The lit-up Washington Monument glowed like something magical, both the tall obelisk itself and the structure's reflection which stretched across the Lincoln

Memorial Reflecting Pool. The base of the 555-foot tall structure was surrounded by fifty flags, one for each state.

I stopped flying, hovering high in the air over the monument.

Here are some fun facts about the monument, Puck said. *It's both the world's tallest stone structure and the world's tallest obelisk. The upper two-thirds of it is a slightly different color than the bottom third because of a twenty-five year pause in the monument's construction, after which time they got the marble for the rest of the monument from a different quarry.*

"Here's a less than fun fact about you: You talk too much. Less talking, more looking. Don't you see that?"

Don't I see what? Rudeness is not visible to the naked eye.

"That," I said, pointing. The base of the monument glowed.

Those are called spotlights, Puck said, speaking slowly, as if I would not understand him if he spoke normally. *They're used to light things up at night.*

I shook my head in irritation. "I'm not talking about the spotlights. There seems to be a glow coming from underneath the monument itself."

Maybe, Puck said dubiously. *Or maybe you're so anxious to find the Spear that you're starting to imagine things.*

It's not my imagination, I said, though I was already starting to wonder if Puck was right. The glow was so faint, it could have just been my overly sensitive imagination exerting itself.

I closed my Third Eye. The magical world faded away. Though the Washington Monument's night lights were still on, the faint glow which had seemed to come from under the structure had disappeared.

I started to get excited. "That's not my imagination," I said triumphantly. "Maybe it's the Spear."

Maybe. But let's not count our chickens before they use the Spear's tip to hatch.

"Only one way to find out." I opened my Third Eye again. The glow at the base of the monument reappeared.

I dove down, toward the ground. I passed through the stone base of the monument as if it did not exist.

I was underground. Even down here, colorful eddies of magical current swirled around me. Straight down, hundreds of feet below the monument, was a whitish-gold glow. From up here, it looked like the light at the end of a tunnel.

Okay, now I'm cautiously optimistic, Puck said.

I continued straight down, toward the glow, passing through the ground like I was some sort of superpowered earthworm. If getting paid for finding the Spear did not work out, I could always try gold mining.

I passed through countless tons of soil and rock before arriving at the source of the glow.

Whatever it was, it was big, the size of a very large room. It was vaguely ovoid, shaped somewhat like an egg. It glowed, though its light was not blinding the way the light from the Ark fragment had been. The glow did not seem to emanate from the surface of the thing itself, but rather, from inside the thing. It was as if a lit candle had been sealed inside an egg, making the egg's shell luminesce.

That's certainly not the Spear of Destiny. Unless the Spear of Destiny is a supersized ostrich egg.

"It might be inside, though," I responded. Increasingly excited, I continued to descend, intending to see if my optimism was justified.

"Ow!" I exclaimed. My head had bounced off the surface of the glowing thing like I was corporeal again and had done a swan dive into an empty pool. The collision hurt and startled me so much that I struggled for a moment to maintain my spirit's mystical tether to my physical body.

"How did I not pass through this thing?" I asked Puck once I recovered sufficiently. "I thought I could go through anything in my astral form." I poked at the glowing thing cautiously with a finger. My finger met with solid resistance; there was no give whatsoever. It was like poking a brick wall.

I have no idea, Puck said. His voice was filled with wonder. *I've never even heard of anything that can keep out somebody's astral form. And I've heard of just about everything. This thing must be enspelled with some next-level kind of magic.*

I slowly but carefully flew through the ground around the massive ovoid, running my hands over it, probing for any kind of opening.

When I finally finished, I concluded there was not one. If the Spear of Destiny was inside—and I didn't know what could cause this kind of Third Eye glow if it wasn't a holy Relic—I couldn't get to it.

If the Spear is inside, it might as well be on the dark side of the moon for all the good it'll do us. As much as it pains me to admit I don't have any idea how to get inside, I don't.

"I do," I said grimly. I started to rise, heading back toward the surface. I needed to get back into my body and make a phone call.

I sighed, not looking forward to the call. I hoped the world appreciated the sacrifice I was about to make for it. As I had thought when I didn't fling my Louboutins at Willow, I wondered when someone was finally going to show up to hand me my much-deserved humanitarian award.

* * *

Ghost carried me in his arms as he flew high in the air toward the National Mall. He was covered from head to toe in his usual off-white costume and cape. I wore all-black, except for Puck. Ebony and Ivory, the Dynamic Spear-Retrieving Duo. I doubted the title would catch on. It hardly rolled off the tongue.

The wind screamed in my ear like a banshee. My hair whipped into my eyes, and the bright sun and rushing wind made me squint. I wished I had thought to bring a scrunchie and some sunglasses. Better yet, goggles like the ones early aviators wore when they flew planes with open cockpits. In my defense, I had never flown before. Well, not without either an airplane around me or me casting an astral projection spell. I did not like it.

Weee! Puck exclaimed. *This is fun. Flying's the best!*

I did not respond. I had already told Ghost too much about the magical world without adding a telepathic 600-plus year-old magic cape to the list. Besides, I did not share Puck's enthusiasm. I felt like Lois Lane in Superman's arms as Ghost zoomed toward the Washington Monument. I had become a cliché. It was mortifying. I've always empathized with Superman more than I ever did Lois. The powerless chick who needed some big strong man to come save her was not my cup of tea.

Before I rendezvoused with Ghost, I had told Daniel I had a lead on where the Spear might be, but I had not told him where. The argument we had about me saving the students at Howard still troubled me.

"Let me see if I've got this straight," Ghost said. He almost had to shout to be heard over the wind despite the fact I was inches away from him. I already had my cell phone and leather gloves in my pocket; I'd have to add an ear trumpet along with a scrunchie and goggles to my hanging with Heroes pre-flight checklist. "In exchange for you helping me locate Millennium, you need me to phase you deep under the Washington Monument and into a hidden chamber which you believe contains an ancient spear that pierced the side of Jesus Christ as he hung from the cross."

"Repeating it over and over isn't going to change my answer," I said, irritated not only by the fact I was doing a Lois impersonation, but also by the fact I had been forced to ask this Heroic kidnapper for help. If the Boston Strangler had the Metahuman power to move through solid matter, I would've called him instead. "Yes, that's what I need. You want me to draw you a picture to make it clear so you'll stop asking me?"

Maybe you should be nicer to the guy who could drop us like a girlfriend who won't put out, Puck suggested nervously. *If you go splat, I'll feel it too.*

"I'll demur on the picture and settle for an explanation," Ghost said. "Whatever happened to you not knowing anything about magic and magicians?" Thanks to Ghost's featureless mask, I couldn't tell if he was looking at me or looking where he was going. What if he hit an airplane while not watching the road? Uh, I meant the sky. What if I became a smear on an airplane windshield on my way to save the world? Embarrassing.

"Circumstances change," I said. "I've decided this is an instance where I need to look out for others before I look out for myself. Though I must admit I'll get into even more trouble than I'm already in if you tell people I'm the one who told you about all this stuff, so I'd appreciate it if you'd keep it under your hat."

Cowl, Puck corrected me. I wanted to tell him to be quiet so badly it was a physical ache.

"Tell people?" Ghost laughed. "Who in the world would I tell? If I told people a magical holy spear was hidden under the Washington Monument, the Heroes' Guild would relieve me of duty and send me to a psychiatrist. Believe me, I'll keep this between us." Ghost paused. "On an unrelated note, that's an interesting cape you're wearing."

"It's a cloak, not a cape."

Darned right I'm a cloak. Set him straight Sage.

"Sometimes I get chilly," I added. "Thin blood, you know." My cloak cover story would have made a lot more sense if it weren't the middle of summer.

"Uh-huh," Ghost said noncommittally. "It's strange, but your cloak bears an eerie resemblance to a Japanese artifact that was recently stolen from a nearby art gallery.

For some reason, the security footage from the night of the theft all got erased."

I'm not Japanese, Puck said derisively. *Not that there's anything wrong with that.*

Finally, the Conclave's Suppression Division was doing its job right, I thought. If only it had been more on the ball when those gargoyles attacked. Maybe I wouldn't be in the arms of a Hero right now. *Big, muscular, sexy arms,* I thought wistfully, before chiding myself. Betrayed by my man-hungry glands yet again.

"Is that a fact? Wow, what a coincidence." I gave Ghost my best wide-eyed innocent look. It was a hard look to pull off when you were squinting, not innocent, and had mostly forgotten what innocent looked like.

"Uh-huh," Ghost said again. I didn't have to see his face to know he wasn't buying what I was selling. "A couple of nights ago, a masked woman who wore a red cloak and matches your description was seen putting out a fire at Howard University. She appeared to have superpowers. She saved a lot of lives. But I suppose that's just a coincidence too."

"You took the words right out of my mouth. It's just a coincidence." I was not going to tell Ghost any more than he needed to know about the magical world or my recent exploits. He'd likely pat me on the back for saving lives and then turn me in for stealing the Cloak of Wisdom. I knew his type. Literally super sanctimonious.

Ghost said, "There's an expression in my line of work: If there's more than one coincidence, it's not a coincidence."

"Oooh, super sleuth aphorisms," I squealed in my best breathy Willow Wilde impersonation. "Tell me more Mister Detective Man."

The fabric around Ghost's mouth twitched. "You know, I can't decide if I really like you or if I really despise you."

"I get that a lot."

I gotta be honest, Puck said. *I wouldn't have guessed you knew the word "aphorisms."* Fortunately, due to Ghost's presence, I did not have to dignify that with a response.

We arrived at the Washington Monument. We hovered high in the sky over it, but underneath the cloud cover. The tourists who swarmed the Mall looked like ants from up here.

So we would not freak people out when we dove down toward the Washington Monument, Ghost turned us invisible. Or at least he said he did. From my perspective, we were still as visible as my donut top was when I pulled my shirt off. I wondered if Puck knew a chub reduction spell. Only the deluge of mockery I would open myself up to kept me from asking.

Ghost plunged straight down. We dropped next to the tall marble monument like it was a plumb line. It felt like we were going to splatter on the ground like a dropped watermelon. Though I knew we were in no danger, it was hard to stifle a scream. Millions of years of human evolution had programmed my instincts into believing falling from a great height was a very bad thing.

We passed through the ground like it was made of thin air. We plunged into complete darkness. Ghost had warned me about that. There was no light underground, after all.

I'm not having fun anymore, Puck said, sounding nervous. *It's dark and scary down here. It reminds me of where I go when you take the cloak off. I want off this ride.*

I opened my Third Eye. The glow I had detected deep under the monument flicked on like it had been turned on by a light switch. The glow was not as vivid as it had been in my astral form, but now that we were deep underground, I could see it, albeit very faintly. I never would have spotted it from aboveground if I hadn't figured out how to astrally project.

I still felt Ghost as he cradled me in his arms. He was as tangible as he had always been. The rock and soil we passed through was not tangible, though I vaguely felt it as we passed through it. It felt like someone gently blowing on my hand, except all over, even on my insides. It was creepy.

We were right on target to hit the glowing structure. Since I couldn't speak to Ghost while we were intangible, and he could of course not see the underground structure, I squeezed his right arm in the pattern we had worked out while flying to the Washington Monument.

As per my non-verbal instructions, Ghost slowed his descent. We were almost on top of the glowing ovoid structure. Thanks to my earlier collision with the structure in my astral form, I halfway expected us to bounce off the glowing structure like a dropped ball.

We did not bounce off it. We passed through the surface of the structure just as easily as we had slid through the dense earth.

CHAPTER TWENTY-ONE

The egg-like structure was hollow. Once we were through its wall, blinding and painfully bright magical light stabbed at me like thousands of razor-sharp daggers slicing through me. I gasped in pain. It was like when I had looked at the Ark fragment with my Third Eye, only more so.

I hastily closed my Third Eye. The searing light disappeared.

"Are you all right?" Ghost asked. I realized he had already asked a couple of times, but I had been so overwhelmed by the magical light that had slammed me, Ghost's concerned question hadn't registered.

I also hadn't realized Ghost had brought us to a halt. We were standing. I leaned against a wall of the hollow structure, with one hand on the wall, and the other on Ghost's broad muscular chest.

Embarrassed, I snatched my hand away from Ghost. "I'm fine," I said. I shook my head, trying to clear it of the fireworks still going off in my head. I knew not to open my Third Eye in here again. It felt like if I did so, the overwhelming magical power here would burn a hole through my brain. It was no wonder the chamber containing this potent magic had been visible to my astral form even from high in the sky.

When you looked at the Ark fragment, I said it felt like a truck had hit us, Puck said, his voice woozy. *Now it feels like a jumbo jet slammed into us. If the Spear of Destiny isn't here, I'd hate to be around when you actually find it. I don't think my aching head'll be able to stand it.*

My vision was clearing. "I'm pretty sure we're in the right place," I said.

The chamber we stood in was about twice the size of my apartment's tiny living room. The walls were spherical, forming a dome over the perfectly flat floor Ghost and I stood on. The walls and floor were made of a whitish-gold substance. Looking at it, I would have said it was metal. Touching it did not feel like touching metal, though. It was warm and pliable, like a fine leather that had been left out in the sun.

Directly under the apex of the dome floated a massive, thick, wooden cross. The cross was perhaps seven feet tall, and its crossbeam was equally long. It was on fire, like one of those crosses the knuckleheads in the Ku Klux Klan burned. The light from the fire was the only illumination in the room. Despite the size of the fire and the enclosed space, the air was fresh and easy to breathe. The fire produced no smoke or sound. It did not seem to consume the wood of the cross.

It was magic. Hercule Poirot had nothing on me and my deductive powers.

The main reason I thought we were in the right place was below the hovering burning cross. Seven small mounds of the same substance as the floor and the walls were under the cross. They reminded me of the circular bases of microphone stands. In six of the seven mounds stood spears of differing designs. The ends of their shafts rested in the mounds, with their tips pointed straight up toward the ceiling.

One of the seven mounds near the middle of the array was empty. I was so busy taking the chamber in, it took me a few moments to realize where the seventh spear was.

It was on the floor, on the other side of the chamber from where we stood. I walked over there. Ghost followed.

The spear that had apparently been removed from the empty mound was clutched in the hand of a tall man lying faceup on the floor. I didn't need to consult a coroner to know the man was dead. Even Stevie Wonder could have seen it.

The man's eyes were hollow and lifeless. His hair was the color of sun-bleached straw. His mouth was stretched wide in a silent scream. His skin was as gray as a storm cloud, and tight around his bones. He was literally skin and bones, like an incredibly powerful vacuum cleaner had sucked everything out of him, including the water in his body. Looking at him was like looking at a mummy. A well-dressed one. He wore a navy-blue suit, a tieless white shirt, and shiny brown shoes. The clothes, while old-fashioned and years out of style, were so spotless it was as though they had been made ten minutes ago. With the man's body being in the condition it was, it was as if the clothes were worn by a scarecrow.

Ghost and I stared at the man, then at each other.

"I'll be honest," Ghost sad. "I halfway didn't believe what you told me about why you wanted to come down here." His face turned up to the burning cross hovering silently overhead. "But seeing is believing. What do you think happened to this man?"

I warily eyed the metal-tipped spear in the desiccated man's hand. "I'd say he came here to do what we're here to do—retrieve the Spear of Destiny. There are seven spears to pick from. I'm guessing this guy chose the wrong one. A booby trap. Be careful to not touch anything." I remembered how difficult it had been getting Puck out of the Sackler Gallery. "I should have known retrieving a

Relic wouldn't be as simple as strolling down here and grabbing it."

I bent over, peering more closely at the man on the floor. "Could this be Millennium?"

Ghost bent over as well. "I've seen pictures of Millennium without the brown helmet he wears as part of his Hero costume. But this man is so disfigured, I wouldn't be able to tell if he was my own brother." Ghost straightened back up. "Even so, I say this isn't Millennium. Millennium is shorter than this unfortunate gentleman. And also, remember that Millennium's hands got chopped off during a battle with a Hero. This man's hands are intact."

I'll tell you who this guy is, Puck said. *He's Mr. Creeping Me Out, that's who he is.*

"The fact he figured out how to get down here means he's a powerful magician, whoever he is. Was," I corrected myself. "If his out of fashion clothes are any indication, he's been down here for decades."

Other than us, the dead man, the burning cross, and the seven spears, the large chamber we were in was empty. I had not expected there to be a sign telling us which spear was the true Spear of Destiny, but it would have been helpful.

"I wonder why there are seven spears," I said.

"I have no idea," Ghost said.

She wasn't talking to you, you big galoot, Puck said. *It's probably because the number seven has a lot of significance in the Christian faith. Genesis says it took God seven days to create everything, if you include his day of rest. Why an omnipotent being would need a rest day is beyond me. There are seven sacraments in the Catholic church. Noah was instructed to bring onto the Ark seven of every kind of clean animal—whatever that means—and seven of every bird. According to the Book of Joshua, God instructed the Israelite army to march around the city of Jericho seven times over seven days before they blew their horns, blowing down the city's walls. I could go on.*

"Don't. We'll be down here forever."

"I didn't say anything," Ghost protested.

"I wasn't talking to you." I crouched down next to the spear clutched in the dead man's hands. I balanced on the balls of my feet and examined the spear, being very careful to not touch it. I had no interest in becoming mummified like the dead man.

Before Ghost had picked me up, I had looked up pictures online of the so-called Spear of Destiny housed at the Hofburg Palace in Vienna, Austria. When I'd first met Daniel, he had told me the Austrian spear was a replica of the real spear. I'd figured that before I came down here with Ghost, I'd better know what the Spear looked like. Score one for thinking ahead. Perhaps I was finally beginning to plan ahead instead of acting on the fly all the time.

The spear in the man's hand looked identical to the pictures of the Austrian spear I saw online. Like the Austrian spear, the tip of the spear on the floor was a brown metal, and over a foot and a half long. Shiny gold leaf that looked a little like angel's wings was wrapped around the middle of the metal tip. In the online pictures, the Austrian spear was missing its shaft. The spear in the dead man's hands had one, though. The shaft was a dark, smooth wood.

"Doesn't this look like the pictures we saw online, Puck?" I asked, wanting a second opinion.

"Who's Puck? Who do you keep talking to?" Ghost demanded. I waved at him to be silent. I wished I had a sign that read *Quiet! Sorceress at Work*.

Yep. Puck's voice was thoughtful. *I don't understand why this dude's dead if this is the right spear.*

"Me neither." I stood. "Let's check out the others."

One by one, I stood in front of the spears sticking out of the floor, careful to not touch any of them. They were all exactly the same length, about six feet high. One of the six upright spears matched the one on the floor of the chamber. Five of the others were gem-encrusted and had shafts or tips made of precious metals; they were weapons fit for royalty. The last of the six spears was plain, with a head made of rusting iron and a shaft made of a medium-brown lumpy wood. Ash, maybe.

Puck said, *Two spears here match the one in Vienna. I guess one's a replica, and the other's the real McCoy. Obviously, Mummy Man picked the replica. It's Darwinism in action. Only the fit shall survive. Sucks for him, but great for us. Grab the real Spear, and we can get out of here.* Puck made a vivid image of dark walls closing in on a red cloak flash in my mind. *I'm not claustrophobic, but if I stay down here in the bowels of the earth much longer, I'm gonna be.*

"I suppose you're right," I said. I had misgivings, though. Something nagged at the edge of my mind, trying to get my attention.

Pushing my misgivings aside, I reached for the upright spear that matched the one Puck and I had examined online.

My hand hesitated before it touched the smooth wood of the spear's shaft. I pulled my hand back. I started to undo the eagle clasp on Puck.

Hey! What are you— Puck's voice in my head cut off mid-sentence as the clasp came undone and I released my hold on the spell which kept me connected to Puck.

I carefully folded Puck up. I handed him to Ghost. "I know this sounds crazy, but this cloak is a friend of mine. One of the few I have. I don't want something bad to happen to him if something bad happens to me when I touch the spear. He's grown to be too important to me."

I thought of whom I could entrust with Puck if I was about to do a female reboot of *The Mummy*. Daniel was the first to spring to mind. Then I dismissed him as a possibility. I had too many unanswered questions about him. "If something happens to me, give the cloak to Oscar Hightower. He's my boss at Capstone Security. Tell him the cloak is a Relic of great power. An ancient and valuable one. He needs to be safeguarded, and a good home needs to be found for him."

Ghost held Puck gingerly, like an insane person had just handed him a rattlesnake. "I'll tell him. But I must admit I do not fully understand what is going on."

"Join the club," I said. I hesitated. I had the sudden, inexplicable impulse to lift Ghost's mask and kiss him. Whether goodbye or for luck, I did not know. I guess him cradling me in his big powerful arms had appealed to me more than I wanted to admit. That or I had an unexamined fetish for masked men who liked to tie me up. Maybe I had seen *Fifty Shades of Grey* one too many times.

I turned away from Ghost before I gave into the temptation. Focus, Sage, focus. What was next? Me texting my BFF about how the barrel-chested Hero who had whisked me off my feet was *Soooooo dreamy*, followed by a string of heart emojis? Staring potential death in the face had apparently turned me into a hormonal adolescent again.

I again reached for the spear Puck and I had picked out.

Again, I stopped before touching the spear. I dropped my hand. The nagging thought at the edge of my consciousness had leaped to the front of my mind and grabbed me by the lapels.

Something about this whole situation was wrong. As Daniel had pointed out to me on more than one occasion, I was no Biblical scholar. But I did know enough about the Bible to know the people who crucified Jesus did not think he was the son of God. To them, he was just a common criminal. Surely the Roman soldier who used his spear to pierce Jesus' side had not been an elite soldier. He'd be some low-level grunt who had been stuck with the unpleasant task of dealing with the men who had been crucified.

Why would such a grunt be armed with a spear as nice as the one I'd been about to grab? Maybe it, like its replica in Vienna, was fake. Just like the five spears here which were fashioned from gems and precious metals. The magicians who had hidden the Spear of Destiny here were trying to trick the unwary and the careless.

Besides, even if I was no Biblical scholar, I was something of a scholar of action and adventure movies. One of my favorites was *Indiana Jones and the Last Crusade.* In that movie, Indy and his antagonists searched for the Holy Grail, the cup Jesus drank from at the Last Supper. It turned out that instead of the cup being ornate, it was a plain cup someone who was a carpenter like Jesus would drink from. Indiana correctly deduced that when he picked the true Grail from a lineup of counterfeits.

My jaw clenched with resolve. If the logic was good enough for my boy Indy, it was good enough for me.

I stepped away from the spear I had been about to grab.

I instead reached for the spear with the lumpy shaft and the rusty iron tip.

CHAPTER TWENTY-TWO

In the wild and reckless years I went through after Dad died, I experimented with illegal drugs. One of my favorites was cocaine. After a few snorts of coke, I felt on top of the world, like I could do anything.

Touching the spear with the rusty iron tip was like that times a billion.

The spear throbbed under my touch, beating like a heart. As I hoisted the spear out of its holder, my mind expanded, disgorging thoughts, ideas, and feelings like an overstuffed suitcase I had never bothered to unpack.

I felt the currents of magic here and everywhere all around the world. It felt like all the magical waters of the world were dammed up and ached for release.

And I was just the woman to do it.

Why had I been afraid of the wererats? My former fear puzzled me. My anxiety about rodent Otherkin seemed foreign now, like the emotion belonged to a different person. A weak person. With a simple Word, Wave, and exertion of Will, I could teleport into their midst. From the Rat King on down, I could slaughter every one of them. I could erase their species from the face of the earth. I could use their blood to write my name in the sky to remind everyone who looked into the heavens to never threaten me again. It would not only be easy, it would be laughably easy.

My money problems? Why was someone like me living the life of a pauper, hounded by her money-grubbing landlord and creditors? I could raze my entire neighborhood, and erect my palace in its place. The world was my oyster. I merely needed to crack open its shell. I could do that easily now. Everything was free if you were strong enough to take it. Money was unimportant and irrelevant.

Millennium? People thought he was the most powerful sorcerer in existence. Hah! What a joke. A simple spell would summon him to me, wherever in the universe he might be cowering from his pursuers. I could squash him like the bug that he was. Show him and the world true power.

The Conclave? I had no need for their certification, no need for their approval. I dared them to question me and my actions now. I was to them what a goddess was to chimpanzees. I could make them my pets. Willow I could make my slave. I looked forward to whipping her morning, noon, and night.

I glanced at Ghost. I had thought to steal a kiss from him, though for the life of me I could not remember why. He was puny. Weak and worthless. Not worthy of my presence, much less my affection. I could have any man I wanted. Gifted, Otherkin, Metahuman, mundane—to the woman I could easily become, they were all the same. I could slake my thirst with thousands of men if I so chose. Millions. I could have the pick of the litter. And if they did not submit willingly, I could bend them to my will.

With my magic and the Spear of Destiny—for it was obvious that was what I held in my eager hands—no one could stand against me.

I could have anything.

I could have everything.

I could be a god. I could make the world worship me.

I wished my father were still alive to see me now. I would make him worship me too.

I suddenly shuddered. Thinking of Dad shook my delusions of grandeur.

Killing? Enslaving? Become a modern-day magical Hitler? That wasn't who Dad had raised me to be. That wasn't me.

And it wasn't who I would let myself become.

I dropped the Spear of Destiny like it was a red-hot poker. It clattered on the floor. I stepped back from it. Before I knew it, my back was pressed against the wall.

I found myself panting like I had just run a race. Everyone had dark thoughts from time to time, but holding the Spear of Destiny had taken mine and amplified them a thousandfold. If I wielded the Spear, I knew I could make those dark thoughts a reality.

If this was a holy Relic, I'd hate to see an unholy one.

"Are you all right?" Ghost said. His voice was filled with concern.

"No." I was still breathing hard. Now I understood why the magicians who had hidden the Spear here had committed suicide afterward to try to keep its whereabouts a secret. The Spear's power should not be allowed to fall into the wrong hands. It shook me to my core to know I was one of those wrong hands. I knew I wasn't perfect, but at heart I'd thought I was a good person. The dark thoughts that lurked in my mind, unknown until now even to me, disturbed me. I thanked heaven Hitler hadn't been Gifted. He had done enough damage to the world with the Spear as a mundane.

What they said was true: Power corrupted, and absolute power corrupted absolutely.

I reached into my pocket. With shaking hands, I pulled out my gloves. I didn't know how I knew, but I somehow knew I could handle the Spear safely if it didn't touch my skin.

I picked the Spear up with gloved hands, careful to not let the Relic touch any of my exposed skin.

"Let's get out of here," I told Ghost. "We have what we came for."

And more, I feared, than I had bargained for.

CHAPTER TWENTY-THREE

I leaned against a tree on the edge of a small circular clearing deep in Rock Creek Park. Rock Creek Park was the over 1,700-acre green space that ran roughly north and south through the District. I came here sometimes when I wanted to get away from the hustle and bustle of the city.

The sun was bright in the cloudless blue sky. Nature's canvas. Cicadas and birds chirped in the surrounding trees. Nature's symphony. Horseflies and mosquitoes kept landing on my face and neck, trying to get a sip of Sage cocktail. Nature's vampires.

Gnats buzzed around my damp face. Sweat trickled down my spine. Though I was in the shade of a vine-entangled tree, I was still hot and sticky. I didn't know how D.C. residents survived the summer before the invention of air conditioning in the early 1900s. Maybe they didn't; maybe they all had spontaneously combusted.

The fact I wore long pants, a long-sleeved shirt, gloves, and Puck did not help. Other than my head and neck, none of my skin was exposed. I didn't want to chance touching the Spear of Destiny with my bare skin again, not even by accident. It lay on the ground in front of me.

Puck said, *If somebody told me a few hundred years ago that I would one day be hanging out in the wilderness waiting for a fallen angel to show up to claim a magic spear while being pooped on by birds and sweated on by a sorceress, I would've called them a filthy liar. Back when there was still slavery in this country, there were house slaves and field slaves. Well, I'm what you'd call a house cloak. Being out here is for the birds. Literally. You need to get me back inside before I drown in sweat.*

"I don't sweat. I glisten."

Your glistening reeks. Have you considered changing your diet?

A rustling in the undergrowth across the clearing saved Puck from my withering retort. Daniel stepped out from the shadows of the tree line and into the light of the clearing. He was dressed more appropriately than I for the hot weather in cargo shorts and a plain gray t-shirt. He carried the Ark fragment. The same old duffel bag Daniel had pulled money out of when he broke into my apartment was slung over his shoulder.

Daniel spotted me and headed toward me. I picked up the Spear with my gloved hands. When Daniel was within earshot roughly in the middle of the clearing, I called out to him. "Why don't you just stay there."

He stopped, frowning. "Why?"

"I want to talk to you before I give you the Spear. It's why I had you meet me out here, away from everyone."

"Don't be silly. We'll talk face to face. I'm not going to yell a conversation with you like some kind of savage." He started walking toward me again.

"Terra," I said, waving my free hand in the pattern of the spell as I exerted my will.

The ground erupted under Daniel, climbing up his legs like green and brown snakes. In the wink of an eye, the ground covered him from his waist down, immobilizing him.

The duffel bag slid off his shoulder as Daniel squirmed and sputtered, demanding to know what I was doing. The bag hit the ground next to him. A separate earth spell made the ground under the bag ripple like a rope whose end has been picked up and flicked. The ground's ripple carried the bag across the rest of the clearing to me.

I bent over and unzipped it. Even a cursory glance made it clear there was more in there than the thirty-five thousand Daniel owed me for recovering the Spear.

Seeing the questioning look on my face, Daniel said, "I decided to pay you extra for recovering the Spear. It's not like I need the money. Though I'm regretting my generosity now. I take it you trapped me here to verify I had the money before you give me the Spear?"

"Not exactly."

"Our deal was I'd pay you the rest of the money in exchange for you giving me the Spear. You have the money. Now give me the Spear."

"Perhaps I will in a minute. But first, I want to talk without you getting too close to me with the Ark fragment. If there's one thing I've learned in retrieving the Spear, it's that it should not fall into the wrong hands. Convince me you're the right hands."

"How many times do we have to go over this? Millennium is looking for the Spear. If someone doesn't safeguard it, he'll eventually find it."

"So you say. But, I haven't seen hide nor hair of him since this whole crazy excursion started. Nor has anybody else. And I know for a fact there are some determined people all over the world looking for him." I shook my head. "All I have for proof that Millennium is looking for the Spear and that he knows it's here in the city is your say-so. And that's not good enough anymore. Though I've always been a little skeptical of you, how you reacted to me saving those Howard students the other night turned my skepticism to full-blown doubt. What kind of a person, much less an angel, gets upset about the fact I acted to save lives? Plus, you and your money showed up in my life right when I needed it the most due to my tangles with the gargoyles and the wererats. Maybe that's just a coincidence.

But, as someone recently said to me, if there's more than one coincidence, it's not a coincidence.

"It's almost as if someone was conspiring behind the scenes to push me into searching for the Spear. Since you're the only person I've encountered in a lather to find the Spear, I have a sneaking suspicion that person was you."

Daniel just stared at me for a bit, blinking. Then he smiled at me indulgently, like a parent at a child who had just told the parent two plus two equaled four. "You are not nearly as foolish as I had first supposed," he said.

Me neither, Puck agreed. Lovely. It's good to have people in your corner.

"You'll forgive me if I don't swoon at the backhanded compliment," I said to Daniel. Since I had him trapped, I had the Spear, and he couldn't touch me with the Ark fragment, I had the upper hand. And yet, Daniel smiled at me like the cat who had just eaten the canary. His inexplicable confidence made me nervous. "It was you who animated the gargoyles and sent them to the Institute of Peace, wasn't it? I'm guessing with the Ark fragment. And it was you who hired the wererats."

Daniel nodded. "When I became aware the Spear was in this area, I knew I needed the assistance of a magician, someone naïve enough to help me, powerful enough to find the Spear, and selfless enough to not keep it for herself. I told you the truth when I said I had been observing you for some time. You seemed to fit the bill of what I needed. I correctly surmised that, thanks to your fundamentally good nature, you would risk exposing your magic for the sake of protecting those people from the gargoyles. That in turn would get you into trouble with the Conclave, which would pressure you into agreeing to steal the Cloak of Wisdom. Hiring the wererats put financial pressure on you to further goad you to help me."

"And what if the gargoyles or the wererats had killed me?"

"Then you would have proven yourself not strong or resourceful enough to help me." Daniel shrugged. "I eventually would have found another magician who was. I was not lying when I said I am immortal. Time was on my side."

"You're immortal, but not an angel, I'm guessing. Unless you're the world's worst one." I was beyond disgusted. "People at the Institute of Peace died because of you."

"Billions have died in the millennia I've walked the earth. A few more won't matter in the grand scheme of things. And no, I'm not an angel, fallen or otherwise. I am as human as you. Have you heard of the Wandering Jew?"

Holy crap, Puck whispered in awe.

Clearly Puck knew something I did not. "The plant?" I asked Daniel.

Daniel looked startled for a moment, then gave me his smug, indulgent smile again. "Sage, you're an interesting woman. You have oases of unexpected brilliance surrounded by deserts of breathtaking ignorance. No, not the plant. I am the Wandering Jew. Though the plant is named after me.

"I was born over two thousand years ago in Jerusalem and, when I grew up, I worked there as a cobbler. I was a contemporary of Jesus Christ. As Jesus walked through the streets of Jerusalem, struggling under the weight of the cross he was forced to carry to where he was to be crucified, he stumbled and fell." Daniel's eyes were distant now, as if he saw the scene playing out again in his mind's eye. "I didn't know who he was. I just thought he was some criminal who deserved the punishment he was getting. I kicked him and said, 'Hurry up and get off the streets. Decent folk are walking here.'

"I'll never forget the look in his eyes when he turned and looked up at me. His eyes seemed to burn like fire. 'My journey on this world will be over soon,' Jesus said, 'but yours shall not end until the world does.'"

Puck cursed. I didn't admonish him. I felt like cursing too. *That explains those coins Daniel is always playing with. Centuries ago I read some ancient Christian texts about how the Wandering Jew was forced by God to carry around five Tyrian silver shekels everywhere he went to remind him of the five wounds suffered by Jesus, namely the one on his side from the Spear of Destiny, and the four on his hands and feet from where he was nailed to the cross. Those texts also said the Wandering Jew could speak every language in the world.* Puck cursed again. *It never even occurred to me to connect the Wandering Jew legend and Daniel.*

Daniel was still talking. It was hard to follow both him and Puck. "Since then," Daniel said, "I've been cursed to wander the world. Never allowed to stay in any one place for long, never allowed to put down roots, and never allowed to die until the world ends.

"At first, it actually wasn't that bad. I was immortal. I've been an eyewitness to some of history's greatest events. Other men have dreamed of what God cursed me with. But over time, I grew to hate my existence. If I got close to someone, I was inevitably forced to leave them thanks to the divine compulsion God forced on me. I've married and had children more times than I can even remember, yet my compulsion to wander always forced me to abandon them. On top of that, I outlived them all. Can you imagine what it feels like, looking down on a newborn baby boy, knowing you can't watch him grow up, knowing he will wither and die long before you ever will?

"After a while, I gave up on forming relationships with people. Century after long century, I lived the life of a hermit wanderer. It was hell on earth, like solitary confinement with no end in sight.

"I turned all my attention to finding a way to end my punishment. Eventually, I learned that if a part of Noah's Ark was destroyed, God's covenant to man to never flood the world again would also be destroyed, triggering the end of the world. The end of the world would mean the end of my punishment. The problem was the only thing I knew of that was powerful enough to destroy an artifact like the Ark was the Spear of Destiny. And I didn't know where it was.

"I've spent centuries looking for the Spear. Eventually, I traced it here. Unfortunately, I had to wait for many years before my divine compulsion to wander brought me to this area. I already had obtained this fragment of the Ark thanks to my association with the Smithsonian as I already explained to you. All I needed was the Spear. And now, you've acquired it for me. My long torment is finally near its end."

"You're the poster boy for counting his Armageddon chickens before they're hatched," I scoffed. I still didn't understand why Daniel was so confident and why he so readily confessed his true motivations. "I have the Spear, you're trapped way over there, and there's no way I'm going to give it to you."

"As I said, you're sometimes brilliant, but more often than not you're simply ignorant. I'm not surprised you don't know holy Relics have an affinity for one another."

The Ark fragment shimmered in Daniel's hand. The Spear of Destiny was ripped out of my grip like an invisible giant had come along and grabbed it.

The Spear whipped through the air. It smacked into Daniel's empty hand.

I felt an external, implacable force push against my will, like a finger pressing into a fragile soap bubble. My will maintaining my earth spell collapsed. The dirt holding Daniel in place dropped back to the ground.

Daniel gave me his canary eating smile again.

Uh-oh, I thought.

Uh-oh, Puck said.

"Surprise," Daniel said.

CHAPTER TWENTY-FOUR

I flung a ball of spellfire at Daniel. Before it got halfway to him, Daniel moved his hand holding the Spear of Destiny in a gesture that seemed almost contemptuous.

The fireball dissipated, instantly disappearing like it had never existed.

Before I could get another spell off, the vines dangling from the trees behind me grew like someone had sprayed them with magical Miracle-Gro. Fast as lightning, they wrapped around my arms and hands, tightening around my limbs like countless little anacondas. Despite my strength, I couldn't free myself

The vines spread my arms far apart. My shoulders howled in protest. The vines yanked me off my feet. I dangled several feet off the ground. Vines also whipped around my ankles. They spread my legs just like my arms had been spread. My joints were on fire. I felt like a human wishbone.

Despite struggling, I could not free myself. Thanks to my hands being bound, I couldn't cast a spell.

Daniel walked closer until he stood just a few feet away from where I dangled.

"It's a real shame things had to end this way," he said. He seemed genuinely regretful. "I have grown quite fond of you. Despite your flaws, you're a good woman. There are too few people like you in the world. If things were different, we could have been good friends. Perhaps even more. I would have preferred to end the world without you knowing the truth about me. It's strange, but after all these years, I find myself caring what you think of me."

He put the Ark fragment on the ground. With both hands around the Spear, he lifted it over his head, with its iron tip aimed at the Ark fragment.

Thrashing, I struggled futilely against the vines binding me. "Daniel, don't do this. There are billions of people in the world. You can't kill everybody. I've spent a lot of time with you. I know you're not a bad person. You're better than this."

Daniel looked up from where he focused on the Ark fragment. His eyes met mine. I saw resolve and determination within them. "I once was better than this. I was a good man." He shook his head. "But that was a very long time ago. Not anymore. My punishment ends today."

The Spear of Destiny descended like a guillotine.

"No!" I screamed.

The tip of the Spear bit into the Ark fragment. The fragment exploded with a deafening, deep, bell tolling sound I more felt than heard.

A barely visible shockwave expanded from where the Ark fragment had been. It passed through me, taking my breath away and making every fiber of my being tingle.

The shockwave grew up and out like the mushroom cloud of a nuclear explosion. It reached high into the clear blue sky.

Like a button had been pressed on Photoshop, the sky instantly got dark, changing from a bright blue to an angry gray. Storm clouds quickly rolled in, covering the sky. It was like watching time-lapse footage of a gathering storm.

I felt my hair stand on end. A bolt of pure white lightning lanced down from the sky. It struck Daniel.

Blinded, my eyes squeezed shut. The afterimage of the lightning strike seemed burned into my retinas. A thunderclap hit. It made my insides shake, like I was at the epicenter of an earthquake.

I forced my eyes to open. It took a few moments for my vision to clear.

When it did, Daniel still stood before me. Though he appeared unhurt by the lightning strike, the strike had burned off all his clothes. He was as naked as a newborn. The silver coins he always carried were on the ground at his feet. The scars on his body danced on his skin like they had come alive.

Daniel's arms were outstretched. His face was turned up to the heavens. He had a beatific smile on his face. For the first time since I had known him, the sorrow that hung around him like a dark cloud was gone.

The heavens opened up. Perhaps literally, in this case. Sheets of rain began to fall. It was though we were suddenly in the middle of a monsoon. The world became as dark as a closet with the door left ajar. The rain sounded like countless pans of frying bacon as it hit the ground and the surrounding vegetation. I had been damp from perspiration before, but now I was drenched, like I had dived fully clothed into a swimming pool.

At first I thought it was my imagination, or that I couldn't see right because of the darkness and the pounding rain. Then I realized it was definitely not my imagination:

Daniel was melting. The water flaked away his skin and flesh like he was made of salt. In seconds, Daniel's bones were partially exposed.

"It is done!" Daniel shouted, his bones and teeth flashing white in the darkness. "Forgive me!"

I had no idea if he was talking to me, the world, or someone else entirely.

Daniel, entirely skeletal now, fell backward. His bones separated from each other and flew apart when he hit the wet ground. The Spear of Destiny rolled out of the bones that had been Daniel's hand.

I felt the vines that bound me relax. The tension had gone out of them. I steeled myself, then heaved, bringing my arms and legs together in front of me like a high diver.

The vines snapped around me, freeing me. I went tumbling. With a splash of water, I landed heavily on the ground on my side. Though the fall jolted me, I had not been very high up. I was unhurt.

I blinked mud out of my eyes. It was hard to believe how hard it was raining when the sky had been clear minutes ago.

Splashing on the already soaked ground, I got to my feet. I pulled my cell phone out of my pocket. I pulled Puck over it, using him like a canopy so I could read my phone despite the pounding rain.

Hey! I'm not an umbrella, Puck said indignantly.

"Now's not the time," I said tersely as I tapped my phone. I checked social media. It confirmed what I already knew in the pit of my sinking stomach: Storm clouds bringing torrential rain had appeared out of seemingly nowhere everywhere around the world.

"How long did it rain in the Noah's Ark story?" I asked Puck.

Forty days and forty nights. The floodwaters allegedly covered the highest mountains.

"And how long before all life will be destroyed if it keeps raining like this?

What am I, a meteorologist specializing in the Apocalypse? How should I know? I'm guessing not long, though, at the rate this water's coming down. Days, maybe. Weeks, certainly.

A small bone floated by my foot in a small stream of water.

Ewww! I think that's one of Daniel's metacarpals.

"Forget about that," I said, though the sight made my flesh crawl too. This was all my fault. I never should have confronted Daniel. Since I was already suspicious of Daniel when I ventured under the Washington Monument, I should have left the Spear right where I found it.

Too late. It was all water under the bridge now. Literally. I had to fix this.

"Do you know any spells that can stop this from happening?" I asked Puck.

A spell that will counteract the effects of the destruction of a holy Relic? His voice was incredulous. *Um, no. I know a lot of stuff, but that kind of magic is way above my pay grade. It's way above everyone's pay grade.*

"I was afraid you'd say that." I started to peel my gloves off. Soaked, they were hard to remove.

What are you doing?

"I'm good at elemental magic. Including water and air. That's exactly what this storm is: water and air. I'll try to dissipate it."

Are you insane? You're not powerful enough to control the weather on a worldwide scale. Nobody is.

"On my own, you're right. But I won't be on my own. I'll use the Spear."

It took me a couple of minutes to find the Spear in the rain and gloom. Puck spent the time giving me a hundred reasons why my plan wouldn't work, saying that it wasn't a plan at all and just wishful thinking, that I'd just wind up tearing my body apart and frying my brain, and that we needed to take this problem to the Conclave's Inner Circle and maybe they could figure out a way to deal with it.

I tuned him out. I had created this mess. I was going to clean it up.

Or die trying.

My groping hands finally found the Spear. As soon as my flesh touched the Spear's wood, my mind expanded, exploding like a mental Big Bang was occurring in my brain.

I grasped the Spear firmly. I stood upright. How dare Puck question my abilities. Of course I could reverse what that suicidal fool Daniel had done. I could do anything.

I strode into the center of the clearing. I hardly realized I repelled the rainwater from me as I walked. The water sloughed away from me without touching me, as if I were surrounded by an invisible force field.

The Spear was in my right hand. Shifting so I grasped the end of its shaft, I lifted the Spear over my head. Using the Spear as a conduit, somehow my mind probed the raging storm. My mind examined it not merely overhead, but all around the world.

I had magically condensed water and created wind many times in the past. To stop the storm, I needed to simultaneously trigger both air and water spells, only in the reverse of what I normally did, and on a much more massive scale.

If you want my advice, what you need to do— A flick of my wrist, a murmured Word, and an exertion of Will cut Puck's voice off like he had been muzzled. He was a fool, unworthy of being bound to me.

My left hand moved in an unfamiliar pattern that still somehow felt as familiar as brushing my teeth. I was creating a brand-new spell, one that was an improvised riff on the standard air and water spells I knew so well. Normally, creating a new spell took weeks if not months of research, testing, and refinement.

With what I wanted to accomplish firmly in mind, I finished the new Wave, spoke several complex sentences that were the new Word, and unleashed my Will as my left hand came to rest on the Spear above my right one.

A blue light shot out of the tip of the Spear, stretching at the speed of light into the sky. It was so bright it lit up the clearing and beyond.

The blue light hit the dark clouds above, piercing them like a laser. Where the light hit the clouds, the clouds thinned and disappeared, like the morning sun dissipating a lingering fog.

As I continued to channel my Will through the Spear, the hole I poked through the clouds expanded, exposing the sun. The hole chasing the clouds away continued to grow. In seconds, the rain had stopped in the clearing. Several seconds after that, I sensed the dark clouds over the entire city dissipating, leaving behind a clear blue sky.

I kept at it. The hole destroying the storm clouds grew and grew, expanding beyond the city like antibodies destroying bacteria.

Suddenly, I met with resistance. An unexpected opposing will. It was a dark, malevolent force I did not recognize that was still somehow familiar, like the face of someone I had fleetingly glanced at in a crowd years ago.

The force pushed against me. Some of the dark clouds I had erased returned.

Annoyed, I increased my efforts. The opposing will matched me, stopping me from progressing further.

Enraged that anyone would dare stand against me, I drew on magical and mental reserves I didn't even know I had. The blue beam of light grew blindingly bright, into a second sun.

Whatever it was that fought me howled almost bestially in rage, frustration, and a hint of fear. I felt it withdraw into the deep, dark shadows it lived in.

All resistance to my Will gone now, the hole I caused which chased the storm clouds away rocketed around the world, evaporating the rain clouds created by Daniel's destruction of the Ark fragment.

In minutes, it was over. The rain was gone everywhere. I had done it.

I relaxed my Will. The blue light flicked off. I lowered the Spear of Destiny. I cradled it in my hands. I had been foolish to reject it before. I looked at it with satisfaction and anticipation.

I had saved the world. Now it was time for me to rule it.

Let it go, Sage. Let it go. This is not your path, came a voice in my head. For an instant, I felt a warm, loving hand caress my cheek.

The voice in my head was not Puck's. I knew whose voice it was:

It was my father's.

Though much of me didn't want to, the rest of me forced my hands to let go. The Spear plopped into the mud at my feet.

I staggered backward, almost falling. Dazed, I felt like I had just awakened from a dream.

Though the ground was wet and muddy, the clearing was as bright and sunny as it had been when I had arrived. There wasn't a cloud in the sky.

Puck was jabbering in my mind.

That. Was. Awesome!!! he crowed. *Omigod, look!*

Still stunned and bewildered, I blinked, focusing my eyes.

A breathtaking rainbow curved from the middle of the clearing, up through the sky, into forever.

CHAPTER TWENTY-FIVE

C'mon Sage. We've been practicing for hours. You said I could watch South Park. You promised, Puck whined.

I sat in the middle of my living room floor with my legs crossed. "I said you could watch it after I levitated successfully. I haven't yet. I've almost got it. I can feel it."

At this rate, I'll be ten thousand years-old before I get to binge-watch season two, Puck muttered darkly. *I wanna find out if they killed Kenny.*

"Did you say something?"

I was saying how you're right on the cusp of flying like a bird, Puck said in a fake, cheerful, saccharine tone. *I've got all the faith in the world in you.*

I grinned, then got back to business. I closed my eyes and began to cast the levitation spell for the umpteenth time. I could easily float by creating air currents under myself of course, but if I was going to get certified as a Master Sorceress, I needed to be well-versed in all disciplines of magic, not just elemental magic. I was trying to levitate by making my body lighter than air.

The sooner I could try for my certification, the better. It felt like an invisible clock was ticking. I was surprised I had not been contacted by the Conclave regarding my

First Rule violations already. My only chance of saving myself was to get my certification.

It was over a week since Daniel had died. As crazy as it sounded, even to me, I felt sorry for him. I knew what it was like to be filled with such despair that you wanted to take your own life. I had felt that way for years after I caused Dad's death.

That's probably why I had cried over Daniel while I buried his bones in the clearing in Rock Creek Park. I had buried the five silver shekels with him. If I had known who his descendants were, I would have instead sent his remains to them so he could finally rest in peace, surrounded by family. As it was, I knew I would visit his unmarked grave from time to time. I would be his family.

With Ghost's help, I had returned the Spear of Destiny to the chamber deep under the Washington Monument. If I knew how to destroy it, I would have. It was better for everyone if an artifact like that did not exist. I had made Ghost swear he would never tell anyone about the Spear, just like he had made me swear to never tell anyone the Heroes' Guild had a secret space station. I also made him swear he would never take anyone back into the chamber under the Washington Monument. Even me. Some things were best buried forever.

As for Millennium, I would follow through on my promise to Ghost to help him locate the Hero turned Rogue. I didn't know how just yet, but I'd figure something out. I had given Ghost my word.

Besides, if I had a chance to spend more time with Ghost, I could figure out if I really wanted to kiss him.

I used the money Daniel had given me to cancel the wererat contract on my life. When I delivered the gold talents, the Rat King told me to contact him personally should I ever decide to put a price on someone's head. I told him I would keep him and the wererats in mind.

I would not.

I had thoroughly cleaned my apartment. It was now as neat as a pin. I had even eaten a healthy breakfast the past five out of seven days. I thought of those two chocolate filled days as cheat days. Though I was trying to turn over a new leaf, I figured I still needed to enjoy myself every now and then. I was a sorceress, not a nun.

Two things still bothered me about me wielding the Spear in Rock Creek Park. What was the evil force that had tried to stop me from preventing the world from flooding? And, who or what was that voice in my head that had gotten me to drop the Spear?

Was it my imagination? My subconscious? The angels of my better nature? Or, somehow, some way, did Dad still live, perhaps on a different plane of existence?

That caress on my cheek had not felt like a figment of my imagination.

I chided myself for my errant thoughts. It was no wonder I couldn't levitate. I was too busy distracting myself with non-magical thoughts. I tried to refocus. I needed to get ready for the Conclave. Everything else had to take a backseat for now.

My supposedly locked door exploded open. Startled, I scrambled to my feet.

Someone stepped through my doorway as if all the protections on my threshold did not exist.

Run Sage! Puck's voice was suddenly as serious as a heart attack. *I personally designed the wards I had you cast on the door. Few can rip through them like that. My Spidey sense detects some major league bad juju approaching. This is bad news with a capital B. Run!*

Someone stepped into view. It was big trouble. The Conclave was here.

Is that fire and brimstone I smell? Don't try to stand your ground. No one's more impressed with how you handled the Daniel situation than I, but discretion is the better part of valor. Run!

I stayed right where I was.

By Thor's hammer! Have you gone deaf? Run! Get outta here!

The intruder stood in front of me. She stared down her nose at me. I did not look away. I forced myself to look directly into arctic blue eyes that were mirror images of my own.

"Hello Mother," I said.

Mother! Puck was thunderstruck. *Holy shit!*

The End

AUTHOR'S NOTE

Thank you so much for reading my book. I hope you have enjoyed reading about Sage as much as I've enjoyed writing about her. I lived in the Washington, D.C. area for over a decade, and it was fun exploring my old stomping grounds again.

When I started writing this book, I only knew the three main characters (Sage, Puck, and Daniel), how I wanted the book to begin, and how I wanted it to end. Everything in between was as much of a surprise to me as it was to you. I started each morning in front of my computer with only a vague idea of what was going to happen next. It's both an invigorating and terrifying way to write. I wrote a murder mystery novel the same way once. As I told a friend when I was about three-fourths of the way through, the lead detective had no idea who the murderer was. The problem was, I didn't either.

As you know if you follow me on social media, I'm a full-time writer. This would be no surprise to my ninth grade English teacher, who told me way back then I should write for a living. She even invited a professional author friend of hers to school to talk to me about being a writer. Thanks Mrs. Driscoll! But, before I followed Mrs. Driscoll's sage advice, I tried out several other careers first. I've been a newspaper reporter, a lawyer, and a small business owner, among other occupations. I even considered running for public office before I came to my senses. If this writing gig doesn't work out, maybe I'll take a page out of Sage's book and try stripping next.

I mostly write superhero novels. *Sorceress Super Hero* got its start when I had the itch to write urban fantasy. Since I already have two superhero series set in the same fictional universe, namely the *Omega Superhero Series* and the *Superhero Detective Series*, I thought it would be fun to add magic to the mix in that universe. Some of the superhero characters referred to in *Sorceress Super Hero* make an appearance in those other two series. The superhero Omega, for example, is the main character in the *Omega Superhero Series*. The Hero Myth who Sage spotted on the space station Ghost took her to is also a featured character in that series. And, Ghost makes an appearance in both series, but especially in the last two books of the *Superhero Detective Series*.

A list of the books in those two superhero series follows. Be sure to check those other books out if you're jonesing for some superhero action.

Sorceress Super Hero is, to be frank, an experiment. A testing of the literary waters, if you will. If the book crashes and burns sales-wise, I'll return to writing about superheroes, especially since fans of the *Omega Superhero Series* want the upcoming fifth book in the series right away, and preferably yesterday. If *Sorceress Super Hero* does well, however, I'll write a sequel. You no doubt noticed how I set up a potential sequel in the last chapter. I also populated this book with characters I intend to explore further in a sequel, if there is one.

If you enjoyed reading about Sage and want me to continue her story, there are a bunch of ways you can help:

First, you can tell your friends about my book and urge them to read it. Heck, tell your enemies and strangers on the street too.

Second, you can leave a review on Amazon. Reviews are huge in helping other readers who share your tastes find books they'll like.

Third, you can join my email newsletter here: http://eepurl.com/dAZ9Dz. I track where my mailing list signups come from, so if a bunch of new people sign up for my mailing list through this book, I'll know people like it. By signing up for my mailing list, you'll get news of my new releases, sales and discounts regarding my existing releases, and the occasional freebie. I usually send out an email to my mailing list once a month.

Fourth, you can follow me on Twitter and/or Facebook and send me a message:
www.twitter.com/dariusbrasher
www.facebook.com/dariusbrasher

Fifth, you can simply email me and let me know you want to see another Sage story. My email address is darius@dbrasher.com. I love hearing from readers. Unless of course you're a Nigerian prince who only needs $10,000 from me to gain access to a million dollar fortune. In that case, don't email me to tell me about this opportunity of a lifetime. I've already wired tens of thousands to Nigeria, and I expect the investment to pay off any day now. There's no need for me to be greedy by going to the well again.

Lastly, you can support me on Patreon in exchange for cool stuff only my patrons have access to for as little as $1 a month: www.patreon.com/dariusbrasher.

Speaking of Patreon, I want to give a special thanks and shout-out to my Patrons who support my work at the $5 level or higher per month: Michael Hofer, Paul Krause, Flint L. Miller, Kathy Mills, Andrew Jones, Marion Dillon, and Tiffani Panek. Guys and gals, thanks for your support. You rock!

Thanks again for reading. You could have spent your time in thousands of ways, and I really appreciate you having spent some of it with Sage.

ABOUT THE AUTHOR

Darius Brasher has a lifelong fascination with superheroes and a love of fantasy and science fiction. He has a Bachelor of Arts degree in English, a Juris Doctor degree in law, and a PhD from the School of Hard Knocks. He lives in South Carolina.

Other books by Mr. Brasher available through Amazon:

Omega Superhero Series

Caped
Trials
Sentinels
Rogues

Superhero Detective Series

Superhero Detective For Hire
The Missing Exploding Girl
Killshot
Hunted

Made in the USA
San Bernardino,
CA

57061527R00166